Praise for *Main Street*

Winner of the 2017 Golden Leaf Best First Book award
sponsored by the New Jersey Chapter of Romance Writers
of America

Winner of the 2018 Carolyn Readers' Choice Award in the
Romantic Suspense Category sponsored by the North Texas
Chapter of Romance Writers of America

Finalist of the 2018 Northern Hearts Awards in the
Romantic Suspense Category sponsored by the Toronto
Chapter of Romance Writers of America

Finalist of the 2018 Aspen Gold Readers Choice Award in
the Romantic Suspense Category sponsored by the Heart of
Denver Chapter of Romance Writers of America

Finalist of 2018 Southern Magic Award of Excellence in the
Romantic Suspense Category sponsored by the Southern
Magic Chapter of Romance Writers of America

"I dropped my Kindle, threw my hands in the air
yelling oh my god no freaking way! I totally did not see
that coming! And that ending... I need the next book
now!"

— KELLY, AMAZON REVIEWER

"Characters you fall head over heels for, and at least one you turn pages for to see if karma steps in!"

— DENA HAWKINS, AMAZON REVIEWER

"The detail, the description, the visualization is solid and you, as a reader, can see everything that is being expressed."

— HARLAN BRYAN, AUTHOR OF *WOUNDED* & *WILDFIRE* NOVELS

"The work flows from one scene to another flawlessly... The characters are memorable and entertaining with the type of personalities that make a story come to life."

— *THE COZY REVIEW*

"I loved the characters; they were funny, exciting and sexy. The story was fast paced; the mystery was suspenseful."

— TINA C, AMAZON REVIEWER

"This book keeps you hopping. I couldn't put it down."

— LRC, TOP AMAZON CONTRIBUTOR

"Intriguing, romantic, and funny... a perfect combination."

— REBECCA DUKETT, AMAZON REVIEWER

"...action, love, drama, and suspense... I didn't want the book to end."

Joha D, Amazon reviewer

"Dianna Wilkes has created a masterpiece with *Main Street*. Romance and intrigue flow readily throughout the story."

— J Banda, Amazon reviewer

"There are plenty of twists and turns, both emotional and evil."

— The Good, The Bad and The Unread

"...full of mystery, suspense, romance, and balanced out with humorous real-life moments."

— Lea Kirk, *USA Today* Bestselling Author

Praise for *Towne Square*

"This book perfectly balances the mystery surrounding these characters with the personal relationships both romantic and familial that everyone loves to read."

— Anthony Avina, author of the Nightmare Wars Series

"The characters are loveable and the drama kept me turning the pages."

— Victoria Gale, Goodreads

"... intriguing and fast paced. I liked the warmth that Dana and her extended family generates."

— Jo-Ann Carter, Goodreads

Praise for *South Pointe*

"...a tender book about loss and love and hope..."

— Bunnyhop, Amazon Reviewer

"...just what I needed after a hectic week at work..."

— Wild About Books!

"The characters are vividly realistic and relatable making it easy to fall into the story. An intriguing story that is sure to stay with you long after reading."

— Truly Trendy PR

ALSO BY DIANNA WILKES

Providence Island Series

Main Street, Book 1

Towne Square, Book 2

South Pointe, Book 3

Crossroads, Book 4

Boardwalk, Book 5 (coming 2021)

CROSSROADS

PROVIDENCE ISLAND, BOOK 4

DIANNA WILKES

Cover design: Karri Klawiter
www.artbykarri.com

Editing: Dana Delamar
By Your Side Self-Publishing
www.byyoursideselfpub.com

Formatting: Jenn Oliver
Sidekick Jenn – Virtual Author Assistant
https://sidekickjenn.com

CHAPTER ONE

Joshua Canfield stared out the front window of Carson's Pizza and Sandwich Shop. Fall flowers in large stone urns stood sentry along the street, swaying in the gentle autumn breeze. In a few weeks, it would be Halloween. This time last year, he'd been somewhere cold and rainy on the west coast. Portland? Or had he made it as far as Seattle?

Wherever he'd traveled, the stop had been temporary. Sometimes days, other times weeks. On one rare occasion, he'd spent a full two months on a ranch in Montana. The weather had been bitter cold and the work grueling. But each night he'd slept in the same bed.

Funny the things he'd come to see as a luxury.

The entire past year had been a world away from his former life. An innocent, sheltered life until his father handed him a packet of cash, a burner phone, and an order to leave home. According to James Canfield, their family was in danger. The ultimate threat was to Josh's mother, but as long as Joshua was alive she would be safe.

"Don't call or contact any of us, especially your Uncle Toddy. There's only one person you can trust." More than a year later, Josh still remembered the warmth of his father's hands on his shoulders. "Trust Ben Hampshire."

Trust his life to a man he barely knew?

A good thing he had because Ben sent warnings giving him time to escape before searchers could locate him. Ben taught him how to disguise himself, how to hide his trail, and how to fight.

How to kill.

The only thing Ben hadn't been able to do was save James Canfield's life. As for Uncle Toddy, aka Nathan Stoddard, he was dead too and his body cremated. The final step in sending whatever soul he'd possessed to a much warmer climate.

Josh shoved away those memories. His mother was safe. They were both on Providence Island, and he was putting his own life back together.

He walked to the entrance to lock up for the day when the door opened. Back-peddling, he narrowly avoided a collision with a young woman who halted mid-step.

Her eyes widened, and a blush crossed her cheeks. "I'm sorry. Did I hit you?"

A quick once-over showed she was tall and slim, almost too slender for her height. The plaid jacket looked well-worn, and the jeans were a bit faded, but both were immaculately clean. Smooth skin free of any cosmetics showed a hint of pink from the outdoors. Golden brown hair flowed around her shoulders. What caught his interest the most was the weary resolution clouding her hazel eyes.

A bit skittish too. More so than she should be over a minor mishap. He smiled, sensing she needed the reassurance. "Not a scratch on me. We are closed though."

"I'm here about the Help Wanted sign." Her shoulders sagged. "I'll come back tomorrow."

A year on the run taught Josh how to size up strangers, and

this woman obviously needed a job. "In that case, you're just in time. Come in."

The faintest of smiles appeared, and she stepped inside. Josh locked the door and flipped the sign to Closed. He held out one hand. "Joshua Canfield."

She put her hand in his for a quick shake. "Lila Grainger."

"Glad to meet you." He gestured toward the back of the room. "Have a seat at the table in the back while I grab an application."

The wary expression on the woman's face suggested she'd expected a different reaction from him upon hearing her last name. The Graingers were infamous due to their disregard for a lawful way of life. Josh had a close—and unpleasant—encounter of his own with one of them several months ago. Neither of which meant Lila was cut from the same cloth.

Judge not was his credo.

He grabbed an application from under the front counter then walked to the table where Lila waited. "You can start filling this out. I'll be back in a moment."

He dashed into the kitchen to check on the two current employees. Karen and Rick, both leaning against the main workstation, looked up from their whispered conversation.

"Waiting on our checks," Rick said, straightening.

A quick glance around confirmed the cleanup for the day had not been completed. "You could have finished in here while you were waiting."

Karen smirked. "Past quitting time."

Josh ignored their snickers while he unlocked the office. The slacking and the poor attitudes had gone on long enough. A conversation with owner Paige Carson would be on the agenda when she returned. He picked up the checks from Paige's desk then relocked the door. By the time he returned,

Karen and Rick had walked to the back exit. He handed a check to each.

"Write another check," Rick said. "I'm quitting and want my pay through today."

Josh shrugged. "You should have given your notice sooner. Any hours worked this week won't be paid until next Friday."

Rick took a half-step forward, narrowing his eyes. "Pay me in cash."

Like that's supposed to intimidate me? Josh let the smile slide off his lips. An Eastwood glint flickered in his gaze. "Not happening... and don't ask again."

Rick's tough guy stance sagged like a deflating balloon. "Yeah... well... I better have it next week... or else." He jerked the door open. "By the way, you suck."

"Good luck to you too." Josh touched a forefinger to his brow. He stepped back as Karen reached for the closing door. "I'll see you tomorrow."

She half-turned, not meeting his gaze. "I don't work weekends, and you don't need me to move all this stuff around."

"Yes, we do need your help. You told Paige you'd be here."

"Now, I can't." She waggled her fingers goodbye as she dashed outside. "See you Monday."

Josh shoved the deadbolt into place and grinned. "No, you won't."

Upgrades to Carson's, including the installation of the drive-thru window, meant the restaurant would be closed the following week, a situation that had been explained multiple times to the two employees. He could have reminded Karen of that before she left, but... too late now.

Seeing the leftover food that hadn't been put away or discarded, Josh prepared a quick snack. He needed a break and Lila looked like she could do with some food as well. He carried two bottles of water and a breadbasket to the table.

"Pizza nuggets," he said, sitting down in the chair opposite her. "We're adding them to the menu. Let me know if you like them."

Lila's gaze shifted to the food before she held out the application. "I'm finished."

He nodded toward the tray. "Don't wait on me while I look this over."

Lila plucked a nugget from the basket. She dipped it into one of the sauces and took a bite. Her eyes widened. "This is delicious."

Her joy over such a small thing lifted Josh's spirits, and he smiled. "One of the perks of working here is taste-testing the food." He watched her for a second longer before returning his attention to the application. "Waitress. Cook. Part-time bartender. Six years. Low Tide Bar and Grill." He looked up from the paper. "That's in lower PI, right?"

The wary look returned to her eyes. "On the west side. It's small but stays busy."

"Let me cover what the job here entails so you can decide if we fit what you're looking for." Josh sat back, resting clasped hands on the tabletop. "Currently, we're take-out only. We had delivery service but discontinued it a couple months ago due to a security incident."

He took a long pull from the water bottle, watching Lila lower her lashes. "Incident" was a minor word, considering Harley Grainger had attempted to rob Carson's while holding former employee Megan McCallister, owner Paige Carson, and Paige's daughter Jess at gunpoint. When Josh returned from a bank run, Harley was on the floor, thanks to a well-placed kick in the groin from Megan. Josh held the man down until law enforcement arrived.

He recapped the bottle. "The other reason was logistics. We received so many orders Megan couldn't deliver them without making multiple trips. That took time which cut into customer satisfaction. To offset the loss of revenue from the deliveries, the plan is to expand our hours and open the dining room."

Lila gestured toward a set of doors on the wall opposite the front counter. "Is that the dining room?"

"It is. We're also adding a pick-up window. The restaurant is closed next week for the installation, cleaning, and setting up the dining space. We're bound to get a rush when we reopen, so we'll need everyone full-time. After that, it'll be at least thirty hours a week." He named the hourly wage. "How does it sound so far?"

Her quick inhale gave the answer even before she spoke. "It sounds wonderful, and I'd love to work here."

"Final decision is up to the owner, Paige Carson. We'll be here tomorrow getting the kitchen ready for the installation on Monday. Can you come in around ten o'clock to talk with her?"

"Of course." She shifted on the chair, swinging her legs to one side. "Should I come to the front door?"

"Let me give you a number to call so someone can let you in." Josh pulled a Carson's card from the pocket of his polo shirt and jotted his cell phone number on the back side. He stood, took a step, then stopped. "How about I wrap up that leftover nugget to take with you?"

Lila's mouth dropped open as she stared at the lone nugget in the basket. A flush raced across her cheeks as she tucked the card into her pocket. "I ate more than I realized."

He flashed a quick thumbs-up to soothe away her embarrassment. "Sounds like we have a hit."

They walked to the exit. Lila paused in the open doorway and took a deep breath. "Thank you for staying after hours to talk with me and for the food."

"You're very welcome."

Lila dashed across the street to the bus stop. She moved with a lightness that had been missing when she'd first arrived. Josh grunted, thinking about the remaining work waiting in the kitchen.

At least Paige would be back tomorrow. When the opportunity arose to accompany her new husband, Sheriff Sam Wallace, to an out-of-state law-enforcement convention, she'd asked Josh to fill in as manager. He'd worked at Carson's only since early summer, but with the choice being Rick, Karen, or him—it was a no-brainer.

He headed toward the kitchen when a sharp tap sounded on the front door.

Better not be Rick wanting to go another round.

Deputy Tom Hunter stood outside, one hand lifted in greeting.

Once again, Josh unlocked the door. "Hey, Tom. I don't have any coffee made—"

"I'm not here for coffee." Tom jerked a thumb over one shoulder. "I need you to come with me to the sheriff's office."

In a flash, Josh's blood turned to ice. *Not again.* All the danger to his family should have ended with Toddy's death.

"Did something happen to my mother?"

Tom's stern expression softened. "As far as I know, Mrs. Canfield is fine."

"What's this about?"

The hardness returned to Tom's face. "It's about the murder of Nathan Stoddard, and some questions you might be able to answer."

Josh allowed his surprise to show on his face, a reaction the deputy would note if it were missing. He forced back the acid churning in his gut.

"I'll do whatever I can to help."

He locked the door behind them. They walked across the street to the sheriff's office, one building down from Carson's. Despite his heart racing in a frantic beat, Josh maintained an easy stride and even managed to make a casual comment about sports. The ploy seemed to work as he sensed the tension ease in the deputy's demeanor.

Five murders had occurred on PI in the last year. All but one of the victims had been shot three times—twice in the torso and once in the head, and each one of them deserved it. Toddy died months ago. Had the sheriff's department learned something that put Josh on their radar?

Then again, the summons might be nothing more than a fishing expedition to gather information about Toddy's past and any possible enemies. The man had operated under two personas—Josh's kindly but grumpy Uncle Toddy and the evil Nathan Stoddard. One of those lives was a lie; the other a mystery. He'd answer their questions the best he could and share what few details he knew.

The only thing he wouldn't share was that he'd stood next to Ben Hampshire while he shot Nathan Stoddard.

Josh settled into the wooden chair and stretched out his legs. He hadn't expected comfort, and the interview room didn't disappoint. The temperature hovered at a too-cool-to-be-comfortable degree, and his chair listed to the right, thanks to the shorter leg on that side.

No sign of Sheriff Wallace having returned from the convention. Strange that the meeting hadn't been delayed until his return. Maybe it was a routine follow-up, even if Deputy Hunter was making the most of the opportunity to be top-dog.

The silence was broken by the ominous click of the door, the echo of boot steps, then the rustle of papers as Tom flipped through a manila folder. As an attempt to set the scene for suspense, Hunter didn't have a clue.

Swallowing a laugh, Josh pulled out his cell phone and tapped on the screen. Tom's head shot up, and a scowl creased his face.

"Put the phone away."

"Sure, if you're ready to begin. I was making notes to review with Paige tomorrow." Josh bit back a grin and slid the phone to one side. Nothing like a mention of the boss's wife to throw off Hunter's stride.

The deputy jabbed a thumb on the console to turn on the video display. "I want you to look at some footage from the day Nathan Stoddard was murdered."

The day Toddy almost killed my mother.

Josh pushed that thought aside as a black-and-white video of Federal Street appeared. Seconds later, his own image came into view as he walked to a parked car.

Ben's car.

The passenger window lowered as Joshua came even with the car. He rested both forearms on the open sill then glanced around before entering the car. A few seconds later, the vehicle drove away.

Beginning their search to find Toddy before he could carry out his plan to kill Dana Canfield.

Josh shifted his gaze from the screen to the deputy. "What about it?"

"Where were you and Hampshire headed?"

"To the B&B where Ben's staying. Mrs. Porter needed some furniture moved. I told Ben I'd help."

Tom tapped the console again. The scene changed to the intersection two blocks up the street. The traffic light changed, and Ben's car turned right.

"Seems like he should have turned left to go to Maisie Porter's place."

"Except all the southbound roads on the east side were blocked off due to that house explosion in South Pointe. We headed to my place. Watched a game on TV and ate leftover pizza. Ben called Mrs. Porter to let her know we'd be there once the roads re-opened."

"Uh-huh." A brief silence simmered before Tom continued. "Did you go to Maisie's afterwards?"

"The roads were clear by the time the game was over. We moved the furniture then ate dinner with Mrs. Porter." Josh shifted on the chair. "Why are we going over this again?"

"When did you hear that Mrs. Canfield was in the hospital?"

Josh's throat tightened, and his chest ached with the same pain as it had that day. Racing to his mother's home to save her from Toddy, terrified he'd be too late. Only the sight of Nick Warden's truck in the driveway prevented them from stopping. His mother would be safe with Warden on the scene while he and Ben continued the hunt to find Toddy.

Josh blinked away the dampness in his eyes. "I called Megan to see if she was busy. She told me she was at the hospital and why."

Another nail in his soul. He *knew* but had to pretend he didn't. He'd forced his way into Megan's despair to give himself an alibi.

"But you didn't go to the hospital until several days later in the middle of the night."

"The family didn't need the extra drama." He shrugged. "I wanted Mom to be the first person to know I was here."

"You were here on PI long before Stoddard attacked Mrs. Canfield, weren't you?" Tom tapped one forefinger against the tabletop. "Working the Dog Cart down the street from your mother's office? Then at Carson's, using a fake identity."

"It wasn't fake. I went by Cole after my middle name Colby." Josh drew a long, slow breath. "After my father was murdered, I came here to see if I could prevent the same thing from happening to my mother."

"You and Hampshire seem tight. Did you know him before coming here?"

Time for another evasion. "I work at Carson's, and Ben's addicted to the coffee. As for when he first got here, that's a question you'll have to ask him."

Josh set the heels of his hands against the edge of the table, preparing to push back his chair. "Is that all? I need to get back to work."

Tom glanced at the frozen scene on the screen then back to Josh. "Considering what Stoddard did to your family, you must have wanted to kill him yourself."

"What I wanted was for him to lose his reputation, every cent of his money, and everything that meant anything to him."

Most of all, he *had* wanted to kill Stoddard. No threats. No mercy.

Stoddard's hand went to his jacket. The lines in his face were tight, and his teeth gleamed in an evil sneer. All traces of kindly Uncle Toddy had vanished.

Joshua lifted his gun.

Ben nudged him out of the way and fired three times.

Josh whirled on Ben, his gut raging that he'd been denied the justice he deserved. "Why did you stop me?"

Ben's eyes were killer-cold, but behind that ice lurked a shadow of something else. "You don't need anything else on your conscience."

The answer chafed, but as time went on, Joshua understood. He still remembered kindly Uncle Toddy. The hearty laugh, the snarky jokes, the outrageous stories. A man who'd been a part of Josh's life for as long as he could remember.

In the months since Toddy's death, Josh struggled to reconcile those two diverse personas. How could a man who'd been a part of the Canfield family hide that evil side for all those years? Accepting their love while time clicked away until he could steal a fortune?

Could he have pulled the trigger?

He'd done it before, shooting two contract killers hired by Stoddard to eliminate Ben Hampshire, and giving Ben the chance to take out the third person. If the deaths of those strangers who'd meant nothing to Joshua still weighed on him, how would he have handled the burden of taking Toddy's life?

"You gave up a lot for a woman who isn't your mother."

Joshua stiffened at the intended sting. He fought past the roaring in his ears and the fury blazing inside him.

"I was two years old when my biological mother died trying to kill Catherine McCall. She survived, but Stoddard drugged and manipulated her into believing she was Dana Canfield. All the years I had with her didn't go away because our DNA doesn't match."

He shoved the chair back, a hot glare locked on the deputy. "We're done here."

The cell phone next to Tom's hand buzzed. He gave it a glance then stood. "You can go."

Josh jerked open the door. He tugged the visitor badge from his pocket as he stormed down the hallway. He reached the lobby, and his pace slowed. Ben Hampshire stood at the front desk, forearms resting on the counter as he chatted with dispatcher Molly Kincaid.

Arms crossed over his chest, Deputy Bret Madigan stood

just inside the doorway, a sure sign he'd been the one dispatched to escort Ben in for questioning.

"Give your visitor badge to Ben," Molly said, jotting a note on the clipboard in front of her.

Rather than clipping the badge to his pocket, Ben juggled it between his hands. "Canfield, I have a couple software systems to show you. POS. KMS."

Molly chuckled. "Um... POS?"

Ben turned a mega-watt smile on the woman and winked. "Point of Sale. KMS is Kitchen Management Service."

Josh bit back a groan. Of course, Ben would flirt with the dispatcher. Not because she was single and attractive, but because it was an open secret that Deputy Hunter had his eye on Molly.

"Hampshire." Tom's voice boomed through the room. "Let's get this over with."

"Certainly." Ben turned, walking backward as he continued talking. "Got time today?"

Josh bit back a grin as Bret attempted to speed Ben's pace. "I have work to finish across the street, but I'm free after that."

"I'll swing by Carson's when I'm finished here."

Josh lifted one hand as Ben side-stepped into the interview room. A solid click of the door followed.

His own interrogation hadn't gone the way he'd expected. When Hunter launched the video, Josh assumed Ben was the intended person of interest. The line of questioning quickly revealed it was Josh who was under scrutiny.

Or maybe both.

He looked up to see Molly watching him, her expression soft and sympathetic.

"Molly—"

"I can't answer any questions."

"Maybe just one." He leaned forward, lowering his tone. "Does Sam know Tom is conducting these interviews?"

Molly glanced down the hallway, and a slight pucker creased her brow. "When Sam's out of the office, Tom's in charge."

Josh nodded. The answer revealed nothing he didn't already know but confirmed what he suspected.

~

Floors mopped. Counters wiped. Trash ready to take out the back door. Joshua initialed each completed task on the job board before checking his watch. *Where are you, Ben?*

Considering Tom Hunter's ambition to solve Toddy's murder and Ben's high opinion of his own intellect, there had to be major head-butting going on across the street. Under different circumstances, he and Ben would never have been friends or even casual acquaintances. To say they even were friends was a question Josh couldn't readily determine. More like mutual survivors of war.

Secrets and lies bonded them. Both had committed crimes, though Ben's sins were deeper than his own. However, Ben could leave PI with no ties.

I'm tired of running. Tired of hiding and lying. I need...

Peace. Home. Family.

Something he'd never achieve with this layer of guilt eating away at his conscience.

A buzz sounded. He grabbed his phone and found a text from Paige.

Chg in plans. Reasons. Don't move thgs.

Did the change mean Carson's would open on Monday as usual? If so, they'd need to restock the perishables. No point texting when they could discuss the matter in full tomorrow.

One thing he would do is give Paige a heads up about Lila. No need to mention names at this point.

He typed a quick reply. *Are we still mtg tomorrow mrng?*

Yep

Applicant coming in for interview

Cool. C U then

A second buzz emitted, this time with a text from Ben.

Parked out back. Lets go.

Josh flipped out the lights, grabbed the bag of trash, and headed out the door. He tossed the bag into dumpster then entered the car.

"How did the questioning go?"

"Hunter seemed disappointed that our stories matched. He asked why I wasn't driving the same car as I had that day. Told him both were rentals. When I travel, I turn in one and rent another when I return." Ben chuckled. "He also tried to trip me by asking where we ordered the pizza."

Josh frowned. "I told him it was leftover."

"He was fact checking."

Except their alibis consisted more of half-truths than solid facts.

"Good thing you remembered those security cameras along Federal."

Ben shrugged. "We needed a cover story anyway. Did you get the impression they were considering if you and Stoddard were collaborating?"

"No, but Tom suggested I had reason to want to kill him."

"Speaking of killing, did you dispose of that gun you had?"

"Yes, I broke it down the way you taught me. I took a trip upstate and dropped off pieces along the way." Rest stop. Gas stations. Dumpsters. "What about the one you used?"

A side-eyed glance burned its way across the car. "Taken

care of. Should be interesting to find out what Wallace does with Hunter's suspicions."

"You're getting a kick out of this, aren't you?" Josh twisted in his seat, sending a glare of his own. "This isn't a game. We could end up in prison."

"Take it easy, Sundance. We've covered our tracks. Nothing links me to Stoddard. Hunter's trying to make something out of a ten-second video of two buddies getting together."

Josh glanced out the window. "Where are we going?"

"To dinner. Eddie's work for you?"

Josh snorted. "Ben Hampshire is going to eat at Eddie's Sea-Shack?"

"Don't be a snob, Canfield." A smile tugged at the corner of Ben's mouth. "We'll go over the reports I have on those systems. When Hunter spills his guts to Wallace who in turn asks Paige, she'll confirm our story."

Josh sank down in his seat with a grunt. "One of these days, you won't be the smartest guy in the room."

A laugh tumbled out of Ben's mouth as he flipped on the blinker to turn south at the Crossroads. "Like that's going to happen."

A wisp of something cold washed through Josh's soul, and the memory of odors from a greasy kitchen pushed into his throat.

"It did happen." He turned his head to catch Hampshire's scowl. "That night at the diner when Stoddard set you up."

Ben's eyes widened then he gave a slow nod. "I had my suspicions from the beginning about that meeting. I didn't expect to him to send three people. Didn't expect you to show up either." He gave a short laugh. "Did I ever thank you for saving my ass?"

Josh snorted. "You said—and I quote—'thanks for back there.'"

"Glad I didn't forget. As far as that parody Hunter put on today, forget it. He's on an ego trip and taking advantage of Wallace being out of town. We have nothing to worry about."

Except Tom Hunter's determination to solve Nathan Stoddard's murder put both Ben and Joshua in the spotlight. As brilliant as Ben was, Tom's ambition could prove to be way more dangerous.

CHAPTER TWO

The scent of someone's dinner cooking mingled with the odor from the near-by dumpster. Two more days remained before the next pick-up, and the smell of garbage already made its way halfway across the parking lot. Lila held her breath and quickened her steps to the front door of her apartment.

She sank on the small sofa and kicked off her shoes. Legs outstretched, she closed her eyes and took a deep breath. A light citrus scent made from a mixture of baking soda and orange peels filled the small space.

It wasn't much. One small room with a make-shift kitchen and a bare-bones bathroom, and she treasured every inch of it.

Lila ran her palm over the worn fabric on the sofa. That piece along with a well-worn chair, a bed, and a dresser were all she had left from her childhood home. She pulled the afghan crocheted by her mother from the back of the couch and wrapped it around her shoulders. Snuggled under the soft folds, she imagined it was her mother's arms surrounding her again.

I'm not giving up, Mama. I'm working hard and saving as much as I can so I can leave this place far behind. That was our dream, and I'm going to live it for you.

Leaving PI would take way more money than she'd saved so far. First step was getting the job at Carson's. She crossed two fingers, a superstitious and childish act, but she still made a wish.

Just one time, let me have a break.

Was a decent job too much to ask for? One that wasn't in a cracker box building that should have been condemned by the health department years ago. Smoke so thick, it could be smelled from a half-block away. Drunks with wandering hands. Co-workers stealing tips. At least she wasn't scheduled to work at the Low Tide tonight. Fridays and Saturdays were the best night for tips. Of course, Angie claimed those shifts, and Cousin Jeffy gave them to her because... Angie.

Carson's might have its downside, but it had to be Heaven compared to the Low Tide. Too bad she hadn't thought to ask Joshua if she could tour the kitchen while she was there.

A smile crossed her lips. Joshua Canfield was one handsome man. Not in a slick magazine way, but real life gorgeous. Wavy brown hair, blue eyes, and the athletic build of a runner. And that voice? Warm and rich like hot fudge on a sundae.

The same kind of guy who'd never give her a second glance, and that was okay. She didn't want anything more than a steady paycheck.

Though looking wouldn't hurt, would it?

❧

Paige Carson Wallace bounced on her toes, waiting for Dana to answer the door. As much as she'd enjoyed a week away with Sam—even though his days had been spent in seminars—she couldn't wait to see her daughter.

Goddaughter by birth, Jess became her daughter after the death of Paige's childhood friend Claire last summer. Since starting school, Jess had made the switch from "Paige and Sam" to "Mom and Dad," a change that still thrilled Paige.

"Oops," Sam said, resting his palms on her shoulders. "Forgot the crowbar."

She twisted her neck to look up at him. "Why do you need a crowbar?"

"To pry little Miss away from Nick and Dana."

Nonsense. As happy as Jess was to stay with her honorary grandparents, she had to be counting down the seconds until she was back at home with her own family.

They were barely through the front door when screams of "Mom! Dad!" and canine yips shot down the stairway. Jess bolted out of one of the bedrooms and raced down the steps. Robert, a Jack Russell terrier, scampered behind her.

Jess leaped off the third step from the bottom into Sam's waiting arms. A kiss and a hug were followed by a squirming reach for Paige while the puppy yipped for attention.

Paige blinked back tears as she received her own round of hugs and kisses before setting Jess back on her feet.

Dana gestured toward the living room. "Can you stay for a few minutes?"

"We'd like to, but we're tired from the drive." The puppy circled through Sam's legs before collapsing on his boots. "Is Jess's suitcase packed?"

Paige glanced around to ask her daughter that same question. "Where did she go?" Really, that girl could zip out of sight quicker than a body could take a breath.

"Here." Seated on the living room couch, Jess lifted one hand in a royal wave. She patted the cushion next to her with her other hand. "Let's visit for a while."

Oh, great. Now, her daughter was channeling Dana.

Paige took a deep breath. "We need to get home, baby. Run upstairs and finish packing."

Jess blinked several times. A sure sign she was considering another tactic.

"Granna's fixing chili and cornbread for dinner. Besides, Grandad isn't home from work. I can't leave without telling him good-bye."

"He'll understand." A hint of "don't make me count" seeped into Paige's voice.

Jess pushed to her feet, heaving a heavy sigh. The moan lasted the distance between the couch and staircase where she mounted a mournful trek up the steps.

Sam chuckled. "I've taken prisoners to jail who didn't drag their feet as much."

Paige rolled her eyes then turned to Dana. "We would stay, but—"

A quick side-arm hug from Dana silenced Paige's apology. "I understand. You've been gone all week and want go home."

"I need help with my suitcase." Jess stood at the head of the stairs. Her ponytail swayed side-to-side as she hopped from one foot to the other.

"My cue." Sam slid his feet from under the puppy. "I'll carry everything out to the car."

"Jess's book bag is sitting by the table in the foyer." Dana held up her cell phone. "While Sam is loading the car, would you mind if Jess called Nick to tell him she's leaving? Just a quick call."

Pick your battles, Paige reminded herself. "No, I don't mind."

She waited until Jess opened the door for Sam to carry out the suitcase and book bag. "Jess, come here if you want to talk to Granddad before we leave."

"Yes, please!"

Jess held out her hand for the phone then zipped back to the couch. With a shrug, Paige followed with Dana.

"Hi, Grandad... How's your day going? Did you eat all your lunch without interruption? Uh-huh... Yeah... Did they rotate the tires on Mr. Sims's car? He needs to stop taking those corners so fast."

Paige forced the grin from her face and held up her forefinger in a warning. "One minute."

Jess nodded. "I'm calling because Mom and Dad are here, and I have to go home." A long pause followed. "That's what I meant to say—I *get* to go home. I wanted to tell you good-bye since I'll be gone before you come home from work."

Her head bobbed again. "Okay, I'll see you in church on Sunday. Love you, Grandad!" Her face beamed with a toothy grin as she handed the phone back to Dana. She shifted on the couch, nestling her head against Paige's arm.

"Thank you for letting me call Grandad."

"You're welcome. Time to roll. Dad's waiting."

Jess slipped her hand into Dana's as they walked to the front porch.

"Thank you for visiting," Dana said, exchanging a tight hug with the child.

"You're welcome. Thank you for taking care of me. I love you, Granna."

"I love you too, baby."

Jess dashed toward the SUV, pausing to slap a hand against her leg. "Come on, Robert. We're going home!"

The puppy spun around from the bushes he was examining and scampered after Jess. Paige's heart swelled as Sam lifted Jess and Robert into the SUV.

My family.

CHAPTER THREE

The back door to Carson's swung open, and Paige swept into the kitchen. Arms outspread, she spun in a circle. "I'm back! Gosh, I've missed this place."

Joshua leaned against the prep counter, grinning. The woman was a force of nature from sunshine to storms. Too bad he had to dump bad news on her. Until then, he'd enjoy this happy moment.

"We missed you too. Enjoy your trip?"

"Williamsburg is amazing. It would have been better if Sam hadn't been stuck in meetings all day. I'd love to go back there with Jess." She spun again, this time at a slower pace. "So, catch me up."

The door opened again, this time to admit Rhys and Jamie McCall.

"Morning, everyone," Rhys said. "Any coffee?"

"Coffee and breakfast burritos." Josh glanced over his shoulder. "Tea or juice, Jamie?"

Jamie lifted a travel mug. "Juice. Brought mine with me."

Paige waved both hands toward the kitchen door. "Let's move out front."

They settled at the four-top table located in the back of the restaurant, a cozy spot hidden from the customer area by a half-wall.

"Was Jess upset that you had to work today?" Jamie asked as she selected a burrito.

"Yes, but she got over it when Sam told her he wanted 'daddy and daughter time.'" Paige shifted onto one hip to retrieve her cell phone. "You have to hear this voice mail message from Jess. This is from the second day we were gone." Seeing the look on Rhys's face, she added, "No, she doesn't have her own phone. Dana let Jess use hers."

Paige hit the play button.

"*Mom, it's me... Jess... I wanted to let you know I'm doing better.*" Her voice broke into a whimper. "*I really am... I only cried once at school but it was in the bathroom, so nobody knew. The rest of the day was okay. Granddad took me to school this morning, and Granna picked me up this afternoon.*"

The sob shifted into a short giggle.

"*Grandad's taking us out to eat at Eddie's tonight. You remember Eddie's, don't you? That's where you, me, and Dad went the first time we all went out together. Megan's coming too, but not Uncle Rhys and Aunt Jamie. They're having a date night. Well, Granna and I need to freshen up before we go out. Call me back when you get this message. I love you.*" A sniff sounded, followed by a whispered, "*Bye, Mom.*"

"That is the most hilarious yet heartbreaking thing I've ever heard." Rhys's chuckle morphed into a wince as Jamie jabbed an elbow into his ribs.

"No, he's right. I laughed and cried when I listened to it." Paige sighed. "I'm glad she had a good time even though she missed us."

"I'm glad you're home too," Rhys said. "Now can we discuss

the not-to-be-installation? Because I'm ticked that I have a window that isn't going to be used and a work crew that has to be rescheduled."

"Not yet." She tapped a drum roll on the table. "Josh, I want to hear what's been going on here. Karen texted me twice last night and called once this morning. I didn't want to answer her until I got the scoop from you."

"You didn't read the text?" Josh asked. It was no surprise that Karen went straight to Paige as soon as she remembered the restaurant was scheduled to be closed next week.

"I wanted the glow to last till Monday, but I'm guessing you're about to wipe that shine away."

He held up both hands. "Don't kill the messenger."

She smiled, showing her teeth. "Spill it, Canfield."

"While I was giving out the checks, Rick quit and demanded that I pay him for this week. I shut that down and told him he could pick up his remaining pay next Friday."

Paige huffed. "Good for you, and good riddance to Rick. What's the deal with Karen?"

"She informed me she didn't work weekends and wasn't coming in today."

"Didn't you remind her? She was counting on getting paid for today to offset the restaurant being closed next week."

"She left before I could." He nodded to Paige's phone. "Obviously she's figured it out. You and I need to talk about this last week before you speak with her."

"Ugh. My glow is officially gone." Paige's brow creased as she read the texts. "Says she'll be here around noon. I'll let her know there's been a change in plans and not to come in."

"She'll call or text you back about next week," Jamie said.

Paige shrugged. "I don't even know the answer to that question right now."

Rhys tapped a forefinger on the tabletop. "Can we get started?"

"One more thing to discuss first." Josh slid Lila's application in front of Paige. "She's coming in this morning for an interview. I should have cleared it with you first but with us now being another person short, we need someone as soon as possible."

Paige waved the apology away and picked up the paper. Less than five seconds passed before the explosion erupted.

"Are you *crazy?*" Heat rose in her face, and she drew her hands into fists. "You expect me to hire a Grainger?"

"Lila Grainger has restaurant experience which we need."

"At the Low Tide." Paige pointed toward the front of the building. "On this very street, Buzz Grainger tried to kill Dana by almost running her over with a stolen truck. Maybe you weren't here on PI when that happened, but you were when Harley Grainger held Megan, Jess, and me at gunpoint. Jess had nightmares for weeks after that, and now you expect me to bring another Grainger into our lives?" She threw up both hands. "Hey, at least she won't need a gun to rob me. She can take the money straight from the till."

Jamie's gasped. "Paige, that's not fair."

Paige shot a steaming glare across the table. "I'm not the villain here."

"Neither is Lila." Josh drew a deep breath. "I knew you'd have reservations when you saw the name, but I didn't realize how deeply it would upset you."

The phone in front of Josh vibrated, and he glanced at the display. The number was unfamiliar, but it had to be Lila. "She's probably out front now. I'll meet her at the door and let her know."

Jamie lifted one hand. "Is Lila the same person you called Nick about last night?"

Paige's mouth dropped open. "You asked Nick to give her a job?"

"I asked if he had any openings in his office at the garage, would he consider talking with her."

"Why are you doing this? She has a job."

Josh met her fiery gaze. He understood Paige's anger—and her fear—but she wasn't the only person to be considered. "Because she wants something better for herself."

He was halfway to the entrance when Paige called his name.

"I'll talk with her."

Josh turned, waiting until she nodded.

"I'll keep an open mind." She tipped her head toward the kitchen. "Bring her back to my office."

"Thank you."

He didn't let his smile show until he walked away. Paige hadn't disappointed him. She'd opened her mind to the possibility. It was up to Lila to see if she could open Paige's heart.

❦

No answer.

Lila sank down on the bench by the Towne Square bus stop. Maybe Joshua Canfield decided not to risk his job by giving her application to his boss. Considering he'd been escorted to the Sheriff's office yesterday afternoon—something she'd witnessed while sitting on this same bench— maybe he was in jail. It wouldn't be the first time her boss, real or potential, had been taken into custody.

Buck up, Lila. You're not getting off this rock by sitting on a cold bench. You made it past closing time and a locked door yesterday.

Whatever reason Joshua hadn't answered her call, she wasn't taking 'no' for an answer without someone having the courtesy to tell her to her face. After a quick check for oncoming traffic, Lila bolted across the street. Before she reached the sidewalk, the front door to Carson's opened. Joshua Canfield stepped through the door. He lifted his hand in greeting, and the smile on his face bumped her heartbeat up a notch.

"Sorry for missing your call. I figured you were close, and it would be quicker to meet you at the door."

"Good morning." Her breath stilled as she met his friendly gaze. Yep, he was not only handsome but a gentleman too, holding the door as she entered and asking to take her coat, which she declined. Depending on how the interview went, she might need to make a quick exit.

Her pace slowed as she followed Joshua through the kitchen. The spacious area with the shiny appliances and counters sang to her heart, and her hopes grew a little stronger.

I could be happy here.

She glanced past Joshua's shoulder to see a woman about her age seated at a small desk. Her head was bowed, her eyes fixed on a paper in her hands.

Joshua tapped on the door frame. "Paige, Lila's here for her interview. Lila, this is Paige Carson."

"Josh, close the door on your way out, will you? I'll be with you in a moment, Lila. Have a seat. I'm almost finished reviewing your application."

The glance Ms. Carson spared both of them was so brief she couldn't have caught the frown that flashed across Josh's face.

Lila sat down, waiting silently. With each second, her hopes began to dissolve.

"Ms. Carson, I don't want to waste your time if you have no

interest in hiring me. But I would like the chance to change your mind."

The woman looked up, her expression blank as she slid the application to one side of her desk. "Go ahead."

Lila hesitated, torn between pride and need. What was the use in humiliating herself in front of this woman when it wouldn't change the outcome? Or would it? She expected to see derision on Ms. Carson's face. Instead, the woman's eyes began to glisten and the barest hint of a quiver hovered at the edges of her mouth.

She's afraid.

Whether it was fear of Lila or the Graingers as a group, this was a battle she couldn't win. The hope that had lifted her spirits since yesterday drained away like it had never existed. "I'm sorry I wasted your time—"

"Lila, wait. Don't leave."

Ms. Carson circled the desk to sit down in the chair next to her. A frown creased her brow, her hands still shook, but her gaze was open and honest.

"When I saw your last name, I flashed back to when Harley Grainger tried to rob my restaurant. My daughter was here. She was five years old at the time. After that happened, she had nightmares and for a while she didn't want to come in the restaurant."

Another portion of Lila's anger faded. She couldn't fault a mama for protecting her child. "Is she doing better?"

"She is." A faint smile replaced the frown. "As for my reaction, that's on me. You had nothing to do with what happened. I was rude, and worse than that, I hurt your feelings. I'm truly sorry."

A cool rush of relief swept through Lila, and she nodded. "Apology accepted, Ms. Carson."

"Call me Paige," she said with a broad grin. "Let's talk about the job. How did you find out about the opening?"

"By chance. I was on my way to the bus stop when I saw the sign in the window."

"Are you looking for a full-time position or a second part-time job?"

"Preferably full-time. Even if it's part-time, I'd like to work here. My current job is random hours and low pay. It's late nights, and it's smoky and noisy." She shrugged. "It's the Low Tide."

Lila's hand curled into a ball on her lap. "I'm a hard worker. I'll work weekends or evenings, if that's what you need. I'm honest too. You'll never have to doubt that I'll be square with you."

Paige's gaze darted to the application on her desk then back to Lila.

"How soon can you start?"

Lila fought back the lump in her throat. "I have the job?"

"You have the job."

The knot in her stomach dissolved, replaced by butterflies that flitted a happy dance. Whether the offer was made because of a guilty conscience or as an apology didn't matter. She wanted a chance to prove herself, and she had exactly that.

"I can start immediately."

"Don't take offense at this next part. I said something similar to Megan when I hired her last summer. There's no drug test or background check. They cost money I don't have to spend, and my husband's the sheriff."

"Sounds more than fair."

"Oh, and whatever Josh told you about the job, forget it, because the plan has changed. We're having a meeting in the front office." Paige jumped to her feet, gesturing toward the door. "We'll handle the rest of the paperwork later."

Lila followed Paige through the kitchen. She'd spotted two other people besides Joshua as she'd passed through the front of the restaurant. If she had Paige on her side, she shouldn't be nervous about the other employees. As far as sitting down with Joshua, she wasn't nervous about that.

Not at all.

❧

The "front office" turned out to be the same four-top table where Lila had sat yesterday. Joshua stepped away to retrieve a fifth chair while Paige made the introductions to the other two people.

"This is Rhys McCall. He's co-owner of McCall Construction. We grew up together, so he's practically my brother."

Rhys glared over the rim of his cup. "Which she doesn't hesitate to use to her advantage."

The teasing note in the man's voice along with an upper quirk on one side of his mouth said more about the relationship than Paige's explanation.

"Anyway, glad to meet you, Lila." Rhys nodded toward the burritos. "Help yourself to breakfast."

Lila glanced next at the woman sitting beside Rhys—a gorgeous blonde with startling blue eyes and a welcoming smile.

"I'm Jamie McCall. Married to this guy, and this—" She patted the bump on her stomach. "—is Baby Mac."

"Nice to meet you," Lila replied. "And congratulations."

Josh returned with an additional chair along with a plate which he set in front of Lila. She poured a glass of juice then selected one of the burritos.

"Hey, Josh, can you come by Mom's house tomorrow around noon?" Rhys asked. "She wants to show us the diagram for the furniture placement on Wednesday."

Before Josh could answer, Paige interrupted. "Rhys McCall, did I see you roll your eyes?"

Rhys gave a half-grin. "Maybe. If you'd been looking at Josh, you might have seen another one."

She huffed with pretend anger. "You guys are the worst. Your mother is getting married in four days. Is it *too much* for the two of you to help make her day perfect? Is that *too much* for her to ask of her sons?"

Mother? Sons? Lila blinked, trying to keep up with the back-and-forth banter.

"You need to work on your guilt trip." Rhys nodded to Josh. "Mom could set both of us straight with a crook of one eyebrow. Am I right?"

Josh nodded, but without a smile. "With middle names thrown in for emphasis."

Lila gasped as the connection clicked. "Wait... Are you two brothers?"

The chatter quieted, and Josh shifted on his chair. "Actually—"

"Half-brothers," Rhys said with a wink, a friendly gesture that soothed Lila's embarrassment. He continued his peace-making by changing the subject. "Paige, can we get started now?"

"Yes, oh, patient one," Paige replied. "I thought about the proposed changes while I was out of town and why they wouldn't work. Lots of reasons—"

Rhys twirled his finger in a "move along" motion.

Paige huffed. "Which I won't go into for the sake of time. New plan starts with resuming delivery service. I'm getting a new vehicle but keeping the Jeep. That way we can deliver orders faster and expand our delivery area."

Josh held up one hand. "Who'll make the deliveries, and what's our service area?"

"Aaron Haskell. He worked here for a brief time last summer before taking a job at the Lighthouse Cantina. I ran into him last week, and he asked about working part-time." She threw a quick glance at Josh. "Sorry. Busy. Forgot to tell you."

"Does that excuse work in both directions?"

She wrinkled her nose at him. "Absolutely not."

"Got it. So, Aaron. Part-time. Deliveries." Josh jotted the info into his notebook. "And the coverage?"

"I'm assigning that to you. By Monday is fine."

Josh snorted. "Sure, ask the guy who's only lived here a couple of months."

"I have every confidence in you." Paige pressed a hand above her heart for a brief moment. "Moving on. I'm holding off opening the dining room. People might spend a little more by eating here rather than take out, but they'll also linger which means no turn-over of tables. For now, I'll keep it closed."

Lila frowned at the closed pocket doors. So much for tips. If she'd calculated the dimensions of the room accurately, there might be another way to bring in extra money.

"What about—" She clamped her lips shut as everyone at the table looked at her. Her heart thumped, the beat echoing in her ears.

Josh tipped his glass at her. "Lila, you're fitting in already. Around this group, jump in when you have something to say."

Despite that warm assurance, Lila cast a quick glance at Paige who nodded.

"Have you considered using the space for special events? Baby showers. Birthday parties. Business luncheons."

"That's a great idea," Jamie said. "Think about it, Paige. You'll make money on the food plus rental of the room."

Paige narrowed her eyes as she stared at the door, then nodded. "I agree. It's a good idea, Lila. Let's give it a try." She slapped her palms onto the tabletop. "Which brings me to my brilliant idea. Carson's Classics."

A small smile crossed Rhys's mouth. "From the old Carson Drive-In?"

"Yep. I'll have a different entrée with sides each week. Maybe two. For dinner pick-up only. Ordered and paid in advance. We'll still close the doors at two. This give us time to complete the orders for pickup by... say... five-thirty. Six, at the latest. That gives people who work time to get here and someone doesn't have to stay too late."

"Someone meaning me," Josh said.

"Yes-s-s?"

He chuckled and nodded his head. "I don't mind."

"What about one of us carrying the order to the customer's car?" Lila asked. "The person can add a description of the car to the order. Is that possible?"

"That's a Ben question. Maybe the city will let us reserve two spots in front of the building for pick-up. I'll ask Sam if that's possible." Paige whirled in her chair toward Josh. "Did Ben get info on the software and other stuff I want?"

"I got an overview of it from him last night."

"When can he show it to me?"

Josh pulled out his phone. "Let me check."

"Who's Ben?" Rhys said to Jamie.

"Ben Hampshire. Computer guy staying at Maisie Porter's B&B."

"Oh, yeah." Rhys nodded. "The guy who's dating Stacy."

Squeals from Paige and Jamie sent Josh's phone tumbling from his hands. "What—" He bit off the exclamation and retrieved his phone.

"Stacy Andrews?" Paige tapped a quick beat on the table. "Stacy who works at McCall's? That Stacy?"

A dimple flickered in Rhys' cheek. "I was coming back from lunch one day last week and saw them engaged in a rather hot lip-lock."

Paige's mouth dropped open. "And?"

Rhys shrugged. "I minded my business and went back to work."

"Keep it down, guys," Josh said. "I'm calling him now."

"Josh," Jamie said in a low voice. "Check if he can meet with me Monday morning around ten a.m. It has to do with Main Street."

Paige waved one hand. "Put him on speaker."

He gave an eye-roll then nodded.

"Hey, Canfield. What's up?"

"I'm at Carson's, and you're on speaker. Can you meet with Paige and me on Monday to go over those systems?"

"One o'clock work for you?"

After a nod from Paige, Josh said, "That works. Also, Jamie McCall wants to know if you have time to meet with her on Monday. Ten a.m. at the Canfield building. Main Street stuff."

"I have another appointment at ten, but I can meet with her at ten-thirty."

Josh frowned. "Will you have time to get to her office from your other meeting?"

"Not a problem. It's in the same building with your mom. Got another call. Later."

Josh stared at the blank screen. "He hung up on me."

"Right, another call." Paige snickered. "I heard Stacy in the background."

"None of our... Hang on." Rhys tugged his cell phone from his pocket. A frown creased his brow as he studied the screen. "I need to leave."

Jamie rested a hand on his forearm. "Anything wrong?"

"No idea other than something to do with a job site." He pushed back his chair and stood. "Paige, since the window is a no-go, let me know if you need anything. Josh, I'll see you tomorrow. Lila, good to meet you."

"It was nice to meet you too, Rhys."

He dropped a light kiss onto Jamie's cheek. "I'll give you a call when I know how long I'll be. Sam's picking me up. I'll get a ride home from him."

Paige's mouth dropped open. "Sam's supposed to spend the day with Jess. Who's watching her?"

Rhys nodded to the front of the building. "Don't know, but they're both out front."

⌒

Despite Rhys's longer stride, Paige beat him to the door by seconds. Before she could speak, Sam delivered a quick kiss to her mouth.

"Can't talk. Call you later. Jess is ticked at both of us."

He delivered one more kiss then dashed to the waiting cruiser. Rhys followed close behind.

Paige locked the door then turned her attention to a pouting Jess. Her heart sank as she spied tear-streaks on her daughter's cheeks.

"It's not fair! I didn't see you all week. It's Saturday, and you're working and Dad's working."

Paige crouched, taking both of Jess's hands in hers. "You're with me now, and I'm done with work. How about we head to Main Street? We'll have lunch and get mani-pedis."

Jess gasped, her eyes widening. "Yes, please. Oh, thank you!"

The stress of the upcoming changes faded. Work could wait until Monday. Time with her daughter was more important. She wiped the tears from Jess's cheeks with her thumbs.

"You're welcome. Go tell everyone hello before we head out."

Hand in hand, they walked to the table. Jess climbed onto one of the vacant chairs. "Hi, Uncle Josh. Hi, Aunt Jamie."

"Jess, this is Lila. She's going to be working here."

"Hi, Lila. I worked here last summer. You'll like it."

Lila exchanged an amused glance with Paige. "I'm sure I will."

"Since Sam got called in to work, I'm calling it a day here. Let's regroup on Monday."

"Open or closed?" Josh asked.

Paige heaved a sigh. "I hate to close since we're not installing the window. But there's so much we need to decide and plan, I don't see how we can open especially with Dana's wedding on Wednesday and whatever schedule Ben sets for software systems."

"Closed it is," Josh said. "We'll lose money this week, but we'll make it up with these changes."

"I made notes," Jamie said. "I'll send those to you so you can combine them with yours."

"What about Karen?"

"I'll text her to come in. At least for Monday." Catching the hesitant look on Lila's face, Paige said, "You too, Lila. We need to fill out your paperwork. Can you be here at nine?"

"I'll be here."

"Did Sam say what the problem was at the job site?" Jamie asked.

"No. He kissed and ran."

"Somebody died." Knees on the chair, Jess studied the left-over burritos then wrinkled her nose.

Jamie's eyes widened. "One of the construction guys?"

She shook her head. "Someone they found while they were digging."

Paige's jaw dropped. A fire lit inside her. No wonder Sam was so quick to take off. "Did Dad talk about this in front of you?"

Jess eased back in the chair. "Not on purpose."

"How did you hear it?"

"I was coloring under the table in the big room. I was pretending I was camping and that was my cabin because it's too cold to camp outside in a tent. Dad and Mike and Bret came in and started talking, and I didn't want to interrupt." She gave the platter another look and wrinkled her nose again. "Can we go now? I'm hungry."

"Sure, baby." Paige waited as Jess scrambled down from her chair. "Josh, would you mind cleaning and locking up?"

"No problem."

"Thanks. Okay, kiddo. Let's roll."

Settled in the jeep and heading toward Main Street Village, Paige hummed along with the radio. A quick glance to the back showed Jess bopping her head in time to the music.

"Jess, do you want to talk about what you overheard at Daddy's work?"

A puzzled looked crossed her daughter's face. "No."

"Are you sure? If you're upset or scared—"

"I'm not, Mom. The person is from a long time ago so it's nobody we know." She turned her face to the window and resumed bopping her head.

Paige pushed her worries away. Jess seemed to be handling the news with no problem. As for Sam, it was hardly his fault to think about checking under the table for a curious six-year old.

She turned the volume up another notch. A glance in the mirror showed Jess giving her a thumbs up.

I need this day. Me and Jess doing girl-stuff and having fun. Poor Sam is missing his Daddy Day. Her smile widened. They'd make it up to him tonight with his favorite home-cooked dinner.

CHAPTER FOUR

Lila collected the used plates and napkins, watching under her lashes as Jamie donned a plum-colored jacket, a perfect shade for her blonde hair and blue eyes. She held back a sigh. The woman had been nothing but nice to her. Still, it was hard not to feel envious of someone who seemed to have everything.

Beautiful face. Handsome husband. A baby on the way.

Some day....

"Do you have any plans for the rest of the day?" Jamie asked.

Lila shrugged. "I'm staying to help Josh clean up."

"How would you like to take a ride to Morgan's Wood-works with me?

Lila frowned. "Why?"

Jamie stiffened, her face reddening.

Oh, shucks! That didn't come out the way I intended.

"Jamie, I'm sorry. I didn't mean to offend you or hurt your feelings." She swallowed the lump in her throat. "I don't know why you'd want my company."

The explanation sounded lame as soon as the words left

her mouth. How could someone like Jamie McCall understand her reasons?

"I want to get to know you since you'll be working with my best friend. Plus, I work right down the street, so we'll be seeing each other frequently." The stiffness eased from her stance, and her expression softened. "Most of all, because I know what it's like to be the new person."

"I've lived here all my life."

"New job. New friends." Jamie picked up her purse then handed Lila's bag to her. "What do you say?"

Friends.

A lightness seeped through her veins. Maybe a job wasn't the only wish she was getting today.

"Yes, I'd like to take that ride with you."

"I'm parked out back. We'll let Josh know we're leaving."

Lila glanced at the breakfast remains. It didn't seem fair to leave the job of cleaning up to Joshua especially since he had double-duty last week with Paige being gone.

Both of them gave me this chance. I'll make double-sure neither one of them regrets it.

"I should help—"

"I have it covered." Josh rounded the half-wall, serving tray in hand. "Your official start day is Monday. Head out and enjoy the rest of your day."

Jamie cut in before Lila made another protest. "Thanks, Josh. You do the same, and we'll see you tomorrow at Dana's."

Josh sent a quick glance before returning his attention to the table. "See you then."

Jamie gave a wave then motioned Lila to follow her. They passed through the kitchen to the back door.

Lila settled into the passenger seat of Jamie's SUV, savoring the luxury of the plush leather seats. Moments after the engine started, a warmth spread along her back, and she couldn't hold back a giggle.

"I've never been in a car that has seat warmers."

"Feels good on a chilly day, doesn't it?" Jamie chuckled. "Tell me if you get too hot."

"You have a beautiful vehicle."

"Actually, I don't. This belongs to Rhys. I have a seven-year old sedan. I bought it used, and it's been a good car for the most part. We want something newer and safer for the baby."

Lila gave a silent sigh. Having a car would make life so much easier. No waiting at the bus stops in all kinds of weather. No more toting her laundry to Aunt Nan's or hauling groceries from the market.

She swallowed a gasp. Would Jamie consider selling her car instead of trading it? Her spirits sank. *There's no way I can afford to pay what she'd expect. Even if I could, it would take a chunk out of my savings. Plus, there's the expenses of gas, maintenance, and license.*

Then again, she'd eventually need a car and when would she get another chance like this? Even not knowing how much Jamie's car would cost, it would have to be less than buying from a dealer. Only one way to find out.

"Jamie, would you consider letting me buy your car when you're ready to get a new one? Depending on how much you want for it and if I can afford it?"

"Tell you what, when we finish my errands, we'll stop by home so you can give it a test drive and decide if it's something you do want."

The butterflies in her stomach kicked up a storm. Some tap-danced a happy rhythm while the others swarmed with doubts. She took a deep breath to calm her apprehensions. She hadn't decided, and she wasn't committed.

"Actually, it's my mother-in-law's home. Rhys and I are living with her until our house is built."

"Is it awkward living with your in-laws?"

"Considering I work for Rhys's mother, it should be, but it's not. As welcome as she's made us, I can't wait to get into our own home."

Oh, my. What family drama have I stepped into? I thought Mrs. Canfield moved here last summer to work on the Main Street renovations. If she's Rhys McCall's mother, does that mean she was married to the man who owns the construction company? What about Joshua's father, and who is she marrying on Wednesday?

Lila bit her lip, toying whether to ask about Joshua's family. Maybe it wouldn't hurt to ask one or two questions to avoid an awkward moment situation in the future.

"Jamie, I don't want to pry, but are Joshua and your husband actually half-brothers?"

Jamie sighed. "Technically, they're cousins. I don't know how much you know about Dana's past—"

"I'm sorry. It's none of my business."

"There are some things you need to know since you'll be working at Carson's."

"Whatever you feel comfortable telling me would be helpful. I put my foot in my mouth this morning."

"It was a natural reaction." Jamie waved one hand in dismissal. "The woman we call Dana Canfield was born Catherine Dennison. She married Rhys's father Erik while she was in college."

"Who is Joshua's mother?"

"That Dana Canfield was Catherine's cousin and went by the nickname Dee. When Joshua was two years old, Dee attempted to run Catherine's car off the road over a large trust fund. Dee died, and Catherine suffered a head injury that left

43

her in a coma for several weeks. Their identities were switched at the hospital."

"Wouldn't Mr. Canfield have known the survivor wasn't his wife?"

"I'm sure he did. Why he didn't reveal the reason is something none of us know. There's more, but it's Joshua's story to tell. What I do know is that Dana—our Dana—loved James Canfield, and he obviously came to love her. He died trying to protect her and Joshua." Jamie gave a soft sigh. "It's been difficult for both Rhys and Joshua."

Seems like it's worse for Joshua, Lila thought. Rhys McCall had his father all those years and eventually got his mother back. From Paige's indication of their relationship, he had the support of the Carson family as well. On the other hand, Joshua lost his father, learned his mother wasn't biologically his, and his birth mother was a killer.

On the heels of those thoughts, a wave of shame washed through Lila, and she hung her head. *Here I am judging someone else's pain. All those things Rhys had doesn't make up for losing all those years with his mama.*

"Thank you for sharing that, Jamie. I don't want to say the wrong thing to either of them."

"Rhys would understand. I'm still getting to know Joshua, at least as much as he lets anyone, but I'm sure he would too."

Jamie slowed the vehicle as flashing lights appeared at the side of the road. Two sheriff's cruisers along with an ambulance were parked at the side of the road.

"That's where Miss Emily lived," Lila said. "I wonder what happened."

Jamie darted several glances as they cruised past the property before resuming her former speed. "You knew Miss Emily?"

"My mama used to clean for her. I helped too. I did all the low work."

Lila chuckled at the frown on Jamie's face. "Baseboards, straightening the bottom cabinets and dresser drawers. Anything so mama didn't have to bend over so much. Not that she couldn't do those things, but it made me feel like I was helping."

"You were helping."

"Miss Emily even paid me. I felt so proud earning my own money. Once I saved enough to buy a book for myself then treated Mama and me to ice cream at Dottie's Dairy Bar. I was probably three or four years old when I first met Miss Emily. I was nine when I went to live with my uncle and aunt. I never got to see her again."

"That's a wonderful memory to have with your mother. I never had that with mine."

Lila shifted in her seat, startled by the sad tone in Jamie's voice.

"I have two older sisters who can do no wrong, and I could do nothing right in my mother's eyes. My father was wonderful. He supported me, he inspired me, he made me believe in myself. When he passed, I lost that confidence. I got it back thanks to Rhys, Dana, Paige... so many people helped me heal."

"You mentioned knowing what it's like to be the new person. Did you move here?"

"Last spring." Jamie laughed as she caught Lila's glance at her rounded stomach. "Rhys and I had a whirlwind courtship. Looking back, it seemed like it was love at first sight."

Not likely. It sounded like something out of a book. Real life didn't work that way.

What about Joshua?

Sure, his looks attracted her. But it was his humor and

kindness that appealed to her even more. But love? No way, because a man like Joshua Canfield doesn't fall in love with a woman like her, and she wasn't about to let herself fall into the fantasy of thinking he would.

The stop at the woodworks shop took less time than Lila expected. Jamie traded a check for the crib along with a friendly conversation while Mr. Morgan and his son loaded the cargo. In less than twenty minutes, they were back on the road.

"I can't wait for Rhys to see the finished crib," Jamie said. "We picked out the style and made a down-payment last summer. I want it to be an heirloom for our children and grandchildren. Does that sound like I'm wishing my life away?"

Lila shook her head. "It sounds like you're planning for the future." The same thing she was doing. She could dream about the future, but it would take hard work and saving—just as Jamie was doing—to achieve that dream.

"Something you said earlier gave me an idea." Jamie signaled a turn into the parking lot at Dottie's Dairy Bar. She pulled into a space and shut off the engine. "You once saved your money for a book then had enough for ice cream. Well, I saved for a crib, and you're saving for a car. Sounds like we both deserve a treat. What do you say?"

Words stuck in Lila's throat as she stared at the building. Years had passed since she'd visited the shop. Lack of time or money were the usual reasons given when Lila, as a child, had begged for a trip to the Dairy Bar. As she grew older, she realized it was jealousy on Aunt Nan's part. She'd rather Lila do without that treat than participate in a tradition that Jennie Grainger started for her daughter.

Lila sat silent for a moment, waiting for the sharp pain of loss to strike. Instead, the ache shifted into something softer, a gentle passing into what would become a treasured memory. Was it instinct or compassion that spurred Jamie to make the offer? Either way, in the short length of their acquaintance, Jamie bestowed a kindness that Lila's own family had not.

"It sounds wonderful."

They hopped out of the SUV and met at the shop's entrance.

Jamie reached for the door handle. "I don't know about you, but Baby Mac wants a hot fudge sundae."

"Mmm, yes, and with whipped cream."

Laughing, they walked to the counter to place their order.

Why had she hesitated to take this trip with Jamie? The time spent with Paige, Joshua, and Jamie proved she didn't have to wait until she left PI to make a new life. She had the job she wanted and a chance for a car. Yesterday, one of those things was a wish within reach and the other a dream for the future.

The one thing she hadn't expected to find was a new friend.

<hr />

Seated at the breakfast nook table, Rhys swallowed the final bite of chili. After several long hours spent in the cold air at the Anderson property, he needed that bowl of comfort food. With Mom and Nick dining out and Megan on a date with Deputy Mike Winslow, he and Jamie had a chance for much needed alone time.

"Thirds?" Jamie asked, casting a teasing look at the empty bowl.

"Two's my limit." Tired, warm, and well-fed, he felt the stress of the afternoon easing away. Glancing at her half-full bowl, he frowned. "Are you feeling okay? You didn't eat much."

"I wasn't hungry. Baby Mac wanted a sundae while I was out."

A dimple flashed in his cheek. "Baby Mac wanted it?"

"He was insistent." Jamie nodded, her eyes wide.

Rhys shook his head. "That kid."

"I have to talk to you about something." Jamie slid her palm over his hand. "What do you think about selling my car to Lila?"

His brow creased in a deep frown. "I thought we were going to wait until spring to trade it in for something new."

"I know, but when I mentioned in passing about getting a new vehicle because of the baby, she asked if I'd be willing to sell mine to her. Other than the bus, she has no other transportation. She'll have to stand at a bus stop in the cold and sometimes the dark to get to work and home."

Any protest Rhys would have made faded when Jamie's eyes reddened with unshed tears.

"I remember how it was when I moved here. Dana took a chance giving me a job. Paige took a chance offering me a place to stay with her. Joshua was right when he said Lila wants something better for herself. I want to help her the way I was helped. We came back here so she could see the car and test drive it." Her fingers entwined with Rhys's into a clasp. "I wish you could have seen her face."

"I can't say no, either. But we need to do it in a way to let Lila keep her pride. What about a down payment then let her pay monthly on the balance?"

She gave his hand a second squeeze. "That's a wonderful idea. She wanted to think it over and let me know next week. I'll call her with that suggestion to help her make a decision."

Rhys stood, collecting the used tableware. Jamie followed him to the sink. They worked together to straighten the kitchen.

"Have you heard anything more from Sam about the body buried at Miss Emily's?"

Rhys grimaced. "All that was left were bones. Sam contacted the State Police about getting a forensic crew to investigate the grave. One of the older guys on the crew thought there might be a family cemetery on the property."

"There could be more graves there?"

"If there is a family cemetery, it's located somewhere else on the property. That's something we'll need to confirm. As for this grave, there was no evidence of a casket, not even a wooden one. Until the investigation is completed, the work site is shut down."

Jamie closed the door to the dishwasher. "Does this mean that the person buried there might have been murdered?"

Rhys shrugged. "The body didn't get in that grave by itself."

⁓

Cleaning Aunt Nan's house was the last thing Lila wanted to do on a sunny fall Sunday, but she couldn't say no to the woman who'd raised her since Lila was nine years old. Nothing, though, could spoil her mood after receiving a call from Jamie last night.

Would it help her decision if she could make payments for the car? The word 'yes' spilled out of Lila's mouth so fast both of them burst into laughter. The asking price was better than she expected and would have taken a sizable portion of her savings without Jamie's generous offer. Granted, she would be earning more at Carson's, but there was no guarantee the hours Joshua quoted to her would remain steady.

I never thought when I asked for a break I'd have so many blessings delivered.

She hummed silently while dusting the living room. Nan settled onto the couch as she flipped through a collection of magazines.

"Should have done this sooner, but never enough time. Can't throw things out if you don't know if you'll need them." The worn springs on the couch squeaked as Nan half-reclined, one leg stretched across the cushions, the other foot flat on the floor. Almost six-feet tall and two hundred pounds, she was more muscle than fat and still as tough as the Army sergeant she'd once been.

"Jeffy says you quit your job at the Low Tide. What's up with that?"

The word got around faster than Lila expected. Considering more than half of her hours for the next week had been switched to Angie's schedule, it shouldn't have been a surprise that she had quit.

"That's right. I got hired at Carson's downtown."

The couch squeaked again, followed by a grunt. "Not smart. You got yourself in with the wrong bunch of people."

Lila dropped the dust cloth onto the table. "Why would you say that? Everyone has been nice and helpful."

"To your face. You need to watch your back." Nan snorted. "That Paige Carson... her daddy owned the drive-in over near Crossroads. Not long after he passed, she ran the business in the ground. Now she's got some hole in the wall joint uptown. Won't be long before she'll shut down there too."

Lila bit back a protest. Carson's lost business due to halting their delivery service, but that wasn't Paige's fault. Nope, it was a Grainger who caused that mess.

Then again, Paige had shifted her plans unexpectedly, leaving Rhys McCall with an unused window and Joshua scrambling to determine an expanded delivery area. But she also had been receptive to Lila's idea about the vacant dining room. Maybe there were other ways she could contribute and prove herself worthy of the chance she'd been given.

"Whether or not that happens, I have a job now that pays more than the Low Tide and more hours too."

"I know Jeffy cut back your hours, but there's no need to get snippy. He's trying to help Angie get on her feet." Nan tossed the magazine onto the table. She sat up, raking fingers through tousled stands of blonde hair. "If you're not going listen to what I have to say about that Carson woman, maybe you'll pay heed to what I tell you about Joshua Canfield. He works there too, don't he?"

An exasperated huff shot out of Lila's mouth. "How do you even know Joshua Canfield?"

Nan lifted one over-arched brow. "This come straight from Birdie Marcum. You remember those four people who got shot last year?"

Lila sank down on the opposite end of the couch. "Of course, I do. One of them was cousin Buzz. He tried to run down Mrs. Canfield in a stolen truck."

After cousin Buzz and a detective from Sutton had been killed the same way, two bullets in the chest, one in the head, rumors raced about Dana Canfield. A few weeks later, another woman died in the same way. The series of murders seemed to end with Nathan Stoddard's death.

Nan waved one hand, dismissing any of Buzz's wrong-doings. "The last one, a man named Stoddard. He was connected to those Canfields. I was working the night shift, and Birdie was working ER. She said he was still alive when they brought him in. Kept saying a 'juh" sound over and over. Didn't make sense at the time, but it does now. He was trying to say the name of his killer. Joshua." She gave a final jut of her chin. "If it's a lie, that's on Birdie, but I believe her, and so should you."

Nan's hand closed around Lila's wrist, and she jumped.

"Don't you worry about that job, child. I'll see if there's any openings in the kitchen at the hospital. Don't figure they need a cook, but you could deliver trays and work your way up." She gave Lila's arm a quick shake. "Maybe we'll even get on the same shift."

"Thank you, Aunt Nan," Lila said, easing her arm free. "But I've given my word to Ms. Carson. I can't walk out without giving it my honest try."

Nan's brow puckered with deep lines of disapproval. "If you won't listen, you have to learn the hard way, and nobody can say I didn't warn you." She shoved to her feet. "Get busy. No point taking all day."

Lila picked up the dust cloth, her thoughts whirling as she completed the chore. In her heart, she believed that Joshua Canfield was incapable of killing anyone in cold blood. But what about the mysterious Dana Canfield?

The story Jamie related was based on what she'd been told. A story that cast the current Dana in the role of an innocent victim. What if she had been as greedy for that trust fund as Dee had been? If Dee even knew about the fund. Maybe she was the innocent one in this tale.

With all the deaths surrounding the current Mrs. Canfield, could she be the killer?

CHAPTER FIVE

Morning fog drifted along the length of the alley behind Carson's. Through the mists, Joshua spied Lila waiting by the door. She wore the same plaid coat but this time with a moss green cap pulled over her ears. Both hands were shoved into her pockets, and her shoulders hunched against the cold.

She looked up as he parked his car. Her cheeks and nose were pink, and her hazel eyes were bright with excitement. A smile broke across her face, and just like that, his day held all the warmth of Spring.

"Didn't expect you to beat me here." He jogged to the door and swiped his card through the security lock.

"I've only been here a few minutes." She bounced on her toes. "I'm excited to get started."

After Rick's belligerence and Karen's careless attitude, Lila's enthusiasm was a welcome change.

"Too long to stand outside. I'll get a pass card for you before you leave. You can put your coat and purse in the closet over there." He nodded to a door tucked in the far corner of the kitchen. "I'll get the paperwork from Paige's office for you to fill out."

Josh started the coffee brewing while Lila completed the employment forms. He glanced over one shoulder when a beep sounded. The back door opened then slammed shut. Feet dragging, Paige trudged her way to the prep island.

"Hey, Josh, Lila. Tell me the coffee is ready."

"Coming right up." Josh switched the carafe for a mug long enough for the cup to fill. He set the mug in front of Paige. "Rough morning?"

Eyes closed, she breathed in the fragrant steam then took a sip. "Just the usual battle with Jess to get moving."

Lila chuckled. "She's not a morning person?"

Paige set the mug down with a thunk. "She may be tomorrow. Sam told her that since she obviously needs more sleep, her bedtime tonight would be thirty minutes earlier. If that doesn't help, we'd move it up another thirty tomorrow night."

Josh winced. "Ouch, tough love."

"You bet." Mug in hand, she headed for her office. "Karen's on her way. When she gets here, we'll catch everyone up. Did you get all the notes from Saturday combined?"

"It's all there, and copies printed for everyone."

"Cool." Paige flashed a thumbs up, pausing as she passed by Lila. "When you finish filling out the forms, I need to make a copy of your driver's license. Oh, and Josh, make sure Lila gets her Carson's shirts."

Lila glanced from Paige to Josh. "Carson's shirts?"

"T-shirt, polo shirt, sweatshirt." He snapped his fingers. "Did you park on a lot this morning?"

"I took the bus, but I may be getting a car soon."

"Let me know when you do, and you can take space number three."

"I won't be taking yours, will I?"

He shook his head. "Paige and Karen have spaces one and

two. Space four is for the delivery jeep. Since Rick is gone, you'll have the third space."

"What about your car?"

"I'll park on the lot next to my mom's building. It's a half-block down the street, and I've already cleared it with her."

The door alarm beeped again. Rick entered, waving his pass card. "Is the boss in?" He glared at Josh. "The real boss."

"What do you want, Rick?"

"Here for what's owed to me. You think I'd take your word for it?" He shifted, glancing behind Joshua.

"Whoa, look who's here. The hash slinging queen of the Low Tide. Canfield, need me to take the trash out while I'm here?"

"That's enough!" Paige stormed across the kitchen. "Not another word out of you, Rick. I'll give you your check but only because I don't want to deal with the likes of you any longer."

A smirk slid across Rick's face.

"I know about that bar fight you got in over the weekend at the Low Tide. You're lucky the other guy didn't press charges. Especially since you're due at boot camp in a couple of days." She jabbed a forefinger at the stool at the end of the counter. "Sit down and keep quiet, or I'll deduct five dollars each time you shoot off your mouth."

Her glare tractor-beamed Rick onto the stool, daring him to move. With a jut of her chin, Paige stormed back to her office.

Arms crossed over his chest, Josh leaned against the opposite counter.

Rick spun on the stool to face him. "Wipe that look off your face, Canfield."

"I'd invite you to do it," Josh said, his grin growing wider, "except you're in time-out."

"I can hear you!" Paige shouted.

She returned seconds later, walking briskly to the exit and opening the door. Josh pushed away from the counter, standing close enough to step in if needed.

Paige held out one hand, wiggling her fingers. "Pass card."

Rick slapped the card into Paige's hand and jerked the check from her other hand. He stopped outside the door.

"One day you won't be able to use your husband as a threat."

Paige snorted. "Don't bet on it."

She slammed the door shut then brushed her hands together. "Good riddance."

"Hey, Paige," Josh said, a soft teasing note filtering into his voice. "Think that technique would work getting Jess up in the morning?"

Paige's scowl held less than a second then she spluttered into laughter. A second later, Lila's giggle joined in. Josh looked around with a satisfied smile.

Yeah, this was going to work.

***

Dana motioned Ben to one of the visitor's chairs then sat down behind her desk. She'd debated the wisdom of asking Ben to trace the deaths of Dennison Trust heirs. Since Stoddard's death, Ben had become a more regular fixture on PI as the IT guy living at Maisie Porter's B&B. If Ben was trying to start a new life, would her request pull him back into a situation he was trying to put behind him?

Before she could speak, Ben shifted forward, elbows on the desktop.

"Is this about Friday? Did something else happen?"

She sat speechless for a moment then asked, "What

happened on Friday?"

"Whoa, sorry. I thought Josh would have mentioned that the two of us were questioned about Stoddard's death."

Dana held back a shiver, remembering that day when Nathan Stoddard poisoned her. Because she was the final surviving heir to the enormous Dennison Trust, Stoddard intended to claim those funds before the trust expired. Months had passed since Toddy's death. Why was this happening now? She pushed away the momentary hurt—and anger—that Joshua had *not* shared that information with her.

"No, he didn't."

"Deputy Hunter found security cam footage of Joshua getting into my car on Federal that day. We'd devised a cover story in advance in case we were questioned. The deputy's trying to score points with the sheriff. Nothing to worry about."

She dropped her trembling hands into her lap. Ben was no longer that six-year old child who'd called her his other mother and claimed Rhys as his little brother. At some point after Catherine's presumed death over two decades ago, Ben ceased to be Cody MacBride, a sweet little boy with an infectious laugh and an open smile. He'd changed his name and closed his heart. Because she had known Ben before, she detected the signs of sorrow and loss that he attempted to hide behind a cool exterior.

Regardless of what crimes Ben had committed in the past, he was the man who'd risked his own life to save both her sons. A man she'd put at risk with her own words, and he needed to know.

"Ben, I've put you in danger."

The concern in his eyes cooled, a keen analytical gleam taking its place. "How so?"

"The day Detective Lansing came to my office, I saw

someone passing the front window. I thought it was Jamie returning to the office."

A shadow fell across the front windows. She caught a glimpse of blonde hair. Jamie? Not Jamie, but who?

"I realized it wasn't her. When the door opened, I couldn't see anyone. I didn't know who was there."

Sunlight spilled into the lobby... The entry wall blocked the newcomer from her sight... Lansing cast a glance over one shoulder... turning toward the unseen person. "What are you doing here, Ham—"

"I gave a partial description to the sheriff. Blond hair and male based on that glimpse at the window. Possibly left-hand because you would've had to step past the entry wall to shoot otherwise, and I would have seen you."

Ben glanced at his left hand then shook his head. "Too vague to be concerned—"

"When Lansing arrived, I started a recording on my phone. When he saw you, he said part of your name. He said 'Ham.' The sheriff has a copy of that recording."

"Damn." A whoosh of air slid through Ben's lips. "I need to hear that recording."

"Sam offered to give me a copy, but I didn't want it. He'll definitely be suspicious if I ask for it now." Another thought struck her. "Would the security cameras on the street have recorded you outside the building that day?"

"They hadn't been installed yet. I cased the area well before then." Ben jerked up in the chair, one corner of his mouth lifting in a half-grin. "Is your phone synced to your other devices?"

"Yes, of course—" She gasped. "There could be a copy on my tablet?"

He held up two crossed fingers.

Dana reached for her tablet when a tap sounded on the

door. "Come in."

The door opened half-way, and Jamie stepped into the gap. "Checking if you needed more time before my meeting with Ben."

"Can you give us two more minutes then I need to head over to McCalls."

"No problem." Jamie stepped back, closing the door.

"So, the real reason I'm here?" Ben asked, the edge in his voice fading.

"I want to set up a scholarship fund using Dennison Trust funds. Danny Price, the attorney, is handling the legalities to set up a foundation. Before I commit those funds, I need to know if there were any legal heirs who should have received a payout."

"Not to my knowledge. At the time I agreed with James to work undercover for Stoddard, you were the final heir. Before that, I have no idea what Stoddard might have done as far as eliminating other heirs. If you can give me some names and history to start, I'll see what I can find out."

Ben rose and walked to the door. He paused, turning. "About the other matter, I could say don't worry because I know you will. What I will say is that I made a promise to James to protect Joshua. I made one to myself to protect you. Those promises didn't end because Stoddard is dead."

She stood, holding out one hand. "Thank you, Ben."

He held her hand for a brief moment and smiled. In that instant, the essence of that little boy she once knew flickered across his face. "You're welcome, Miss Katie."

He walked out of the room, leaving her with one lingering question.

Who'll protect you, Ben?

She would, and she'd start by searching for that voice recording.

The meeting room at McCall Construction was empty when Dana and Megan entered.

"I guess we can sit anywhere," Dana said.

Megan grinned. "You sit at the head. I'll take the other end."

Dana laughed and walked to the opposite side of the table. "I prefer to sit facing the door."

"Good plan." Megan trotted to the other side and plopped down next to her.

How did she get so lucky? In just a few short months, Nick's daughter had claimed a permanent place in her own heart. Technically, Nick was Megan's stepfather, but having been in the child's life since she was seven months old, he had every right to the title of "Dad."

In those same months, Dana's entire family expanded, including a grandson in the near future. She bit back a grumble that neither Rhys nor Jamie would reveal the name they'd picked. Probably for the best. Once they did, everyone would argue or offer an opinion.

"Any idea what this get-together is about?" Megan whispered as voices grew louder in the hallway. Seconds later, the other attendees entered.

"No idea," Dana said. She glanced around the table, trying to read the mood of each person.

Not a clue showed on Erik McCall's face. CFO Kevin Davis barely concealed a smug grin. Rhys appeared to be holding back whatever he was feeling. Stacy Andrews, office manager, had no qualms about voicing her impatience.

"How long will this take? The computer guy is here, and I need to let him know what's needed."

"It'll take as long as it takes," Kevin said. "Longer depending on interruptions."

Stacy tossed her red hair over one shoulder. "Fine, but don't complain when you have to pay him for the time he's here and not working."

Erik tapped his knuckles twice on the tabletop. "Let's get started. The news is McCall is in the process of purchasing Winters Construction. If you're not familiar with the name, they're located in Frostburg. That's forty miles north of Sutton."

"Which is at least ninety minutes or more from here," Stacy said.

Megan snorted. "Longer if the ferry isn't on time."

Kevin cleared his throat. "To continue, Winters overextended and is on the verge of bankruptcy. What makes this deal advantageous is a pending development project for a subdivision with potentially seventy-five residences and other amenities. It also gives us a foothold in expanding operations in that area."

Stacy frowned. "Is this a merger or a buy-out?"

"A buy-out," Erik replied. "Kevin is now part-owner with McCall. In the immediate future, we'll become McCall-Davis Construction. Once that takes place, we'll proceed with the buy-out."

His glance shifted to Dana. "You're here with a potential offer as the design consultant for the home buyers along with Jamie handling marketing. We'll discuss that in a separate meeting."

The project sounded intriguing and would certainly keep her busy. Her main concern was what was Rhys's role in this new structure.

"Will the company headquarters remain here?" Stacy asked.

"For the current time. However, we'll need our key people at the Frostburg site during the transition. We'll start having regular meetings as the sale proceeds. That's all for today, folks."

Dana remained seated, waiting until everyone but Rhys and Erik had departed. Once the door closed, she confronted her ex-husband.

"Did you give Rhys any idea before this deal was made?"

Rhys held up one hand. "I found out a few days ago."

"So, it was a done deal before you told your son." She cast a fierce glare at Erik. "How much of the company did you sell?"

"None of your business."

"In other words, enough that you and Kevin can squeeze Rhys out of any decision making."

"Still none of your business."

"Rhys *is* my business."

"Keep it up, Kate, and I'll reconsider throwing any work to your little design company."

"Take your offer—"

"That's enough!" Rhys shoved his chair under the table. It hit with a thump then ricocheted several inches. "Both of you stop. Dad, don't ever denigrate my mother in front of me again. Mom, thank you for the support, but this is a matter between Dad and me. What I need from both of you is an end to this war."

Rhys rubbed the back of his neck as he paced the room. He halted, fixing a firm look at both of them. "Jamie and I are expecting a baby in the spring. The two of you will be my son's grandparents. You have to come to some sort of resolution."

He walked to the door and rested his palm on the handle. "I don't want either of you to leave this room until you've come to terms like the adults you are."

The door clicked behind his departure, and silence reigned for a brief instant.

Erik leaned back in his chair and stretched both arms over his head. "Like old times, huh?"

Dana lifted her nose, exactly in the way she knew irritated him the most. "I don't remember."

"I thought that twenty-plus years of amnesia had passed."

Well, this wasn't settling anything. She switched tactics. "If you expect me to back off on this matter, tell me how much autonomy did you leave Rhys."

Erik heaved a deep breath. "Rhys has twenty-five percent, Kevin has twenty-four, and I have fifty-one."

"Which means you and Kevin could shut him out of decisions."

"Damn it, Kate, Rhys is my son too. Something you prefer not to acknowledge. He's the reason the company is still standing. Towne Square, the Adams property, all the other projects he initiated are keeping us afloat. That can't go on forever. At a certain point, we're back to home improvement and repairs and whatever work the city contracts with us. That'll mean layoffs." He wiped a hand across his face. "I wish it hadn't come to this, but I'm thankful Kevin was willing to invest with us rather than taking that offer to Winters."

Hands clasped on the table, fingers interlaced, he leaned forward. "I promise you any decisions I make will consider our son's interests as well as the company's."

He sounded sincere. Looked it too. Darn it. She was going to have to believe him.

"What about the design job? Was that for Rhys's benefit?"

"Either. Both." He shrugged. "It's up to you. If you're totally against the idea, I need to know now so we can find someone else. Sound fair?"

It sounded totally fair. So unlike the Erik she knew from years ago.

"I'm not opposed to the idea, but I need more details before I make a decision. I will let you know after you give me more information."

"Agreed. Anything else?"

Dana tapped her fingertips against the tabletop. It helped her think, but she also knew it irritated Erik. Her conscience tugged, and she relented. "Do you promise what I'm about to say will never leave this room or be repeated?"

Eyes narrowed, Erik drew an X across his chest with one forefinger.

"I apologize for planning to move back to Connecticut with Rhys after graduation. It wasn't fair to either of you."

"Wow, okay. Under the same conditions, I apologize for not following through at the hospital after I was told you'd died." He nodded. "Your turn."

Hmm. Apologies for all the issues during their marriage could take the rest of the afternoon.

"How about a blanket agreement to leave the past in the past?"

Erik grinned. "With the stipulation that we can still spar on current disagreements?"

"Absolutely." She retrieved her satchel from under the table. "Regardless of the past, we did one thing right. We have a wonderful son."

She had the door partially open when Erik called her name. He stood at the head of the table, hands in his pockets.

"We did a lot of things right."

Her breath caught, and her lips parted. Their gazes met, transporting her thoughts back to that time when they had shared a life together. Speechless, she could only nod and walk away.

Erik walked out of the boardroom, his long strides carrying him toward his office. What was it about that woman that kept pulling him into the past? If it hadn't been for having a child, the relationship would have burned out with each of them going on their own way. Both of them were stubborn and hot headed. How they ended up with a calm, logical son was a mystery. Rhys definitely had gotten the best from both of them.

Hearing laughter behind him, he turned to stare down the hallway. Rhys stood with one arm around Kate's shoulder, his other hand clasped within both of Megan's. Mother, son, daughter. A neat family unit only missing a father. In two days, Nick Warden would step permanently into that picture.

Erik could have a life like that too. All he had to do was propose to April, something he'd planned to do all those years ago before Mitch Davis and his buddies beat the hell out of him. By the time he recovered, April and Mitch were married and living hundreds of miles away.

Then he met Catherine Dennison. She came from money; he was blue-collar. They were both stubborn to the core. If either of them had given a little, maybe things would have turned out differently. His knowledge of construction and her design talent could have made them an incredible power couple. Add in Rhys's architectural expertise, and the three of them would have been unstoppable.

Now he had April back in his life, and her son Kevin was driving McCall Construction to a wider platform. The three of them could be unstoppable.

After one final glance down the hallway, Erik continued to his office and closed the door on all the what-ifs.

CHAPTER SIX

While Paige continued Lila's onboarding, Joshua met with Karen in the front office. Hands clasped on the table in front of her, she eyed him warily.

"Do I still have a job?"

Joshua ignored the defiant tone, focusing instead on the slight tremble of her hands. He gave a reassuring smile. "Of course you do. I want to go over the upcoming changes and get your opinion."

Her upper lip curled. "I could have done that on Saturday if you'd let me come in."

"When you left on Friday, you specifically said you were unable to work weekends."

Her mouth tightened, and she looked away.

Give her a chance. When he'd checked Karen's personnel file, Josh found she'd been an employee at Carson's Drive-In since she was a teenager. She wouldn't have continued working for either Mr. Carson or Paige if she hadn't been a good worker. Whether the problem was due to Rick's influence or something else, he needed to get to the root of the cause before he could give Karen a second chance.

"If there's a problem I can help with—"

"Dale walked out on me and the kids."

Okay, not in the area of topics he'd intended. Definitely not what he expected. Neither of which mattered when the woman in front of him was hurting.

"Fifteen years and two kids in grade school, and he decides it's not the life he wants. Everything falls on me now. I think I'm organized, then the person I count on to drop the kids off or pick them up cancels. I know I've been slacking, but I need this job."

The desperation in Karen's voice tugged at his heart. As uncomfortable as the conversation had become, he needed to find something more than sympathy to offer the woman. He needed to find answers to help her while meeting his responsibility to Paige.

"I'm sorry you're going through this, Karen. How are your children coping?"

"Hurt and mad. Mostly at their father, but also at me because I'm not fixing it back to the way it was." She glanced away then back. "Now that Rick's gone, is there any way I could get a bump in my pay? I don't get much from Dale so even a little more would help. I know I haven't earned a raise, but bills are getting behind. Much more and I won't know how ever I'll catch up."

"I don't know what Paige has in the budget. Things will be tight at first with the changes she's making until we settle into a new routine. Even though Rick is gone, she hired Lila and Aaron. Even if she can't increase your pay rate, you will have more hours available."

The worried look on her face deepened with those words.

One of the lessons he'd learned since the time he'd left home and family was what a privileged life he'd led. Volunteer work was part of his life while growing up, but nothing prepared him for the hardships others endured on a daily basis. He learned to do with less or even without. To give when he had little because someone else had less. Compassion was well and good, but it didn't help Karen's situation.

In the meantime, there was one suggestion he could offer.

"I have an idea that might help with the afternoon pick-ups for your children. We'll all have later hours until we get a feel for customer flow. Paige plans on bringing Jess here after school. Would it help if you bring your kids here too? There's room in this area for another table. They can have a snack and do their homework."

"That would help in the afternoons, especially if you need me to stay longer." Karen drew in a deep breath, and the tight lines on her face eased slightly. "Plus save me the cost of childcare."

"Would starting a half-hour later on your morning shift help?"

"Tremendously." She stared at the remains in her coffee cup. "I apologize for the way I talked to you on Friday. On top of what's going on at home, I followed Rick's attitude into acting that way. That's not an excuse. I was wrong."

She lifted her gaze, meeting his full-on. "It hurt when Paige made you manager while she was gone."

Josh lifted one eyebrow.

Karen's shoulders sagged, and she nodded. "I understand why. I can't put those hours in and I don't want to handle all the business side. But it would have been nice if I had been considered. I've been here longer than any of you. I worked at Carson's Drive-In and was one of the best cooks they had."

"I know that by the number of people who insist that you fix their order because—" He made air quotes. "—Karen knows how I like my food."

A smile drifted across her lips. "I like the kitchen. I like knowing that folks enjoy the food I fix."

"That's why you're exactly who we need helping with the classic meals. You know what the customers like and what sells."

With each change Joshua discussed, Karen's enthusiasm increased. She pointed out negatives that neither he nor Paige had considered, suggested improvements on their preliminary plans, and even proposed several workable additions.

"I don't know about this computer stuff though."

"Ben's coming in this afternoon to discuss options with Paige. Once she decides, he'll do the install and train everyone on the system. If you don't have any additional questions, check if Paige is free. She wants to finalize the new menu items and get orders placed for inventory."

"Will do." Karen rose and headed toward the kitchen, stopping at the edge of the half-wall. "Thanks, Josh. The things you said mean a lot."

Her words touched him. "You're very welcome."

⁓

Seated on a stool behind the front counter, Lila studied the current menu. Was there any point to it with the upcoming changes? Paige thought so. Joshua did too. So, she studied. The new computer system sounded complex too. Big change from scrawled orders on grease-splattered tickets. Communication at the Low Tide kitchen was yelling and pounding on a call bell.

Ben—the computer guy—wasn't the bespectacled nerd she'd envisioned, and shame on her for prejudging him. Tall, blond, and handsome, though his sharp blue-eyed gaze seemed to be constantly searching and evaluating. She gave a silent laugh. Maybe it was his computer brain at work.

Hearing voices approaching, she looked up and hid another laugh. Paige had dogged Ben's footsteps since he'd arrived. Asking questions or offering suggestions, and barely waiting for his answers.

"What about—"

"No more changes." Ben walked behind the counter, poured a cup of coffee, and took a long swallow. "By the way, we haven't discussed my fee."

"No, and before we do, let me just say... *gulp*."

Those analytical eyes narrowed, and Lila could almost see the circuits racing through his brain.

"Cooking lessons. For two. Six lessons."

"I didn't expect that." She fluttered her lashes and smirked. "For two, huh?"

He crooked one eyebrow. "Yes, and let's make that eight lessons."

"Deal. When can you have the system... computer... the stuff ready?"

"I can pick up the hardware Wednesday. Installation plus training on Thursday. That'll give everyone a couple of days to practice."

"You're the best. I need to get back with Karen on inventory. Let me know when you're ready for those lessons."

She spun and dashed out of the room, passing Josh as he entered from the kitchen.

A tap sounded on the front door. Two figures clad in deputy uniforms stood outside. Lila glanced at Josh, surprised to see the look he exchanged with Ben. Paige had mentioned that her husband Sam and the deputies often stopped in for coffee. Or did this visit have something to do with Josh being escorted to the sheriff's office last Friday?

Josh opened the door, greeting the two men. "Hey, Bret, Mike. You here for coffee?"

"Wouldn't mind a cup," Mike Winslow replied.

Bret Madigan sent a wide grin in Lila's direction. "I'm here to get a hug from my cousin."

Lila hopped from the stool. She rushed around the counter, stopping short of his hug. "What happened to your face?"

"This?" Bret gestured toward the dark bruise on his right cheek then to Mike. "Saving his hide."

Mike snorted. "Your aunt packs quite a punch."

Lila gasped. "Aunt Nan hit you?"

"Guess you haven't heard about the squall at the Low Tide Saturday night? Once we got all the he said/she said sorted, it seems Jeff took offense at some flirting that went on between Angie and that guy Rick who used to work here. She claimed she was just being friendly to get a better tip. Jeff accused her of looking for a hook-up. Both guys did some trash talk then took a couple swings at one another. We hauled the two of them to the station to cool off."

Mike took up the story. "We just finished processing them when two women come barging into the station. One of them is dripping wet and reeks of beer."

Heat rose in Lila's cheeks. Mike and Bret might find the story amusing, but she didn't. It was humiliating to have a sordid tale like this discussed in front of her employer. A quick glance under her lashes showed Joshua with his usual calm expression. As for Ben, he had both forearms planted on the countertop, listening with a rapt expression on his face. Poor guy, this stuff had to be horrifying for someone who lived in a logical world free of violence.

"Nan got to the bar right after we left. She decided Angie's to blame and poured two pitchers of beer over her head. Except the woman she doused wasn't Angie."

Lila's hand went to her lips. "Oh, no."

"The woman files an assault charge, so Mike and I track Nan down at her home. When she comes to the door, this yahoo—" Bret jerked a thumb in Mike's direction. "—says the three words you *never* say to her."

Mike held up both hands, palms out. "I didn't know."

"Looks right at her and says 'Hannah Jane Grainger?' I saw her fist come up and pulled Mike out the way." A from-the-gut laugh broke loose. "She went flying across the porch and slammed into the post. I made the mistake of trying to help her. That's when she slugged me."

"Now, Bret, she did apologize for that. Swore it was an accident then cussed out both of us while we cuffed her."

"Is she still in jail?"

"Jeff tried to bail her out after he and Rick dropped the charges on each other. The woman was an out-of-towner and dropped the charges on Nan. Sam kept her overnight for striking a deputy."

"Why the reaction over her name?" Josh asked.

Lila sighed. "According to her, it sounds girly and weak. She hated it so much she erased it from the family bible and wrote 'Nan.' If you look close enough, you can see the original name."

Bret snapped his fingers. "Jeff said to tell you he fired Angie, and you can have your job back."

"No, thank you." Lila shuddered. "It was good to see you, Bret, but I need to get back to work."

"We're here for another reason." Mike set his cup on the counter. "We need you to come across the street with us."

Lila's mouth dropped open. She took one step then

another away from the deputies. "I haven't done anything. I wasn't even at the Low Tide."

Joshua stepped forward. "What is the reason?'

His arm brushed against her, and Lila slipped her hand into Joshua's palm. She didn't know why, only that she felt safer having done so. Especially when his fingers curled around hers.

"There's some items we're hoping you can identify." Bret glanced at Mike, and with his nod, said, "They may have belonged to Aunt Jennie."

"You have something that belongs to my mother?" She shook her head. Why did he say 'belonged' as if...?

The person was already dead... They found the body while they were digging.

That same day she'd told stories about her mother to Jamie, never suspecting what was happening when they passed those flashing lights.

Her heart thumped, and she stiffened to halt the quivers running through her body. "Was it my mother you found on Miss Emily's property?" Her voice cracked. "Tell me!"

Bret nodded, a faint redness rimming his eyes. "Looks like it might be."

"We found several personal effects that we need you to identify," Mike said. "The remains have been sent to the state lab. We need to provide a DNA sample from you to confirm the identity."

Effects. Remains. DNA.

Each word slapped her. Hard and furious and worse than any blow Aunt Nan could deliver. She swallowed back the tears that would never stop if she allowed the first drop to fall. Her throat ached, leaving her voice just above a whisper. "I'll come with you."

"Do you want me to go with you?" Josh asked. "Or maybe Paige?"

A deep fog rolled through her brain. She heard his words but struggled to make sense of them. Finally, she shook her head. "No, thank you. I'll manage."

Bret cupped a hand under her elbow. "I'll take care of her, Josh."

Lila counted the steps between Carson's and the sheriff's office. A mindless task to keep herself from breaking down in the middle of the street. The sun taunted her with its brilliance. The cool autumn air whipped her hair around her face like a shroud. Her stomach churned, and she fought back the rising nausea.

She flexed her hand, remembering how safe she'd felt when Joshua held it in his, and she wished she hadn't said 'no' when he asked to stay with her.

CHAPTER SEVEN

Joshua stood sentry at the front window. How long did it take to have Lila look at a few items? Were they questioning her about her mother? According to Karen, Lila had been a child when her mother disappeared. Unconfirmed but popular rumors claimed she deserted her child for the attentions of a man, leaving PI without a word of good-bye.

What if Lila had collapsed? No sign of an ambulance or EMT though all the deputies would have been trained in emergency first aid.

A hand brushed his shoulder as Paige joined him. "I'm going over there if she doesn't come back soon."

"I was thinking the same thing." He glanced at the clock over the counter. "Time for you to pick up Jess?"

"I called Dana. She said she'd take care of it. Karen's already left to get her kids. By the way, thank you for talking with her. I wish she would have said something."

"She was embarrassed. She probably wouldn't have told me except she felt desperate. I should have run my suggestions past you first."

"I'm in agreement with her kids coming here and the start time. I just need to figure where to get another table and chair."

"I can check the resale shop on Main Street. Morgan's sometimes has seconds. I'll look there too."

"Karen's coming in tomorrow to work with me on the food for Dana's wedding reception along with finalizing the new menu items. Can you take care of running the errands for the wedding along with table hunting?"

"I can. Lila will probably want to keep busy. If she insists on working, I'll take her with me."

"Good thinking. She shouldn't be alone." Paige craned her neck further. "I fixed food for her to take home. A couple containers of soup. Sandwiches. Chips. Cookies. I wasn't sure what she'd like or feel like eating."

He dared a glance away from the window. "You're a good person, Paige."

"I thought I was." A hint of sadness flickered across her face. "But I wasn't willing to give Lila a fair chance until you stood up for her."

"I gave a push. You did the rest."

"Here she comes." Paige lifted onto her toes, grunting. "I can't believe neither of those guys walked back with her."

"She probably refused."

Seeing Lila's bowed head, her arms wrapped around her middle, the slow, robotic walk, he wanted to charge across the street and rip into both deputies. His shoulders slumped, pulled down by a wave of guilt. He'd done the same thing by letting her leave by herself.

They stepped back from the window by the time Lila opened the door. She jerked to a stop when she saw them.

"I'm sorry I took this long. If we're done for today, I'd like to leave."

"Of course it's okay," Paige said. One hand fluttered as if to pat Lila's arm then dropped to her side.

Lila picked up her notebook from the counter. "I need to get my coat and purse so you can lock up behind me."

Josh exchanged a quick glance with Paige and pointed to his chest. She nodded.

"I'll drive you home, Lila," he said.

She shook her head and walked toward the kitchen. "The bus is due in ten minutes. No need to go out of your way."

The door didn't have a chance to swing all the way shut before Paige and Josh followed. They met Lila as she rushed out of the coat closet.

"You're one of us." A tremor coursed through Paige's voice. "We take care of one another."

Josh took the jacket from Lila's hands, holding it so she could slip her arms into the sleeves. "No need to stand in the cold, and it's not out of my way."

"Thank you," she whispered.

He could see Lila was near the end of her energy when she allowed him to help her to the car. Paige set the bags with the Carson's shirts and the food she'd prepared in the floor of the back seat.

Josh lifted a hand to Paige who returned the gesture then stepped back inside.

"You need my address," Lila said as he started the car.

He had that information from her application, but he let Lila tell him. Head bowed, hair blocking her face from his view, she fell silent afterward.

Her heart had to be broken in as many pieces as his had been when he'd learned of his father's murder. He gave a silent sigh, wondering at how much had changed in just a few days.

Paige had been dead set against even talking to Lila. If she hadn't changed her mind, where would Lila have been when the deputies gave her that news? Would anyone have cared if she had food to eat or a way home that didn't involve sitting on a bench in the cold?

A smile tugged at the corners of his lips. Paige called it right. Lila's one of us now, and she won't be alone through this.

⤙

The drive from town to Lila's apartment took minutes but seemed longer due to the silence. Joshua apparently didn't know what to say, and she couldn't bear to speak.

She hopped out of the truck as soon as Josh pulled into one of the parking spaces. "Thank you for the ride. I'll see you tomorrow." She closed the door, fumbling for her keys as she rushed across the parking lot.

"Lila, wait!" The slam of a door followed the shout, then the pad of running soles against the asphalt pavement.

I need to get inside where I can cry.

Why wouldn't people leave her alone? Calm and professional questions from the sheriff. Plastic bags that held the belongings of her mother's final day. Sympathy from a woman who two days ago had almost declined to talk to her. Now, Joshua refusing to recognize the boundary she'd set for her own protection. She was too used to harsh words and blunt reality for kindness to be a comfort. Still, she couldn't dismiss the man who'd treated her not just with compassion, but with respect.

She hovered in the open doorway as Joshua covered the distance from the truck in long, even strides, a Carson's shopping bag in either hand. His features were solemn, but the softness around his mouth offered a comfort she hadn't expected.

"Shirts," he said, lifting one bag then the other. "Soup and sandwiches."

A glance over her shoulder suggested an offer to invite him in. She stepped inside, allowing him to pass. She closed the door. Lock turned. Deadbolt engaged. An unfailing habit.

"Would you like some soup? Or a sandwich? We could split one."

The casual normality of the question soothed her more than any obvious expression of sympathy. Her gaze shifted to the afghan neatly spread across the back of the sofa, and she reached out to stroke the woven stitches.

"Why would anyone want to hurt my mother? She was kind and good."

He placed his palm next to hers. "Because there's evil people who do bad things to good people."

A flood of tears broke free. She cried for her mother. She cried because her last hope for a reunion was lost forever. She even wept for Joshua Canfield whose voice held the pain of someone who'd also suffered a shattering loss.

Joshua wrapped an arm around her and eased both of them onto the couch. He pulled the afghan around her and held her as sobs racked her body. At last, a deep breath overtook her, and her muscles relaxed.

She dozed, coming to awareness just as dusk was surrendering to dark. Her head rested on Joshua's chest, and his arm nestled her. Being here like this was wrong. She should move.

But she didn't.

Through the remaining light that sifted through the window, she studied his features. Handsome was a shallow description that failed in comparison to his heart. There was where his true beauty lay.

He worked in a small-town restaurant, never complaining but ready to take a stand for others. His family had money, but he wasn't a snob. He certainly hadn't peeled out of the parking lot after seeing the exterior of this crummy place.

She eased free of Joshua's protective arm and switched on the table lamp. He roused instantly, looking around.

"What time is it?"

She glanced at the display on the microwave. "Almost seven."

He sat up, rubbing his eyes with the heels of his hands then ran fingers through his thick hair. Rumpled looked good on him while she was a mess. Wrinkled clothes, messy hair, face stiff with dried tears.

"I need to wash up."

Lila turned toward the bathroom as his yawned "okay" followed her. She washed her face, brushed her hair, and accepted there was nothing she could do about her clothes. She rested her palm on the door handle then took a deep breath.

It was time to send Joshua home.

※

Joshua filled two bowls with re-heated soup. No doubt Lila had purchased the microwave. Unlikely the owner of the apartments would have provided an appliance small enough to be carted off by a parting tenant. He set the bowls, spoons, and several packages of crackers on the small table in front of the couch then closed the window blinds.

He looked up when the bathroom door opened. "Feel like eating?"

A faint smile touched her lips. "I could manage soup."

They sat next to one another, eating in a comfortable silence broken only by the occasional rattle from the dumpster or the slam of a car door.

Lila set her bowl on the tray and shifted on the cushion to face him. "Thank you for staying with me. I didn't think I needed company, but having you here helped."

"You're welcome." He hesitated then had to ask, "Do you want to talk about any of it?"

Her head dipped for moment, and he thought she'd decline to answer. Instead, she straightened her shoulders and meet his gaze full-on.

"No one knows this—except now the sheriff and his men —but my mother and I were planning to leave PI the night she disappeared."

Josh stiffened. "Were the two of you in danger?" He'd lived that life. Running, hiding then finally, confronting it.

"No, but she taught me to keep my business to myself when it came to the Grainger family. Maybe you haven't been here long enough, but they take family to a new level. No matter what one of them does, there's a code of silence. It didn't help that the previous sheriff, a man named Rayburn, was related to us."

"What happened that night?"

"I don't know. Mama had been saving money and making plans for some time. We'd leave here and make our wishes come true and find happiness. One morning she told me this was the day we were leaving. We packed the car after dark so none of the neighbors would see." Her gaze drifted upward as if she could see those events again. "She looked so pretty in a new dress, cream colored with tiny flowers. New pink shoes too. She worked so hard and rarely bought anything for herself. She bought a dress for me too. New clothes to start a new life. She said she had one errand to do before we could leave. I wanted to go with her, but she told me to take a nap. We planned to leave on the last ferry out. She didn't want me to be too sleepy and miss seeing it."

Her shoulders drooped. "That was the last time I saw her."

He stayed silent, letting her talk when and as much as she wanted. When she took his hand, he threaded his fingers through hers. And he listened.

"I ended up sleeping through the night. It was early when I woke up and couldn't figure out why we hadn't left. I couldn't find Mama anywhere. I wondered if her errand took her off PI and she missed the ferry coming back. It didn't make sense since we were going to leave on the ferry. I even worried if she'd had an accident. Maybe she didn't have her purse with her or someone stole it, and the doctors didn't know who to notify."

Josh's breath caught in this throat as he pictured Jess in that situation. Alone and scared. Something no child should go through. Lila's grip tightened, and he gave a gentle squeeze in return.

"Aunt Nan came by looking for Mama. She had a cleaning job lined up for her. She called Sheriff Rayburn. He's the one who started the story that she must have taken off with a man, leaving me behind." Her lips pressed into a tight line. "I was nine years old, but I knew there was no man in her life. Everything she worked for went toward our future. She would never have left me on purpose."

A moment or two passed before Joshua broke the silence. "Why does Sam think the person was your mother?"

"You mean the remains? That hit me the hardest when Deputy Winslow said that. There wasn't enough left to call a body. Nothing was left of her but a few items they called effects. A scrap of cloth from her dress that hadn't decayed. Her shoes. Pieces of her wallet. Driver's license but no money. One earring. I wish they could have found her wedding rings. I would like to have something that Daddy had given to

Mama." She gave a harsh laugh. "Remains and effects. All that's left of Jennie Lynn Grainger."

Her voice trembled then steadied. "After that I went to live with Aunt Nan and Uncle Mick."

He loosened his hand long enough to tuck the afghan around them. "What was that like?"

"Horrible. I went from a clean, quiet home where books and music were valued to a rowdy house with loud people who got louder the more they drank. I was the only girl of all the cousins, meaning the so-called woman chores landed on me."

"What about Hannah Jane?"

Lila nudged an elbow in his ribs. "Bite your tongue. Aunt Nan made it her mission to toughen me up. Life was hard and would walk all over me."

"Don't believe anyone who says you're weak. Lila Grainger, you're one of the strongest women I know."

"I'm getting there. I've been rattling on and keeping you here. Especially on a work night."

"Nope. Paige said there's no need for either of us to come in tomorrow. She and Karen are going to work on food for the wedding and the new menu items."

"I was going to help with that. Oh, no!" Eyes wide, she bolted upward. "I made such a scene today. In front of you and Paige was bad enough, but the computer person too. Ben must have been horrified."

"Ben was very sympathetic."

A broad translation of Hampshire's remark of 'Poor kid. Whoever did that needs a bullet between both eyes.'

"I need to keep busy. Would she mind if I went in?"

"How about giving me a hand instead? My mom is getting married on Wednesday, and I could use help with the to-do list Jamie and Paige gave me."

The first genuine smile since early afternoon danced across her lips. "Of course I'll help."

Josh picked up the used dishes and carried them to the kitchen area.

Lila nudged her way to the sink. "I'll wash those. You've more than done your share."

He stepped aside, admitting he'd pushed his way into her home and her life. Lila had accepted his gestures, but that didn't give him free rein over everything. Boundaries, he reminded himself.

Back planted against the counter, he glanced around the small apartment. "I lived a couple of weeks in a place similar to this. Smaller and no kitchen."

She rinsed a bowl and set in the drainer to dry. "Here on PI?"

He racked his memory. So many places melding into another. Idaho? That was it. He'd stopped briefly traveling between Washington and Montana.

"Little place in Idaho. I was on my way to a job at a ranch in Montana."

"You were a cowboy?"

That note of excitement in her voice amused him. If that's what it took to impress her, he'd accept it. "Ranch hand."

He frowned as a shadow crossed in front of the window. Not crossing. Lingering. Shifting as if trying to see into the room. A second later, the doorknob rattled.

Joshua bolted across the room, fumbling with the locks. Flinging open the door, he caught the fleeting glimpse of a person bolting around the corner of the building.

"Who is it?" Lila cried, grabbing the back of his shirt.

No point in pursuit. The person was gone or in hiding. Besides, it could have been a ruse to make him to do that very thing, leaving Lila unprotected. He shut the door, reengaged the locks.

"Someone was looking through the slats in the blind then tried to open the door."

She stumbled back a step, color washing from her face. "Someone had the wrong apartment."

"A visitor would have knocked. A tenant would have tried a key. Has this happened before?"

"No." She shook her head. "Someone made a mistake."

He closed the gap between them, cupping his hands around her upper arms. "I'm not trying to scare you. Something bad happened—"

"What happened was fifteen years ago!"

"And it came to light Saturday. Maybe it was a mistake. Maybe it was a warning or a threat. It's too coincidental to take a chance after what you learned today."

"I could go...." Her voice trailed off.

He gave a silent snort. Go to crazy Aunt Nan's? Or her doofus cousin Jeffy? At this point, could Bret Madigan be trusted?

"How about one of these options? I'll stay here and sleep on the couch. Or you can stay at my place. I have a garage apartment on Donaldson. Or I can call Paige."

"I can't impose on Paige. She has a child." She gazed around the room, no doubt realizing what little protection the ancient door and two flimsy locks provided.

He gave himself a mental kick in the rear for scaring her. Lila had been through too much trauma already. However, his own experience plus what his mother had gone through taught him not to take risks.

"If you're sure, yes, I'd like to stay with you."

The knot in his chest eased just a smidge. "Gather what you need for tonight and tomorrow."

That was close. I can't stay parked here much longer. Didn't expect Lila to have a guy over, especially tonight. Would've thought she'd be curled up in a ball, crying over her dead mama.

Somebody sure wasn't going to be pleased with that news.

CHAPTER EIGHT

Lila yawned, stretched and rolled over to dappled sunlight shining through the window. How glorious to wake up and see blue skies and the brilliant splash of autumn leaves rather than the brick wall of the next building. She couldn't remember the last time she'd slept so soundly. Or so late.

She threw back the covers and sat up, taking a moment to wiggle her toes in the soft rug next to the bed. A tap sounded on the bedroom door, and she jerked the sheet over her bare legs.

"Checking if you were awake," Joshua said through the inches wide opening.

"I just woke up. What time is it?"

"A little past nine. No rush. The places we need to go don't open until ten. The bathroom's yours whenever you want."

"Thanks. I'll be right out."

Lila waited until the door closed before standing and tugging the borrowed t-shirt into place. Her mind had been so scattered last night, she'd forgotten to pack a sleep shirt. She eyed the hastily packed bag sitting on the chair by the window and hoped she'd hadn't forgotten any other essentials.

She gathered her clothes and toiletries and headed out of the bedroom. She paused in the doorway to the living room where Joshua sat on the couch, tapping away on his tablet.

"I forgot my shampoo. Would you mind—"

He looked up with a grin. "Help yourself to whatever you need."

"Thank you, and don't worry. I remembered my toothbrush."

Lila closed the bathroom door on the heels of his chuckle. After a second of hesitation, she turned the lock. The shampoo and body wash were drugstore purchases, much like her own only with a more spicy scent.

She wiped the steam from the mirror to study her reflection. Eyes clear, no shadows. A wonder since she'd cried herself to sleep last night. Her hand paused in the middle of combing the tangles from her wet hair. Not a tear shed this morning. She sank down on the edge of the tub.

Am I that heartless? Her world changed yesterday. Except it hadn't.

Jennie Grainger had been out of Lila's life for over fifteen years. What changed was knowing that her mother hadn't deserted her.

Living with Aunt Nan and Uncle Mick taught her to hide her feelings but couldn't take away her dreams. Years passed, but Lila never forgot the pledge her mother had made and vowed to find the happiness that had been denied them.

She'd gathered the strength to move out of Nan's house and stake her claim for independence. Even after the move, she was still tied to the Graingers. Working at the Low Tide. Helping Aunt Nan. Throughout those times, she clung to those promised words.

Her mother was gone forever now, but it didn't mean Lila couldn't proceed with her exit strategy with a real-life goal.

New life. Good job. Love. Happiness.

She'd go back to her own home tonight. Joshua meant well but he wasn't responsible for her, and she wasn't going to take advantage of his kind heart. Things would remain strictly business between them.

Could she stick with that promise? The past few days had opened her heart, and she didn't know if she could close it off again. If she didn't, it meant breaking her promise to her mother for something that might never happen.

❧

Joshua shifted the car into gear and headed toward the streets leading to the Crossroads. Then again, the authorities may still be examining the grounds at Miss Emily's. Better to take Old Main. With the fall foliage still on the trees, the scenic drive might improve both their spirits.

"Our mission today is the dry cleaners, the party store, Caine's Jewelers, and Morgan's Woodworks." Before he could continue, a call signaled on the console. He tapped a button on the steering wheel to answer. "Hey, Paige. You're on speaker, and Lila's here with me."

"Great. What do you have done so far?"

"Nothing. The shops don't open for another fifteen minutes. We're on our way now."

"Oh, right. We've been at it since eight-thirty and seems like it should be later. Will you still have time to check on the table and chairs?"

"On the list. Anything else?"

"If something else comes up, I'll let you know."

"I'm sure you will. Later." He tapped the button again. "I think Paige is more wired over this wedding than Mom is."

"How do you feel about your mother remarrying?"

"I hate it." He winced over his blunt honesty. His heart felt like a rock in his chest, and he heaved a deep breath as if that might relieve the weight.

It didn't.

"I'm sorry. That was none of my business." Her hand brushed the sleeve of his jacket.

"Nick Warden is a great guy. He loves my mom, and she loves him. He even asked for my blessing. How could I say no to a guy who saved her life the first day they met?"

Another curious coincidence between the Graingers and Canfields. Though, what acts Buzz and Harley committed had nothing to do with Lila.

"Did you get the furniture plan worked out with your mother?"

Josh chuckled. "It took all of fifteen minutes."

Lila's eyes bugged. "She made you come to her house just for that?"

"Of course not. She had all this incredible food made, and we ended up eating on the terrace outside."

"How many were there?"

"Besides Mom, there was her fiancé Nick, his daughter Megan, plus Rhys and Jamie. After that, I went home and washed the truck. How was your Sunday?"

"Nothing special. I cleaned Aunt Nan's house for her."

"Are you and your aunt close?"

"In some ways, I'm closer to her than others in the family. Probably because she can count on me when she needs something." Lila sighed. "She took me in when I was nine years old. I don't know what would have happened to me if she hadn't."

He wasn't judging but from the little he did know about Hannah Jane, it was a safe bet she'd received more than her due from Lila over those years.

"Does your aunt work?"

"She works per diem as a nurse at the hospital. She said your—" With a soft gasp, Lila fell silent.

Josh shot a quick look in her direction. "She said something about my family?"

The tip of her tongue traced her lower lip. "It was about that man Stoddard. She repeated something that the ER nurse told her."

Josh took a deep, steady breath, an attempt to calm the thumping of his heart. "What did the nurse say?"

"She said Mr. Stoddard was still alive when he was brought in."

His hands tightened around the steering wheel. "That doesn't seem likely since he was shot three times."

Plus, Ben would never have left the scene if Toddy had been alive.

"I didn't mean to upset you."

"You didn't, and thank you for telling me. I hope this nurse isn't spreading this story around."

"To be fair, I don't know if Birdie did tell that story or if Nan made it up."

"Why would she make up that story?"

"Because Jeffy wants me to go back to work at the Low Tide. Nan also wants me to work there and move back to her house until she gets me a job at the hospital."

"In other words, she doesn't want you working at Carson's?"

"Yes, and that's why I shouldn't have mentioned that tale."

"Let's forget all that for now. "Josh eased the truck into a space on the Village parking lot. "Ready to do some walking?"

Lila's face beamed, showing more excitement than a list of routine errands should evoke. "I'm ready!"

This wasn't a date.

Lila repeated the warning several times as they strolled along Main Street. Window shopping and browsing alternated with completing the wedding tasks. Confirming delivery of flowers for the next morning. Doing the same at the bakery for the cake. Picking up more decorations than seemed needed for a small at-home wedding. Still, what would she know about that?

The opened-mouth stare from Rhoda, one of the mean girls from high school, when she saw them exiting Caine's Jewelry thrilled Lila to the point she almost felt ashamed.

Almost, but not quite.

She'd never laughed as much over minor things. Never looked in shop windows just to see what was there. Never known the contentment of strolling with a good-looking man who treated her like a lady. All things so normal to others, but ones that made the day magical for her.

"Next stop," Joshua said, opening the door to the dry cleaners.

"Hey, Lila!"

They stopped, turning to see Bret Madigan strolling in their direction, one hand lifted in greeting.

"Go ahead with your pick-up while I chat with Bret," Lila said. Seeing the wavering look on Joshua's face, she brushed her hand across his wrist. "I'll watch the bags."

"I'll be quick." He handed the shopping bags to her then darted into the building.

She took a few steps away from the entrance. "Good morning, Bret. Are you on patrol today?"

"I make rounds here a couple times a day." He nodded to the bags. "Taking the day off?"

"Running errands. Carson's is catering a wedding tomorrow."

Bret leaned one shoulder against the building. "Who's getting married?"

"Joshua's mother." She leaned forward, lowering her voice. "Have you heard anything more about those test results?"

"The lab said the DNA results should be ready by Thursday. I knew it was Jennie even before we found the driver's license." His mouth tightened as he stared over Lila's shoulder. "Pink shoes."

Her breath caught as she pictured those shoes. Dressy enough to match Mama's new dress, casual enough for jeans. She'd tried them on, and they'd laughed as Lila clomped around the room.

"There's nothing else to tell you at this point." He ran his palm from her shoulder to elbow. "I know it's impossible to put it out of your mind, but please try."

She nodded, fighting back bitter thoughts. A few seconds, sooner or later, and she would have missed Bret. Would have had a few more hours of what was normal to other people before returning to the reality of her own life.

Bret shot a quick glance over Lila's shoulder then took a step closer.

"I want you be careful around Joshua Canfield."

Chin jutted, she glared up at her cousin. "Joshua—"

"Did you know he was brought in for questioning for Nathan Stoddard's murder?"

... he was still alive... trying to say the name of his killer... Joshua

Lila shook away those treacherous thoughts along with the memory of seeing the deputy escort Joshua to the sheriff's office.

"Joshua didn't kill that man."

"You don't know—" Bret clamped his mouth shut as Joshua exited the dry cleaners.

"Ready to go?" Joshua called as he walked toward them. He shifted the plastic covered garments to hang over one shoulder.

"My cue to get back on patrol." Bret tapped his forefinger to the brim of his hat.

Lila pivoted, avoiding Joshua's keen gaze. "That's everything on our list, isn't it?"

"Are you all right? Did Bret have more information about your mother?"

She seized onto that excuse. "He said the DNA results would be back on Thursday. I don't want think about any of that today."

"I understand. Are you ready for a break? It's a little early, but how about lunch?"

"Don't we need to stop at Morgan's? We shouldn't take time—"

"There's plenty of time. If we were at work, we'd stop to eat."

Lunch. What normal people did. What she was going to do. "Sounds wonderful."

He transferred several of the shopping bags to himself. "Pick a place. Anywhere you want with the exception of the Garden Tea Shoppe."

"You don't like tea?"

"I can take or leave it, mostly leave it. Right now I need more than rabbit food."

"You wouldn't mind eating outside, would you?"

A smile crossed his lips. "No objections."

"Great. Let's take everything to your car then we can hit the...?"

He caught the teasing glance she cast in his direction, returning it with a full-fledged grin and a hopeful note in his voice. "Taco truck?"

She bumped her shoulder against his. "You got it."

Sharing another meal with Joshua seemed like a natural and easy thing to do. She pushed away the momentary shadows from her conversation with Bret and held on to the moments she'd shared today with the man beside her.

Because moments can be stolen away in a heartbeat.

∽

Minutes later, they sat at small wooden table, a cardboard tray of paper wrapped tacos and drinks in front of them. When Lila placed a five-dollar bill on the counter to cover her half of the meal, he hesitated only a second before adding his own money. Paying for both their meals might be a generous offer, but not when it stole Lila's dignity.

The air was cool, the sun was warm. They talked, and sometimes ate in silence. With one taco remaining, Lila nudged the box in front of Joshua. He eyed it, then claimed it.

"After we finish lunch," Lila said, "let's check the resale shop for the table and chairs Paige wants."

Josh wiped his mouth on a paper napkin. "I hope we can find something suitable there. It'll cost less than even a slightly irregular set at Morgan's."

"I'm an ace at refinishing old furniture. If we find something that fits the space, I can make it look good."

He didn't doubt that at all. "You'll have to show me so I'll know how."

Blatant skepticism crossed her features. "You intend to refinish furniture?"

"Why not? I like older furniture. Not older as in antiques but the kind like grandparents would pass down."

A teasing smile played around her lips. "*Your* grandparents?"

"Okay, definitely not mine." He lifted his hands in surrender. "Let's leave it at I like traditional pieces that can be made to look new again."

"I'm your girl." On the heels of those words, Lila's eyes widened, and she clamped her mouth shut.

He couldn't help teasing in return. "I'm counting on it, especially if it involves a trip to the hardware store."

"I promise it won't hurt." The pink in her cheeks receded to a paler shade. "Depending on the condition of the tables, we might need an electric sander. If the hardware store doesn't rent those, would your brother have one we could borrow?"

Josh shook his head. "Who—oh, you mean—Yeah, I'm sure Rhys could get one."

"I'm sorry. I wasn't thinking." She ducked her head for a moment. "While Jamie and I were together on Saturday, I asked if you and her husband were half-brothers. She didn't go into any personal details other than how you two are related. I didn't want to say the wrong thing like I did at the restaurant... and right now."

"You said nothing wrong."

Lila relaxed as if she'd been forgiven even when she'd committed no offense. The concern on her face was evident, but more so was her patience. A serenity that soothed his jangled edges. No pressure. No demands. No judgement.

"If you don't mind, I'd like to fill in the rest. Warning, it's a sordid story."

She rested one palm on his hand. "I'm a Grainger. I think I can handle it."

He laughed as something eased inside of him. If anyone could understand, it would be Lila Grainger.

"What did Jamie tell you?"

"That your biological mother was killed in a car wreck that she caused trying to run Mrs. Canfield's car off the road. Mrs.

Canfield is actually someone named Catherine and was married to Rhys' father and ended up in a coma."

"In a nutshell." He whooshed out a deep breath. "It was all about money. A trust fund was due to expire, and Mom was the remaining heir. Stoddard needed to eliminate any of Mom's legal heirs before the trust was disbursed. At that point, since he was managing the account, he'd have access to the funds."

"If your father knew this, why didn't he go to the authorities?"

"No idea. Maybe he was working to get proof. To complicate the matter more, it turns out that Mom isn't my biological mother."

"How did that happen?"

"That trust fund I mentioned? At one point there were two living heirs. Dana Canfield and Catherine McCall. They were cousins going back a generation or two. Maybe more." He shrugged. "Nathan Stoddard approached my biological mother first to advise her of the trust. When she found out there was another heir, she made contact with Catherine and tried to kill her. Stoddard paid off someone at the hospital to switch the records. He needed a living heir until the date that the trust expired. Mom was in a coma for several weeks after the accident, probably pumped full of drugs during that time too. She had memories of her own life but was told they were false."

"Your father must have known the difference."

"Exactly. Why did he stay silent? He could have exposed the identity issue from the beginning."

"How old were you when this happened?"

"I was two years old. After she came to PI, she said something that triggered a recollection for Rhys. He found pictures of the two of them and started putting the story together.

Mom wants us to have a relationship, but I feel guilty. He grew up without a mother because I got his life."

"That's not your fault."

"No, it's Nathan Stoddard's fault for putting it into motion. But my father and biological mother bear responsibility for their actions."

"Jamie seems fond of you. Jess obviously adores you."

"They've all welcomed me. I'm getting close to them, too. It's a little harder with Rhys, but I give him credit for pushing like he did on Saturday. I need to do more too." He looked around to see a line forming by the truck, and several people looking around for a table. "We should get moving."

They cleared the table and deposited the trash in a nearby bin.

"Hey, Lila." He caught her hand in his. "Thanks for listening."

"You're welcome." An impish smile danced on her lips. "Come on. I'll show you how to shop for less."

The glow on her face, the touch of her skin against his, was all it took to chase away the sadness clinging inside him. He lifted his face to the warmth of the midday sun.

I'm falling for you, Lila Grainger.

CHAPTER NINE

Dana checked her reflection in the cheval mirror in her bedroom, not with her professional designer eye, but with the gaze of a woman in love. The off-white sleeveless lace dress hugged her slender curves, ending with a scalloped hemline just below her knees. Three-inch stiletto heels with a sling-back strap shimmered on her feet. Twin combs lined with crystals held her hair in a casual upsweep. Diamond and pearl earrings and a matching bracelet completed her ensemble.

Sexy and sophisticated. Just the look she was going for. Her heart beat a little faster, and the corners of her lips turned up in a smile she couldn't hold back.

Nick and I are getting married today.

In many ways, it seemed as if they were a married couple. Living together since late spring. His daughter, her son and daughter-in-law living in the house with them. An extra bedroom set up for sleepovers with Jess.

She seated herself at the vanity, resisting the urge to touch up her make-up. Paige would have a fit if her handiwork was ruined at this point. A tap sounded then the bedroom door eased open a few inches.

"Are you dressed and ready for photos?" Jamie asked. "Robin's finished with the guys."

She and Nick had agreed on a scaled-down wedding. An at-home ceremony and reception with an even dozen guest list. No attendants with the exception of a flower girl, neither of them having the heart to disappoint Jess about participating in their wedding. The one option Dana refused to minimize was the photographer.

After an in-depth consultation and a review of Robin Spencer's portfolio, Dana granted the photographer carte blanche and a generous budget. Flowers died, cake was consumed, but photographs... those were forever.

"Yes, come in. I'm ready."

The door swung open, and Jess wiggled past the others. She raced across the room, stopping at the edge of the vanity where Dana sat. Paige, Jamie, and Megan waited to one side.

"Granna, you look so beautiful."

Holding the child in a one-armed hug, Dana rested her cheek against the top of Jess's head. "So do you."

"Hold that pose." Robin dropped to one knee. The shutter clicked several times. "Now one with just the bride."

She smiled. Crossed her legs. Posed before the cheval mirror. Sat on the chaise lounge. And she wondered what shots she'd captured of Nick.

From the corner of her eye, she saw Paige frown at her watch, her mouth opening. At the same time, Robin lowered her camera.

"Just one more. We're a couple minutes ahead of schedule."

Paige closed her mouth.

"I need the bride—" She motioned Dana into place, then Jamie, Megan, and Jess. "Daughter-in-law, daughter, and granddaughter."

Paige stood behind Robin, a wistful look on her face. Dana lifted a hand, waving.

"Paige, I need all my girls."

A brilliant smile emerged, and Paige skipped across the room. A few more poses and numerous clicks of the shutter followed before Robin lowered the camera again. "Thank you, ladies. I'll be downstairs."

"Let's give Dana a few minutes alone." Jamie stood by the open doorway, waiting until everyone trooped out then gave Dana a quick wink.

Bless Jamie for knowing exactly what Dana needed. She couldn't have wished for a more perfect wife for her son. And perfect daughter-in-law too.

She sank down again on the vanity bench. It wouldn't hurt to touch up her lipstick. Her hand jerked when three raps sounded on the door.

"Come in," she called, her scowl disappearing as she viewed her reflection. Whew—no damage. She swiveled to face the door.

Joshua entered, glancing around the bedroom. "First time I've seen this room. It has your touch."

Her mouth went dry, and her heart beat hard and fast as if she'd seen a ghost. She pushed to her feet and crossed the room, hands extended.

Joshua's mouth tightened, worry sketching across his features. "Mom, are you all right?"

"You remind me so much of your father," she whispered. Cupping her palm against his cheek, she struggled to hold back a sob. "When you walked it, it was like seeing him again."

He blinked several times, fighting back his own tears. "I want to hug you, but Paige will kill me if I mess up your dress or make-up."

She shook her head. Joshua was a grown man, but the

little boy in him could always make her laugh. Taking his hand, she led him to the chaise lounge. She ran her palm along the sleeve of his suit jacket. "I forget sometimes how grown up you are now."

"I must not be too old to have a mom who looks so young."

He was hiding behind a joke and a smile. Something her son had never done before. In the past, he was an open book with never a doubt how he felt. Of course, he'd kept certain parts of his life to himself. Nothing more than what any other teen-age boy would have done. Joshua had been very much his father's son and like his father, he'd always been protective of her. Not so much he couldn't turn to her when needed. Some problems in his life couldn't be solved shooting hoops or jogging with his father. Those times required chocolate chips cookies and mother's touch.

"I know today is difficult for you, but thank you for being here."

"I couldn't not be here." He gazed over her shoulder. "It helped that Nick asked for my blessing. He's a good guy. He cares for you."

She slipped her arm through his, leaning against his shoulder. "Do you realize I've known you longer than anyone else in my life? You and I have spent more time together than I did with my parents. We're the only ones who'll have memories of our holidays, birthdays, and vacations. Everyday life. I loved your father, but I'm also hurt and angry with him."

"So am I, but I'm mad at myself too. I let him send me away instead of staying to protect you. If Dad would have told us the truth, maybe he'd be alive. That year I was away, I grew up in ways I never expected and learned to appreciate all the things I took for granted."

"Did you get the emails I wrote?" From the time Joshua had left home, she'd sent an email every night to him. Chatty notes about her life. Letting him know she loved him, missed him, hadn't forgotten him.

"I read them over and over. They got me through a lot of rough times. Ben set up a redirect to whatever email address I was using at the time. I couldn't risk writing back to you."

"I missed you. You're my son. Without you, there's an emptiness, regardless of how many others came into my life." She squeezed his hand. "Providence has been a place of healing for me. I want it to be one for you as well."

"I'll get there in time." He dropped a quick kiss on her cheek. "In the meantime, I'll let you get back to your primping."

Dana huffed in a mock scolding. "Joshua Colby Canfield, sometimes—"

"There's a surprise waiting for you downstairs." He stopped at the door, grinning that little boy grin. "Love you, Mom."

He pulled the door shut behind him.

"I love you too," Dana said, even though he couldn't hear the words.

That was okay. Joshua always knew he had her love.

Nick's den was the perfect spot for Rhys to hide out. Other than providing muscle when needed, he'd escaped the majority of Paige's directives. Anything for Mom, but Paige had a staff of four including herself to pull off the event.

No TV or music. Just blessed silence and the comfort of a black leather sofa from Nick's old apartment. He leaned back his head, savoring the quiet.

A sharp knock broke the stillness. He sat up, groaning as the door opened and Josh entered.

"Got a few minutes?" he asked.

Rhys waved a hand. "Close the door. Quick."

Josh eased the door shut then plopped down next to him. "Relax. Paige is doing last minute checks. Megan's keeping Jess occupied, and Jamie's greeting the guests. Nick and Sam escaped to the patio."

"Need help with anything?" Despite wanting to avoid the chaos, he was ready and willing to pitch in again if needed.

"Decorations, flowers, food and drink, all covered."

Rhys studied Joshua's features. He seemed calm. No, not calm. Controlled. All of the family were dealing with emotional wounds, but the freshest ones belonged to Joshua.

Maybe that was the reason Mom chose a pared-down wedding. Good guy that he is, Nick willingly agreed to go along with whatever dream wedding Dana envisioned. What she picked was an at-home, simple affair with no attendants. If she'd scaled down her own vision to make things easier for Joshua, Rhys had no objections.

"I need a favor," Josh said.

"Sure. Go ahead."

"I want to escort Mom down the aisle."

Rhys pushed back a smidgen of jealousy and reminded himself that today wasn't about him and his feelings. Before he could agree, Joshua continued.

"Half-way, and you escort her the rest of the way."

Shame kicked jealousy to the curb, followed by an unexpected warmth. "That's a great idea. I bet Mom was thrilled when you asked her."

"I didn't tell her other than a surprise would be waiting." A mischievous grin crossed his lips. "That's why I want to go first so I can see her expression."

Cunning and unexpected. Mom would never see it coming.

Rhys held out a closed fist. "Let's do it."

They fist-bumped in solidarity.

Rhys sat for a moment after Joshua departed. *This is what it's like to have a little brother, even if that little brother is grown-up.* More encouraging was Joshua taking the next step toward that relationship.

Co-conspirators was a good start.

⟡

Joshua's best efforts to hide a smile failed as Dana descended the stairs, bouquet in hand and a slight frown creasing her brow. He leaned forward to whisper in her ear.

"Surprise."

Her dark brown eyes cast a swift glance toward the living room. "Joshua—"

The sound of *Canon in D* floated through the air, and Paige gave the signal for Jess to proceed. Josh tucked his mother's hand into the crook of his arm.

"As we walk down the aisle, Mom, remember how much you love me."

He took the first step, and she had no choice but to follow. Midway into the room, they turned toward the French doors where the reverend and Nick waited. Nick's lips formed a silent *wow*, and he lifted one hand to his chest in a heartbeat motion. Beside him, Jess bounced on her toes, her face beaming.

Halfway down, Rhys stepped into the aisle. Joshua paused, meeting Dana's startled look before kissing her cheek.

Rhys nodded in thanks. Joshua dipped his head in return and took a seat next to Ben and Stacy. Mouth dry, eyes damp, he watched Rhys escort *their* mother the rest of the way, giving her a kiss the same way Joshua had done before resuming his seat.

Rhys seemed at peace with the wedding. Maybe due to all their lost years, he was thankful to have Mom back in his life and open to anything that made her happy. Then again, the animosity between Mom and Rhys's father might have more than a little to do with that.

Josh glanced at Erik McCall, wondering again why the man had been invited or why he'd accepted the invitation. Probably because Mom was friends with April Davis, McCall's... what? Date? Fiancée? Lady friend?

I'm living in a damn soap opera. My mother's best friend is dating her ex-husband who's the father of my cousin who's also now my stepbrother.

At the sound of Nick Warden's voice, Joshua jerked his attention toward the ongoing ceremony.

"I was standing outside my garage the first time I saw you, and my life shifted. That building is gone, but the love that began there will last forever."

Sweat broke across Josh's brow. His heart thumped against his chest. *I can't sit here. I can't listen to this when it should have been Mom and Dad renewing their vows.*

He coughed, covering a choke. Ben's shoulder nudged him, and he glanced to one side. Ben sat in profile to him, his expression calm except for a tightness in his jaw. Another nudge and slight lift of his chin.

He's remembering Dad too.

Joshua pried his mind away from those memories in time to hear his mother complete her vows.

"We bring three remarkable children into this marriage. With them, we'll honor our past and build a future together, and I'm blessed to have you by my side on this journey."

The minister stepped forward. He rested his palm upon

Nick and Dana's hands. A few more words followed before he pronounced the couple wedded.

Joshua's shoulders sagged, and his hands lay limp in his lap.

It was done.

Done but not over. There was still the reception to get through. Champagne, cake, and hors d'oeuvres had been set up on the dining room table. Music played softly in the background.

Joshua lingered at the edge of the kitchen, watching the interaction of the guests. Kevin Davis attempting to talk with Megan, and Deputy Mike Winslow neatly cutting off any chances. Davis moving on and Megan giving Mike what appeared to an earful. His fault. Anyone who could take down Harley Grainger, six-foot-two, two hundred pounds, with one kick didn't need Winslow to fight her battles.

His gaze moved on. Mom and April Davis talking. More like April talking, Mom listening. He held back a grin, recognizing her polite society smile. Wonder what the story was there.

Hmm. Nick Warden and Erik McCall conversing as well. Seemed at ease, an occasional laugh. Regular guy talk.

Now, this was interesting. Jess and Stacy Andrews. The redhead sent out fire under ice vibes which made either an excellent match with Ben or a disaster waiting to erupt. Jess spun in a circle, her dress swirling around her legs, and Stacy clapped her hands. Camaraderie sealed between the two when they began comparing shoes.

Through it all, his gaze kept returning to Lila. She moved with a swift grace. Replenishing the food and napkins. Cutting and plating the cake after the initial slice had been made by the wedding couple. Refilling glasses as the guests mingled. By preference, Karen remained in the kitchen, keeping everything under control there.

An hour later, Mom and Nick stood at the edge of the dining room, ready to make their exit. Nick called for everyone's attention, and the chatter of conversation faded.

"Dana and I are leaving now. We appreciate you being a part of our day."

"Thank you, everyone," Dana said.

The group trooped onto the porch. Seeing the besotted look on Warden's face, Joshua pushed another piece of hurt out of his heart. How could he begrudge his mother having someone who loved her that much?

He fell into step behind Rhys and Megan, walking to Nick's SUV while the guests remained on the porch prior to leaving. Hugs, kisses, and handshakes were exchanged before the couple drove away. Megan dashed back to the house while Rhys kept stride with Josh.

"Give me a hand moving the furniture back?" Rhys asked.

"Sure. No problem."

"Hungry?"

He wasn't expecting that question, but since it had been asked, the answer was obvious. Appetizers and cake kept the hunger away but not for long. "Yeah, I could eat."

"I'll call in a pizza order to the Lighthouse."

A friendly clap landed on his back, and they walked the rest of the way in silence. Another small step down the new path.

~

The furniture was back in place, the clean-up completed. Rhys and Jamie were on their way to pick up the pizza. Mike and Megan retreated to the patio to finish whatever argument was currently in progress. Snippets of conversation between Lila and Stacy filtered in from the kitchen. All the others departed including Sam and Paige, despite Jess's protests.

Which gave Joshua a much-needed moment of peace. No wonder Rhys took refuge in the den earlier. He considered taking that advantage himself when Ben headed toward him.

"You okay?"

"I am now." He bumped an elbow against Ben's arm. "Thanks... for back there."

Ben's mouth lifted in a ghost of a smile. "I knew it was tough for you."

In that moment, Josh realized the purpose of Ben's sympathetic gesture had been for both of them. An act which indicated more than professional relationship between Dad and Ben.

For that matter, why had Ben invested so much time and his own personal safety for the Canfield family? He'd never asked for money though Dad must have made funds available to him. Possibly Ben siphoned off a portion of Toddy's larceny. He was good enough at computers and security to do that without detection.

Whatever the reason, it had to be about something other than money. Right now, there was another issue burning to be discussed. He gazed around the room to ensure they were alone.

"We need to talk."

"About?"

"Is there any chance Toddy was still alive when the EMTs arrived at the emergency room?'

"No."

"What if he didn't die immediately?"

"He was dead." Ben's eyes hardened into an icy glare. "Where's this coming from?"

"One of the ER nurses told Lila's aunt that Toddy was alive when he was brought in."

"Didn't happen. If—and this is a big if—he was alive when we left, it was several hours before he was found. He would have bled out by that time if shock hadn't already taken him out. Where did you hear this?"

"Lila's aunt told her when she found out about her new job. She was concerned Lila was getting into a dangerous situation."

"Compared to the Low Tide?" Ben snorted. "The aunt? Is that crazy Hannah Jane who punched out Madigan?"

Josh snickered. "You mean Aunt Nan? Yes."

"If it was true, the sheriff would have mentioned it to Dana. That nurse was either looking for attention or setting the aunt up to spread a fake story. Or the aunt was lying."

Josh let that theory simmer for a moment. "Do you ever think about Stoddard?"

Ben frowned. "No reason to. Do you?"

"I hate what he did to Mom. He had an entire year to manipulate her emotionally after Dad died. Standing up for her in public but wearing away at her until she was emotionally dependent on him. The poor old man all alone except for her, and how they needed each other. Sometimes... sometimes, it's hard to separate the Uncle Toddy I knew since I was kid from Nathan Stoddard."

"You'll get there. Just keep reminding yourself Toddy was an act, and Stoddard was the man playing that role." Ben glanced toward the French doors at the back of the room. "Looks like they're getting ready to come in."

He walked to the fireplace, hands in his pockets. "As for

your mom, if anyone can overcome what she's gone through, it's Miss Katie."

Miss Katie.

Josh's nerves tingled as if an alarm had been triggered. "What did you call my mother?"

A hint of 'oh, crap' slid across Ben's habitual poker face. "I said if anyone could, it was this lady."

"No, you didn't."

He paced forward. Ben backpedaled. Grabbing fistfuls of Ben's jacket, Joshua slammed him against the wall. "Why did you call my mother Miss Katie?"

"Back off, Canfield."

He slammed him again, relishing the grunt that spilled out of Ben's mouth. "Not until you explain yourself."

"Whoa!" Mike thrusted a shoulder between them, planting his hand on Josh's chest. "What's going on?"

"Just a disagreement," Joshua muttered. He flexed his hands, releasing his hold on Ben's jacket.

"My fault," Ben brushed the wrinkles from his clothing. "I made a comment that was completely out of line. Josh rightly took offense."

"Must have been a doozy to get that kind of reaction."

"I told Josh he has an extremely hot mom."

Mike's eyes bulged. "Dude, you don't talk about a guy's mother like that."

"Which I now understand." Ben extended his hand. "Joshua, I was out of line, and I apologize."

"Apology accepted." Joshua accepted the clasp, adding a bit more pressure than necessary. He stepped back, looking around. "Where's Megan?"

"In the kitchen, taking a break from me." Mike glanced in that direction, missing the emerging grin on Ben's face and Joshua's warning glare.

The front door opened with Rhys and Jamie bearing several large boxes. As if the fragrant aroma hadn't announced its arrival, Rhys called out, "Pizza. Dining room."

Josh fell into step behind Ben, whispering. "We will talk."

Ben glanced over his shoulder, his poker face back in place, and gave a nod.

The mood lightened with the addition of pizza, soft drinks, and beer.

"Where are the honeymooners headed?" Mike asked.

"No idea," Rhys said. "Mom doesn't even know. Nick asked Jamie to pack for her."

Stacy shot a glare at Ben. "Don't ever think about trying something like that."

He stroked the curve of her chin. "Wouldn't dare."

"Stacy, is your pizza okay?" Rhys asked. "Plenty left if you want another kind."

"Veggie pizza is what I wanted. I only eat the toppings, not the crust." She eyed Lila sitting next to her. "Unlike this one who's on her second slice, crust and all. Admit it, you eat whatever you want and never gain weight."

Lila smiled. "Pretty much."

"I officially hate you."

"You're absolutely gorgeous, and I hate you back."

"Now, me." Jamie waved her hands. "Nothing against Baby Mac, but since I soon will no longer see my feet, I hate both of you."

"I have nothing to add," Megan laughed, "but I'll send out some hate vibes to all of you."

"Now that's the way to settle an argument." Mike gestured toward Joshua and Ben. "Unlike these two, about to come to blows."

"Mike," Megan hissed through the other exclamations. "Stop being a jerk."

"No big deal," Ben said. "I made a comment that was out of line. Josh called me out, and I apologized."

A sad shake of his head. A humbled look on his face. Ben gave every appearance of a remorseful man. Joshua would have appreciated the performance if the story wasn't based on a lie intended more to embarrass him than Hampshire.

"He shoved you against the wall."

"I deserved it."

Mike snorted. "Go ahead, Hampshire. Tell McCall what you said about his mother."

Wearing that same repentant expression, Ben looked across the table at Rhys. "I told Josh he has an extremely hot mom."

Josh tensed, waiting for an explosion similar to his own.

"Huh." Rhys kept his gaze locked on Ben for a few seconds then looked at Mike. "Are you saying that my mom isn't hot?"

Mike's mouth dropped open. "I'm going to take a pass on that question."

"Why? It's either yes or no."

Megan leaned around Mike, hissing, "Get him, big brother."

Mike glared at Megan. "In my defense, you don't say that about another guy's mom."

Rhys rolled his shoulders. "Yes or no, Winslow."

Josh glanced at Ben who wore a broad grin. Right now, it was a tie who was the bigger jerk—Ben or Mike.

"Okay, yeah, Mrs. Canfield... Warden... is hot."

"Damn straight." Rhys lifted from his seat, arm extended toward Ben then Joshua for a high five.

"You know," Megan said as Rhys sat down. "Mom would have shut down this conversation with a single look."

"The eyebrow." Josh eased another slice of pizza onto his plate. "Flavored with an on-point comment."

"Ooh, do the eyebrow, Rhys." Megan bounced in her chair, looking around the table. "He almost has it nailed."

Hands clasped on the table in front of him, Rhys lifted one eyebrow then turned his gaze toward Ben.

"Ben, thank you for the compliment." His gaze scanned around the table. "Now that we've covered that subject, let's move on to a more suitable topic."

Four thumbs up, two thumbs down, and Lila abstained.

"Okay. How about this one?" Rhys huffed a long drawn out breath. His tone rose with each word. "Good grief, Mike, you're such a *jerk*!"

Megan burst out laughing. "That was pretty good."

"Right on the nose." Mike chuckled.

Stacy leaned forward, chin rested in her cupped palm. Her full lips teased a smile. "Rhys... do me."

Rhys shook his head, raising both hands in surrender. "Not touching that one."

One arm around Stacy's shoulders, Ben winked. "Damn straight, McCall."

Joshua glanced around the table. Despite Ben's remark and Mike's hammering over that statement, the remainder of the afternoon had turned out better than he'd expected. Credit for that belonged to Rhys. He shared that quality with Mom of making people feel relaxed and included.

The party began to break up as Mike left for the evening shift. Jamie excused herself next to rest upstairs, followed by Rhys.

Josh stood, looking around the table. "Ladies, why don't you relax in the living room while Ben and I clean up?"

Lila hesitated. "I should—"

Stacy linked an arm through Lila's. "You should come with us."

"Alone at last," Ben said as he cleared the uneaten scraps into an empty pizza box.

"You're off the hook for now because the others might overhear. After you finish the installation at Carson's tomorrow, we're having a talk."

"You got it."

Joshua followed Ben into the kitchen and began rinsing the plates. "I want the truth, not some half-ass diversionary remark, or there'll be trouble between us."

"You think I'm scared of you, Canfield?" Ben jerked his head toward the opening between the kitchen and living room. "I still have to explain to Stacy why I think Dana is hot."

Interesting. This time he called her Dana. Yep, diversionary tactic.

"You have yourself to blame for that."

"It threw Winslow off guard. What excuse would you have given?"

Josh stammered for a moment then shrugged. "We'll never know. You're just lucky Rhys took it in good spirits, and yeah, you still have to face Stacy."

Ben shrugged. "I'll apologize, turn on the Hampshire charm, followed by passionate seduction."

"Gag me."

"If that doesn't work, I'll toss back the 'do me' comment she made to McCall."

Josh snorted. "Which will lead to her reply of 'we're talking about you, not me.'" He held up a hand, halting Ben's retort, as his phone beeped. He pulled the phone from his pocket when a second beep sounded. Then a third.

Ben jerked to attention. "Trouble?"

"Not the way you mean. Paige wants to know if you finished the tweaks—her word, not mine—on the software? Is the installation on for tomorrow? What time—"

"Yes, yes, and ten." Ben picked up a small white box holding a slice of wedding cake. "I'm heading out. Thanks for the cake for Maisie."

After a nod to Ben as he exited to the living room, Josh switched on the dishwasher. He leaned back against the island, listening to the conversation in the next room. The rumble of Ben's voice. Stacy's throaty laugh mingled with a higher pitched one from Megan. Within it all, the soft cadence of Lila's gentle tones.

The day had been rougher than he'd expected, but worth it to see Lila relaxed and happy.

CHAPTER TEN

The drive from the Canfield house to Stacy's apartment passed in silence with the exception of several generic comments about the wedding. She didn't *seem* mad. Hot or cold, Stacy wasn't one to conceal her emotions. Either way, Ben wasn't about to bring up the subject of Dana Canfield.

What did prey on his mind was Canfield's comment about Stoddard making it to the ER still alive. The story was nonsense. What concerned him was the reason the story had been told. Was it matter of a night-shift nurse wanting attention? Or was the aunt trying to seed doubts in Lila's mind about her new job? Using it as a ploy to get her unpaid helper to return home?

Lila Grainger seemed like a good kid, which was probably the reason her useless family continued to take advantage of her. Canfield, whether he realized or not, was primed to ride to her rescue.

The Monday night trip he'd made to the Low Tide proved Lila was right about wanting out of that environment. Loose adherence to liquor laws, gambling in the back room, and multiple drug deals involving pot or pills. Plus a visit from

Deputy Bret Madigan with a doofus named Jeffy, which could have meant "I have an eye on you" or "I'm here for my payoff."

All that in the time Ben pretended to nurse a bottle of beer and lost a game of pool on purpose.

He had no doubts Lila was an innocent to any of the illegal goings-on. She probably suspected laws were being broken, but was either too naïve or scared to look for hard proof.

Did Jennie Grainger have proof of illegal acts fifteen years ago? Was she a participant who'd skimmed enough money to attempt an ill-planned escape with her daughter? Or had she been another innocent caught in the crossfires of the Grainger clan?

Ben pulled into one of the empty parking spots outside Stacy's apartment building. He shifted the car into Park to the click of a seatbelt being released.

"Do you still carry your taser?"

Stacy frowned. "Why would you ask that?"

"A bad feeling I have. Something's bound to break loose with that dead woman they found."

"You mean Lila's mother."

Ben accepted the reproachful note in Stacy's tone as deserved. "Yes, her mother."

"You think she's in danger?"

"Possibly. Maybe the killer thinks Lila heard or saw something that night or during the days before or after the murder. The way we're all being thrown together, I want to make sure you're protected."

"I have it right here." Stacy patted her purse. "Along with the handcuffs you gave me."

He ignored the scolding tone. This rebuke he didn't deserve.

"I did ask what you wanted for your birthday."

She rolled her eyes at the teasing comment. "Not what I expected when I said something shiny to go around my wrist."

He stroked a finger over the diamond bracelet circling her wrist, recalling the look on her face when she searched deeper in the gift bag as he'd suggested. She thanked him in more ways than he'd expected as well, looking mighty fine in nothing but that bracelet.

"I want you to be safe. These Graingers can be dangerous."

"Tell me about it. That Denton guy who attacked Erik last summer is a shirt-tail relative to that bunch."

His jaw tightened. "Why didn't you tell me that?"

Stacy pursed her lips, sending an air kiss his way "By the time we met, Denton was already in jail, but you're sweet to worry." She shifted in her seat, tapping a nail against the top of the cake box. "Are you coming back after dropping off Maisie's cake?"

"Wish I could, but I need to run some final checks on the system I'm installing at Carson's. How about tomorrow night?"

"I can't. A group of us are going to Frostburg tomorrow to discuss the buy-out with Winters Construction." She rolled her eyes. "I'm not sure what time I'll get home."

"Any possibility you can take Friday off?"

"I'll check with Rhys. Kevin's still under the misunderstanding he can tell me what to do."

Ben chuckled. "Idiot."

"What do you have in mind?"

"I pick up you after work in Frostburg, and we head over to Richmond for a long weekend."

Her eyes widened, and her lips parted.

"Is that a yes?"

"Of course, it's a yes. We haven't gone away together since last summer, and I really need a break from work." Her shoulders sagged. "With whatever you're doing at Carson's, can you take Friday off?"

"I'll drill everything he needs to know into Canfield's brain. He's smart. He'll get it." He stroked a thumb across her cheek. "So, get packing, lady."

"I hope Joshua realizes what a good friend you are to him." She tugged her keys from her purse. "The poor man was obviously struggling with his mother re-marrying. No wonder, considering the circumstances of his father's death. I know you made that comment about Mrs. Canfield to shake him up. If he was angry, he wasn't dwelling on those other things."

He was off the hook, but for some reason, Stacy's observation rankled him. "You know me that well?"

"Please. I saw you talking with Mrs. Canfield while you were at the office working on my computer. Friendly, courteous but no flirting, and definitely no ogling."

His ego bumped up a notch. "Can't keep your eyes off me, huh?"

"Can't help it. There's something about a nerd, a gentleman, and a tiger all wrapped up in one incredible package that sets my blood racing."

All thoughts soared out his head. Before he could make a move, Stacy slid out of the car.

She leaned down and winked. "I'll sext you after I talk with Rhys and let you know where to pick me up."

"I'll be waiting."

Ben watched as she walked to the entrance to the building. Hair bouncing, hips swaying, a saucy look over one shoulder before she stepped out of sight. A broad grin broke free as he drove away.

Tiger, huh?

His smile faded as he eased one hand from the steering

wheel to confirm the USB stick Dana had slipped to him remained safe in his inner jacket pocket.

One more thing to take care of tonight.

~

Dana kicked off her shoes and wiggled her toes to catch the warm air blowing around her feet. Nick's attention *seemed* to be directed at the road ahead of them, but she could see the smirk hovering on his lips.

"Give up?"

Dana held back a huff. Married less than three hours, and the man was driving her crazy playing 'guess where we're going on our honeymoon.'

"Not yet. We're not flying, so that eliminates Hawaii. We're not leaving the country which rules out Niagara Falls. Not New York, Atlanta, or Nashville since we're not leaving the state."

"Because Virginia *is* for lovers."

She shot a side-eyed glance at him. "But not Richmond or Virginia Beach." The huff exploded. "You win. I give up."

"Fairburn."

"Never heard of it."

"Located along the Chesapeake Bay just south of the Maryland border." He nodded toward the dash. "There's a brochure in the glove box."

She had the pamphlet in hand before he finished the sentence. "The Victoria Inn. Nick, this is amazing. Horse drawn carriage rides. Cruises on the bay. Ooh, and a spa."

"There's shops and restaurants in town too. Best of all, we'll be there in less than two hours."

"That soon?"

"Yep. I didn't want to spend hours traveling after the

wedding. We'll get there in time to rest, check out the hotel, then decide where we want to go for dinner."

"Since Jamie packed for me, did she know where we're going?"

"She did, and she's the only other person who knew. Though she might have told Rhys. It was driving Paige crazy not knowing."

"I know the feeling." She sank back in her seat with a sigh. "It was a beautiful wedding, wasn't it? I can't wait to see the pictures."

"I didn't realize you'd planned on having Josh and Rhys escort you down the aisle."

"Neither did I. Joshua came to our room before the wedding to talk. Before he left, he said I'd have a surprise when I got downstairs. I should have thought of it."

"The important thing is Josh thought of it, and he included Rhys."

She'd couldn't have asked for a better wedding gift. Progress had been slow, but bit by bit, her boys were forming a relationship. The fact they banded together to slip one over her was another matter.

"I noticed you had quite a discussion with Erik. Did he give any indication about proposing to April?"

Nick shot a quick "Really?" look in her direction. "He talked about his boat. Invited me to go fishing. Watch a game. Cars. That sort of thing."

She shook her head. "Amazing how the two of you are bonding."

"He's involved with April. You and April are friends. We need to get along. Not just for Rhys's sake but ours too." Nick gave her hand a quick squeeze. "Besides, I don't like seeing you upset."

She returned the squeeze with a laugh. "Or dealing with it either."

"All part of the relationship."

Dana bit her lip. Nick's comment gave her the perfect opening to a subject she'd mulled over for several days. Maybe she should wait until tonight after he had a chance to rest. No, better to get the matter resolved now. She took a deep breath.

"Nick, I want to pay off the loan on your garage with some of the funds from the Dennison Trust."

He shifted his glance from the road to her then back. "Sweetheart, I appreciate the offer, but no."

"You've done so much for me. Planning our wedding and honeymoon." She rubbed her thumb over her ring. "Even ordering a special ring for me. I want to do something for you. You wouldn't have that debt if it wasn't for selling your garage to Rhys and buying Glenn Thornton's business."

"I *considered* selling to Rhys because you asked me. I *decided* because it was good business opportunity. Besides we're not keeping score here." Another glance. This one with a wolfish grin. "Tell you what. When we get to the hotel, you can do something for me... to me... with me."

She lounged back in her seat, stretching out her legs. "As a businessman, wouldn't you agree that paying off the loan would save a considerable amount of money? Money that could be rolled into the business or savings?"

"Little hard to argue when you shift from emotion to logic."

Her mouth curled into a smile. "And...?"

A long sigh whooshed through his lips. "Okay. It makes sense to pay off the loan."

"Thank you for agreeing. It means a lot to me to do this for you."

"Hard to say 'no', especially when you're not incorrect."

Wait... what?

"Did you mean to say *I'm right*?"

He shook his head. "I said what I said."

Dana rested her palm on his leg, sharing a laugh. What could have been the first argument of their marriage had been solved with humor and respect. Perfect solution. Nick got the last word, and she got to give her husband the present he deserved.

⁂

Lila returned to the Wardens' kitchen just in time to see Josh give a final wipe down to the counters. She flushed, realizing how much work he'd done while she visited with guests.

"I should have been helping." She looked around and found everything clean and in order. "Is there anything else I can do?"

"Vacuuming, but—" he raised his voice, "—that's Megan's job."

Megan raced past them to the laundry room, waving her hands. "I know. I know."

"I should do that."

"Catering was our job, and you've done more than your share." Josh turned as Megan returned, pushing the vacuum. "Tell Rhys and Jamie good-bye. We're heading out."

"Got it." Megan set the sweeper to one side then held her arms out to Lila. "Hugs."

The embrace was swift but sincere, one that Lila felt comfortable enough to share.

"Let's get together sometime and hang out. I'll get your number from Josh and call you."

Before Lila could respond, Megan zoomed into the living room.

"Wow."

"Yeah, wow." Josh handed his car key to Lila then hefted the last of the catering supplies that hadn't been loaded yet into his truck. "Grab your jacket and purse, and let's take off."

As Josh called out to Megan to lock up behind them, Lila rushed ahead to unlock the back of the truck. He set the boxes in the cargo area then settled himself behind the wheel.

"If you're not too tired, how about catching a movie then a bite afterwards?"

Movie? A meal? Did Josh mean this as a date or... What else could he mean? He meant as friends. He offered because we're co-workers going out after work. Except he's the manager.

All the reasons she considered why to say no fell to the wayside to the reason to say yes.

Because she wanted to.

"I'd like that, but I need to change clothes. I don't have anything clean at your place."

"No problem," Josh said, pausing at the end of the driveway to check for traffic. "We'll swing by your place to pick up what you need. I'm ready to get out of this suit."

Josh obviously assumed she'd go back to his place to shower and change. Not that she didn't prefer that option too. Still, she couldn't let Josh continue to make her decisions.

"Or I can clean up at my apartment while you do the same at yours." She held her breath, waiting for his reaction.

"If you prefer to do that, I'll come inside and wait on the couch. If you're not comfortable with that option, I'll wait outside in the truck."

The shadow at the window. The rattle of the doorknob.

Her stomach lurched "You're right. I wasn't thinking—"

"I'm sorry you have to think about those things. Do you still want to catch a movie? If not, we can pick up your clothes then go back to my apartment."

What I want is to feel normal. The way I did on Main Street yesterday and with all of Josh's friends today.

"I'd love to go to a movie. It's been years since I've seen one in a theater."

"That's what we'll do." A smile brightened his face as if her answer had given him something that he'd wanted as well.

While Joshua drove, Lila rummaged in her purse for her key. Her hand brushed her cell phone, reminding her that she'd turned off the ringer while working. Checking, she found two missed calls. Both from Aunt Nan in the past half-hour.

She tapped the first message.

"Lila, get over here now. Trouble's brewin', and I need you."

"What now?" she muttered then bit her lip, ashamed of her resentment. Was it so much to have a day with no arguments or family drama? Maybe the *trouble* had been resolved. She played the next message.

"Lila, I need you here bad." A hiccup sounded followed by a sob.

Heat rushed through her body, filling her with shame for those selfish thoughts.

"Josh, something's wrong with my aunt. I need to check on her. I'm sorry. I can't go out after all."

After a quick glance at the side mirror, Josh switched lanes then turned at the next corner. "I'm sorry too, but it can't be helped. What's the address?"

"One-twenty-nine Marshall," she said, adding a few more directions.

"Did your aunt say what's wrong?"

"No, but she was trying not to cry, which isn't like her at all. It has to be something bad." She tapped again on the phone. "I should call her."

Nan answered on the second ring.

"It's me, Aunt Nan. Are you hurt?"

"They're gone for now. Just get here before they get back."

Alarmed by Nan's labored breathing, Lila asked, "Do you need an ambulance?"

"Just get here."

"I'm a few minutes away—"

The call ended with a beep.

"I don't know if she hung up or passed out. What's if she had a stroke or heart attack?"

"Call 911."

"Aunt Nan would have a stroke if the EMTs showed up." Lila shook her head. "She's an LPN. She would know the symptoms. It's probably something one of the boys did."

"Why wouldn't she want to be checked by an EMT?"

She sank back in the seat, exhausted more from the drama of the past few minutes than the physical exertion of the entire day. "Her business is her business. If she wants someone poking and prodding at her, she'll be the one to decide when and where."

A side glance showed the tight set of Joshua's jaw.

"I know it's ridiculous but she's... well, stubborn is the nicest word I can think of. She's rough and bad-tempered, but she took me in when I didn't have anyone. Mostly because of family, but she does care for me."

"I didn't mean to criticize."

She shot up in her seat as the car turned onto Marshall. "It's the third house."

Josh parked in the one open spot half-way down the block.

Lila pushed away any embarrassment she might have felt over Joshua seeing the worn-down houses and shabby yards. She grabbed her purse in one hand, the door handle in the other.

"I'm coming in with you." Josh turned off the engine. "Just in case."

The three simple words slammed into her heart. With a nod, she jumped out of the truck and raced toward the house, Josh close behind her.

The storm door swung open. Nan stood in the opening, eyes reddened, jaw set, feet planted. Her chest expanded in a deep breath as she extended one arm.

Pointing a gun directly at the two of them.

CHAPTER ELEVEN

Lila halted, rocking on her heels. Josh cupped her shoulders to keep her from falling then eased in front of her.

"Mrs. Grainger, what's going on here?"

"What's going on?" Her voice growled, more threatening than a shout or a scream. "I saw you chasing my niece, and I grabbed my gun."

Lila circled around Josh and climbed the front steps. "Put the gun down, Aunt Nan. This is my boss. He drove me here and wanted to help if you were hurt or in danger."

Nan lowered the gun. Her mouth tugged in a tight smile. "No offense meant."

"None taken, Mrs. Grainger, but you need to be careful when you point a gun at someone."

"I've handled guns longer than you've been alive. I only bring one out when there's a threat to one of mine." She jerked her head toward the sidewalk. "Thanks for bringing Lila home. You can go now."

Heat crept up Lila's face at Nan's rude dismissal. Joshua smiled, but she knew his face well enough to see the crinkles of concern around his eyes and the tight set of his jaw.

"Call me when you're ready to leave." His tone lowered. "Or sooner."

She blinked to let him know she understood. She forced a cheerful note in her voice. "Thank you for the ride. I'll see you tomorrow at work."

Joshua walked to the sidewalk, then turned. "Have a good evening, Mrs. Grainger."

A slow nod of her head was her only response before she motioned Lila into the house.

"Have a seat on the couch while I put this gun away." Nan opened a drawer on a small table next to the couch. She set the gun down and slid the drawer shut. "There, safe and sound."

Lila mentally shook her head. The location of the gun wasn't a secret. Neither were Nan's threats of bodily harm on anyone who touched the gun or anything else on her property.

"I need a beer," Nan said, walking toward the kitchen. "You want one?"

"No, thank you."

"You won't believe what all I've had to deal with today." Nan's voice rose and fell as she moved around the kitchen. "Trouble never seems to stop, does it? Here I am fretting my heart and walking the floor, and you're not answering my calls."

I wish I hadn't returned the call. It didn't seem as if anyone had died or gone to jail, which meant someone ticked off Aunt Nan, and she needed a sounding board. Moving out hadn't stopped Nan from demanding on-call attention, and it needed to stop.

I have to set boundaries and not jump every time she calls.

A glint of gold on the coffee table caught Lila's eye. She

eased off the couch to her knees and picked up the ring. A gold ring with a ruby setting exactly like the one her mother had worn. Fueled by a rage that would have made even a Grainger quake with fear, she pushed to her feet, fingers curled around the precious ring.

"Where did you get my mother's ring?" Her fist shook with each word.

Nan stood in the doorway to the kitchen, a deep red racing across her face. Her chest heaved, and her fists tightened. Beer spluttered from the opening in the can, splattering onto the floor. Feet planted, shoulders lifted, she was a bull about to charge.

"You watch your tone with me, girl."

"I want the truth. Why do you have my mother's ring? I found it on the table."

Nan shifted the can to her right hand, shaking the liquid from the other. She hauled in one deep breath after another until all the red left her face except for twin blotches on her cheeks.

"I don't hold with backtalk from anyone. I'll give you a pass because of what happened this week." She slugged back a swallow of beer. "That ring didn't belong to Jennie. Mick gave it to me."

"The exact same ring?"

Nan plopped onto the couch. "It wasn't the only one like that. Sit down, and I'll tell you a story about the rings." She set the beer can on the table then held out her hand. "Let me show you."

Lila eased her hand open.

Nan plucked the ring from Lila's palm. "This goes back to your great-granddaddy's time. Back then, there was a mercantile store called Marcum's in what used to be downtown. It had been around years before then. That's where women went to get their dry goods, ready-made clothes, shoes, furniture. Even had a lunch counter. Now, you're wondering where this story is going, aren't you?"

Lila nodded, not daring to speak and break the mood. She'd never known Aunt Nan to be this talkative about the past.

"They sold jewelry. Nothing like that fancy, pricy stuff Bart Caine sells down on Main Street. Marcum called it fashion jewelry. They got in a stock of birthstone rings right at spring-time, just when all the weddings would start happening. A lot of the men decided to buy those for engagement rings. Your granddaddy bought an emerald. That got passed down to my brother John, your daddy."

"An emerald? Mama's ring was a ruby like this one."

Nan waved away the protest. "Seems all the boys bought rings whether they were fixing to marry or not. Which made a predicament when they gave their sweetheart a ring with stone she didn't like. They decided to pool the rings and the next one to get engaged would get his pick according to what the woman wanted." She rolled back on the couch, slapped her knee and hooted. "Those rings changed hands so many times, it's hard to remember who bought which one. Don't know what's happened to most of those but you might remember the one Carol Sue used to wear."

"The sapphire ring. She always said Cousin Dirk picked it out because it matched her eyes."

"That's what he told her. Your daddy, Dirk, and another fellow, can't remember who it was, played poker for first pick of the rings. John won and took the ruby. Said it was Jennie's favorite stone. The other fellow won the diamond, leaving Dirk with the blue stone. I laugh myself silly every time Carol Sue tells that story."

"Didn't any of the women object to having a ring that had been passed around?"

Nan snorted. "This part of town, we were thankful for what we got. If a gal made enough fuss, the man might give in and buy the chick a new one. I never cared for this one. Too flashy but I took it because Mick gave it to me. It meant something to him because it came from his granny."

She slipped the ring onto her left pinky where it stuck above the knuckle. "I wore it on a chain around my neck while I was at work. Tried to put it on one day and my fingers had gotten too big. I put it away for good after Mick passed."

They sat in silence for a moment then Lila rested her palm on Nan's arm. "I like talking with you this way. Hearing family stories. It makes the people I knew only by name seem real."

Nan's chin quivered. She sucked in a deep breath and fumbled for Lila's hand. "I've been hard on you at times. You probably don't want to hear a bunch of 'I'm sorrys' so I won't say them."

Lila wanted to reassure her aunt she understood. But she couldn't. Nan may have felt she'd done her best, but her actions hadn't shown it.

"John was my brother, but he was nothing like the rest of us. Thought more about books and talking rather than hunting and fishing and living life. He and Jennie raised you in that kind of household. Both of them were dreamers, always had their head in a book or listening to music. Dreams don't get you anywhere. It's hard work that does. When I brought you here, I knew I had to teach you what real life was like. Otherwise you'd stay in that shell." Her chin quivered again. "I didn't want to lose you too."

"I'm here now." Lila stroked her thumb across the work-roughened skin on Nan's hand. "What happened to make you so upset?"

Nan pulled her hand free and reached for the beer can. She took a gulp then swallowed back a belch. "Jeffy proposed to Angie."

Lila's mouth dropped open. "I thought they had a fight at the Low Tide." She clamped her mouth shut, remembering Nan's part in the uproar.

"They're all made-up again. Lovey-dovey like they haven't split up a half-dozen times before."

Her gaze dropped to the ring on Nan's pinky. "He asked you for the ring?"

"He did. Told me they were moving in here. Angie didn't want to live in the apartment over the bar. Like she hadn't stayed there more nights than I have fingers and toes and then some." Nan huffed. "I'm going to sit both of them down and lay out the rules. If they don't like it, they can go elsewhere."

"Are you going to let Angie have your ring?"

Nan closed her hand, turned it to view the ruby stone. "I thought I could. Thought it would prove I was making an attempt to accept that bleached blonde hussy. Can't believe that woman's going be a Grainger."

"Aunt Nan, you're a Grainger. Why didn't you take Uncle Mick's last name when you married him?"

"Told him flat out I wasn't going through life with the last name of Fink. Wasn't going to saddle any kids with that name either."

Lila hid a smile. Poor Uncle Mick never stood a chance with a woman like Nan. Maybe that's why she married him.

"He must have loved you very much to agree to those terms."

"You won't believe this, but I was quite the looker back in the day." Nan winked and wiggled her shoulders.

Lila giggled at Nan's unexpected playfulness. "I'd love to see a picture of you and Uncle Mick when you were young."

"Those albums are put away in one of the closets. If I do let Jeffy move in, I'll need your help cleaning out one of the bedrooms."

"You should make both of them help you."

"Too much personal belongings stored in the closet. I don't want either one of them snooping to see what's there." She nudged her elbow into Lila's arm. "I trust you."

"What about the ring?"

Nan whooshed out a slow breath. "I'm not ready to let go. Not after seeing it and holding it again. I might wear it on a chain for awhile." She snickered. "Right out in plain sight for everyone to see."

"Please don't let those two upset you again. If they don't like the rules, they can find a place of their own."

"Darn right. If Angie don't like it, she can ride the business end of my broom out the door."

Lila held back a groan, foreseeing another round of hostilities. Time to make her escape before Jeffy and Angie returned. She pulled the strap of her purse over one shoulder and stood.

"I have work tomorrow so I need to get home. I'm glad you're feeling better."

Nan pushed to her feet. "I wish you were the one moving in here. By the way, I'm keeping an eye on the job posts at the hospital."

Lila shoved aside the wave of irritation that surged through her. Time for her to set boundaries of here own. Firmly. Kindly.

She dropped a kiss on Nan's weathered cheek. "You have plenty to handle without worrying about me. I love my new job, and I'm happy there."

Nan gave a quick jerk of her head. "Go on then. Catch your bus."

Refusing the guilt trip, Lila trotted down the steps to the sidewalk. Half-way down the block, she turned to wave. As expected, Nan's gaze was scouring the street from one end to the other. No doubt looking to see if Joshua was waiting.

Dusk had shifted into darkness, stealing the last bit of warmth from the air. Shoulders hunched, she shoved her hands into the pockets of her coat and wished she had her knit cap as well. She turned the corner, hoping to find Joshua waiting for her. The truck was nowhere in sight. She pushed back her disappointment and decided to walk to Stone's Corner Market. Two blocks away and well lit, it was a safe place to wait.

She pulled her phone from her pocket to call Joshua who answered immediately

"Hey there."

"You said it would be all right to call you for a ride."

"I see you walking this way. I'm parked in Stone's lot."

He was there. Waiting for her. Window rolled down, one hand lifted in a wave.

"Wait there. I'll—"

She broke into a run, unable to hold back a wide grin. By the time she reached the truck, he'd leaned over and opened the passenger door. She hopped into the cab and pulled the door shut. Phone to his ear, a grin on his face, Joshua said, "—drive down and pick you up."

As those words echoed out of her phone, Lila laughed. She disconnected the call and shoved the phone into her coat pocket. "Tell me you weren't waiting here all this time."

"I went home to change then drove here." He hesitated then said, "I didn't want to be too far away in case you needed to leave in a hurry."

"Aunt Nan was checking the street as I was leaving."

"That's why I parked here. Some kids were getting rowdy in the store, so I hung around inside for awhile until they left. I bought a cup of coffee and asked if it was okay to stay parked outside."

"I'm sure he appreciated your help."

Joshua chuckled. "Especially when those kids came back about fifteen minutes later, thinking I'd left."

"Poor Mr. Stone."

"His grandson is coming home from college in December to help out. The guy plays football at Clemson."

Lila shook her head. "You have a knack for making friends."

"I like talking with people." He started the engine and gave a nod in her direction. "Buckle up."

She glanced at the clock on the dash while latching the belt. Almost seven-thirty. "Seems like it should be later."

"Feels that way when it gets dark so early. Of course, we've been on the go most of the day."

"With a noon wedding, your mother and her husband got an early start on their trip."

"Mom texted a little over an hour ago to let us know they made it to the hotel."

"Already?"

"They went to a place somewhere on the Chesapeake Bay. It's about two hours away, not counting the time on the ferry." He shifted the truck into gear and drove off the lot. "We don't have time to make the next movie, but how about dinner? You hungry?"

She shouldn't have been after all the pizza she'd eaten, but there was a slight gnawing in her stomach. Besides, riding at night in a big, bad truck with a good-looking guy teased her senses, and she wasn't ready to go home.

"I could eat." She brushed a hand across one pant leg. "Maybe some place casual?"

"Is a burger and fries casual enough?"

"Dottie's?"

"Yep."

He winked, she smiled.

"That's a yep from me too."

⁓

Eating at Dottie's proved impossible with the Friday night influx of teenagers. Not wanting to wait in line to order food then drive back to his apartment to eat, Joshua suggested an alternative. He deliberately neglected to mention the location of the fast-food restaurant was in Sutton until they reached the terminal to board the ferry.

At expected, Lila protested the time and expense when a simple meal could be fixed at home. His heart had thumped a double-beat at her admission of his apartment as 'home', and he fell a little further for her.

Joshua overrode each objection, fervently convincing her of his yearning for seafood, how it was worth the trip, and she'd enjoy every minute of the trip.

After docking in Sutton, they made the trip from the terminal to the restaurant and back in time to catch the next ferry. As it was the next to last sailing of the evening, Joshua's truck was one of only four other vehicles returning to Providence Island.

The ferry pushed through the water at an even pace as they sat at a corner table in the small lounge, eating their meal. The lights were low, and they had the area to themselves. For an impromptu idea, he couldn't have planned it any better.

"Finish my hush puppies?" he offered.

"No, thank you. I am stuffed, but it was good."

"So you enjoyed yourself, huh?" He gathered the trash and tied the bag for quick disposal in one of the trash bins.

Lila gave him side-eyed glance at his teasing. "Yes, I enjoyed the food and the ride."

She gazed around the small area then back to him. "It seems like we're a world away from everything, doesn't it?"

"We both needed it." He gave a short laugh. "My mom hadn't planned on having me escort her down the aisle. Rhys and I decided to surprise her."

"She looked so happy." She hesitated then continued. "Joshua, I told you about my mother last night. Would you like to tell me about your father? Not about what happened, but about being father and son?"

Joshua's breath caught as the memory of his father swept through him. Strong and vivid as if James Canfield was sitting next to him. So much of what was discussed now focused on those last two years and the fallout since then.

"You're the first person who's asked me that. When I talked with Mom before the ceremony, she told me how much I remind her of my dad. She almost cried. Heck, both of us almost cried."

"Whatever you need to talk about, I'll listen."

Joshua opened his mind, releasing all those memories he'd locked away for his own protection. Maybe the grief wouldn't be so devastating if he shared those remembrances, one by one.

Lila waited, not rushing him to a decision. Despite the dim lighting in the lounge, he saw the warmth and compassion in her eyes.

We're the only ones who'll have memories of our holidays, birthdays, and vacations.

That was true only if those stories were never shared.

A mischievous grin broke free. "I was ten years old…"

He felt ten years old again as he told the story. Lila listened with rapt attention, and in those next moments, James Canfield lived again.

CHAPTER TWELVE

"No more stalling." Josh eased into a chair opposite Ben in Carson's front office. "Paige, Karen, and Lila are running through those test scripts which mean you and I are going to have that talk."

Ben tapped several keys on his laptop before looking up. "You're not going to let this go, are you?"

His jaw dropped. "You called my mother 'Miss Katie' with a familiarity that makes me very suspicious. You think I'm going to let that pass?"

Ben rested an elbow on the tabletop and grinned. "I was hoping to keep you busy enough so I could scoot out before you had a chance."

"You're busted, buddy. So spill it."

Ben's gaze shifted over Josh's shoulder then he lifted his forefinger slightly in warning. A signal they'd used in the past. Josh nodded just as Paige rushed to the table, plopping down next to him.

"Everything tested out perfectly. Can we go live now?" Before Ben could reply, she drummed her knuckles on the

141

table. "Jamie's ready to email my customer list, and Aaron's going to deliver fliers."

"If you're certain, I'll move the production site live. Do you want to keep the development site active through the weekend so your team can continue practicing?"

"Yes-s-s?"

Josh chuckled "I think Paige is asking what happens if both sites are available."

Ben shrugged. "Nothing. On the dev site, you have access to both interfaces. Anything you do there has no impact on the production site. Remember this is only for your current menu. I need answers back from on you the Classic menu. After that's locked down, I'll finish the mobile app."

Paige gave a short gasp. "Oh, yeah. That email you sent. I'll get right on that. One more thing. The production site is the live site, right?"

"Yes. The live site is where the customers view the menu and place orders. Those orders are received on the back end. Lila and Karen have user roles on that platform. You and Canfield have user and admin access."

Josh frowned. "What role do you have?"

"Supreme Overlord."

Josh rolled his eyes. As if Ben's ego wasn't inflated enough.

Paige's giggle was fleeting. "I'm nervous about the changes, especially since you won't be here tomorrow."

"Canfield has it nailed down. If there is a problem, he'll handle it. If he can't, he'll call me. I'll log in remotely."

She heaved a deep breath. "Perfect. I'll put all the worry on Josh's shoulders and go pick up Jess from school."

"Nothing to worry about," he said. "Enjoy your evening."

Paige bounced to her feet. "You're awesome. Let me know when you're ready for those cooking lessons."

"Will do."

Paige made it as far as the divider wall then pivoted. "One more thing."

Leave, will you? Josh swallowed a grunt, scowling as Ben tapped his watch.

She wrinkled her nose. "This is for Josh. Karen's leaving now too. Lila's still here. She's in the pantry working on inventory and shopping lists."

"Thanks. I'll tell her to scoot out when I get ready to leave."

"Okay, I'm out. Bye, guys."

With a quick wave, Paige whirled, speed-walking into the kitchen. Seconds later, the slam of the metal back door sounded her departure.

Arms crossed over his chest, Josh watched as Ben closed the lid to his laptop. "Talk, Hampshire."

"Let's talk first about you and Lila."

"What about Lila and me?"

"I saw the flirty looks between the two of you. That bunch is nothing but trouble."

"Tell me about it. I dropped Lila off at her aunt's house yesterday after leaving Mom's. She met us at the front door with a gun. Claimed she thought I was chasing Lila." He glared at Ben. "As for Lila, she's not like the others."

"Never thought she was." He leaned forward, lowering his voice. "I checked out the Low Tide. There's a lot going on behind the scenes and in plain sight."

"What sort of things?"

"Underage drinking. Pot and pills. Gambling. I don't doubt there's a hooker or two doing business there too. The night I visited, Madigan stopped by."

Josh mulled over that piece of information. "Maybe he was there to give Jeffy a warning about cleaning up the place."

Ben snorted. "And being an upright citizen, he'll jump right on that. You need to be careful."

"I need to be careful? You're the one taking chances going to the Low Tide by yourself."

"Low risk for me. You, on the other hand, might have been recognized."

"Are you going to report what you saw to the Sheriff?"

"The place might be on Wallace's radar already. If not, I don't want to stir up any trouble until we find out more about Jennie Grainger's murder."

"Why do you care about this?"

"Lila seems like a good kid. She deserves answers. Plus, she's working here which might put Paige in jeopardy."

When did steel-hearted Ben Hampshire turn into a compassionate crime-stopper?

"Whatever you've got planned, let me in on it."

"Deal." He slid his laptop into a brown leather satchel. "I'm heading—"

Josh slapped his hand on the top of the bag. "No, you're not, and back to the original subject. I want answers on why you called my mother 'Miss Katie.'"

All signs of Ben's habitual cocky demeanor disappeared, replaced with... sadness? Grief? He scrubbed both palms over his face then leaned forward.

"I knew Dana when she was Catherine McCall."

"You...what?" Josh swallowed the rising tide of acid rolling through his gut.

"My mother and I lived in the same student apartment building as Miss Katie." A faint smile washed across his lips. "She used to baby-sit me when Mom had classes. My mom did the same for her."

"You knew Rhys."

Ben nodded. "I was two years older than him. I called him my little brother, and Miss Katie was my other mother. I adored her. One day—" He grabbed the bottle of water by his elbow and took several deep swallows. "Rhys's father came one day. Packed up all their stuff before telling my mother about the accident. Rhys was crying to stay with us. Mom was crying. So was I. I begged Mr. McCall not to take my brother away."

Ben scrubbed his face again. When he lowered his hands this time, his eyes were rimmed in red. "I lost my family that day."

Josh's mind rolled as he struggled to piece Ben's story together with everything else he knew. Those details explained Ben's devotion to protecting Joshua and his mother. Still, there were more missing pieces.

"How did you meet my father?"

"Several yeas ago, I saw a picture online of your parents along with several other people. The caption included Mr. and Mrs. James Canfield. I couldn't get over the woman's resemblance to Miss Katie. I thought she might be a relative, and I could reconnect with Rhys." His mouth tightened in a grim smile. "It threw your dad for a loop when I asked if he knew a Katie McCall. He put me off, but I knew he was hiding something. A couple days later, he contacted me. I gave him enough details that he finally believed me. From that point, we worked together to take down Stoddard. I wanted to kill him before anyone got hurt. James wanted to put him behind bars. I should have listened to my instincts."

"You were willing to kill Stoddard based on what my father had told you?"

"My first hit was the three men who killed my fiancée just before we graduated college. I had no problem doing whatever was necessary to protect a woman I once considered my family."

"Why didn't you tell me this before now?"

Ben's gaze cooled. Not with the gleam of a cold-blooded

killer, but the sympathetic look of a friend. "Because that would have meant telling you Dana Canfield wasn't your biological mother." He bowed his head for a brief moment. "I'm sorry Stoddard was the one to tell you."

And took pleasure in doing so.

"Ben didn't tell you? Not even after all the bonding you two have done? He didn't once mention that Dana isn't your mother? That she's an imposter who took over your dead mother's life after that car accident when you were just a toddler? Makes you wonder just who was the responsible party behind your father's murder, doesn't it?"

"Part of the agreement I made with James was that he'd come clean with you and your mother after we took down Stoddard." Ben's shoulders sagged. "I'm sorry I couldn't save him."

Bitterness rose into Josh's throat, and his hands closed into fists. "He should have gone straight to the authorities."

"Stoddard had a lot of people in his pocket. People like Detective Lansing. James could have gone to higher authorities, but there was always a potential risk." Ben nudged the back of his hand against Josh's fist. "He made mistakes, but he loved you and your mother."

Anger faded, replaced by an understanding that while his father's actions had been flawed, his heart had been true. Seeing Ben's restless shifting on the chair, he rushed to ask one more question.

"Does Mom know who you are? Didn't she recognize your name?"

"I told her while she was in the hospital after Stoddard's attack. As for my name, I changed it after I left home at eighteen."

"Does Rhys know?"

"He hasn't said anything if he does, and I doubt that she told him."

"I don't know what else to say except thank you."

"If you want to thank me, give me a coffee to go." He stood, shoving the chair into place.

"Coming right up."

Josh walked toward the front of the restaurant. He filled a large cup to the sound of Ben's hands drumming on the counter. The tapping stopped abruptly.

"Here comes trouble."

Josh whirled, thankful he'd sealed the cup before turning. A glance out the window showed Deputy Bret Madigan walking toward the building. Since it was Bret rather than Tom Hunter, odds favored this visit was related to Jennie Grainger's murder.

"My cue to leave." Ben tipped the cup in salute and headed for the exit. He paused for a second at the doorway. "Call if you need me."

Josh nodded, though from the look on Madigan's face, it would be Lila needing someone in a few minutes.

⁓

Lila closed the door to the pantry. Paige had set up an excellent organization for the staples and other supplies, but a few tweaks might make things more efficient. After their first initial conflict, Paige had shown Lila the same respect and camaraderie as she did to Joshua and Karen. Suggestions from a new employee, though, might not be as well received. Better to run them past Joshua first. From what Lila had picked up so far, Paige intended for Joshua to manage the operations while she concentrated on the food side of the business.

Fair enough.

Notebook in hand, she crossed the kitchen to the main room. She halted in the doorway, staring at her cousin Bret leaning against the front counter, talking to Joshua.

"Hey, cuz." A wide smile crossed his lips.

Lila forced a smile of her own. If Bret followed the same pattern as his previous visit, he'd start the visit with a friendly chat before delivering the bad news. Not this time. She walked behind the counter to stand next to Joshua.

"Did you stop in for coffee, Bret, or—"

He cut her off before she could finish. "Coffee would be great."

Lips pressed together, she plucked a to-go cup from the stack, then filled and capped it. She slid the cup in front of Bret, eying him steadily. "You didn't come just for coffee, did you?"

Bret straightened, resting both palms on the countertop. "No, I didn't."

"Go ahead and say it, though I probably know what it is."

He stroked a finger down the side of the cup, not meeting her gaze. "So did I."

"Where's Sam?" Josh asked. "Shouldn't he be the one here?"

"We thought it would help if Lila heard the updates from someone close to her."

"Except you're not close. You've been gone since before her mother disappeared. You came back last summer and didn't come by to talk with her until a few days ago."

Bret took a step back from the counter, one hand resting on the gun holstered to his hip. Josh drew himself to his full height, shoulders set. Lila's head swiveled, watching the tension build between the two men. She bolted around the counter, pushing between Bret and the bar.

"That's enough. I don't need the two of you going at each other. Tell me what you came here to say."

A long moment passed before Bret lowered his hand. He shifted positions, cutting Josh out of his line of sight. The heat in his eyes faded, softening into a sympathetic gaze.

"We received positive ID back on the remains. It's Jennie."

She stood silent and still. The words should have shattered her, crushed her under the weight of their meaning. In her mind, she'd known the truth when she'd viewed the few remaining effects the sheriff's department had recovered. In her heart, she had known—but denied—the truth from the beginning.

She stepped away, half-turning. "Thank you for letting me know, Bret."

He reached out a hand to comfort her. She ignored it and walked to the end of the counter. Joshua stood on one side of the wooden structure, Bret on the other. Two men. Two sides of her life.

"The cause of death—"

Her hand sliced the air. "I don't want to know."

Not here. Not now.

Bret nodded. "The remains should be released—"

"I have to think—"

Lila pressed a hand to her throat. Her heart pounded a furious beat. So hard as if it would burst through her chest. She sensed rather than saw Joshua move to her side. He slid his palm down the length of her arm, and it was his hand, his touch that provided the comfort she craved.

"One more question, Bret," Josh said, stepping in the distance between Lila and her cousin. "Lila said your family left PI when you were fifteen and only returned here one or two times."

Why is he asking Bret about that? What does it matter? For whatever reason Joshua had asked, it seemed to matter to him. Her stomach churned and her breath quickened. She gripped the lip of the countertop as her knees began to tremble.

Bret's eyes narrowed. "So?"

Joshua cast a quick look in her direction. A sad-eyed look of apology for whatever was coming next. His jaw tightened as he turned his attention back to Bret.

"How did you know about Jennie's pink shoes? The way I see it, the only way you would have known that was if you were there that night."

Madigan sucked in a deep breath through his teeth. "You don't know what you're talking about, Canfield. Better you pay mind to keeping yourself out of jail."

Lila bolted for the door, blocking Bret from exiting. He glared down at her, but the anger she expected wasn't there. It was fear she saw there. Good, he deserved it.

"Joshua is right. You told me that you knew it was my mother as soon as you saw those shoes." She stabbed a finger into his chest. "Tell me now, or I'll go across the street and get the sheriff. And you will answer his questions."

≈

If asked—which he hadn't been—Josh's vote would have been to call Sam to the restaurant ASAP. From that point, the sheriff could escort Madigan across the street for a formal interview. Instead, Josh was seated now at the front office table to hold his second Come-to-Jesus meeting in one day.

Madigan slumped in his chair, his face drawn in weary lines while Lila shivered from nerves or rage. Probably both.

"Start explaining, Madigan," Josh said.

"I swear to you, Lila, I didn't hurt Jennie." He took a deep breath. "I was supposed to meet the two of you in Charlottesville the next day."

Lila shook her head. "Mama never said anything about that."

"No one else knew. Jennie asked my parents if they'd consider letting the two of you stay at their house until she could save enough for a place of her own. Dad agreed but Mom flat out said no. Said she'd made her escape from the Grainger clan and wasn't getting pulled back into any drama. Later, I saw Dad slip some money to Jennie before you left our house."

He pounded a fist on the table. "I couldn't believe they wouldn't help, especially with a child involved. When the two of you got ready to leave, I walked out to the car. I was home on break from college in Morgantown and had a small apartment off campus. I told Jennie to let me know when she was ready to make her move, and the two of you could stay with me. I lived far enough away that no one would think to look in upstate West Virginia. I doubted that any of the Graingers would go looking. If they did, it wouldn't be on a university campus."

"I told you about the shoes," Lila said, her eyes widening with recall. "I was sitting in the back seat of our car. I was excited about our new clothes. Then Mama reminded me it was a secret. She didn't seem to mind too much because it was you."

"You were bouncing on the seat when I told you about the mountains and other things we'd see and do." A softness appeared in Bret's eyes, and a smile touched his lips. "And Jennie... she looked at me as if I'd given her the world. She told me not to call her in case she had to postpone leaving. She deleted my number from her phone so no one could find a connection between us. A couple weeks later, Jennie called to say the two of you were leaving that night. We had a meeting place set up. When she got there, she'd sell her car, and we'd continue on in mine."

"Why that day?" Josh asked.

"What do you mean?"

"Why did Jennie pick that day to leave? Why all the secrecy?"

"Isn't getting away from the Graingers enough of a reason?" Bret shrugged then looked to Lila. "Do you remember anything particular?"

"Because she'd saved enough money, I guess." Lila gasped, bolting up in her chair. "That's where she went that night. To get the money she'd saved."

"The bank would have been closed at that time."

Lila sniffed. "Mama didn't trust the bank. One of the aunts worked there, and she didn't want anyone in the family knowing how much money she had or when she made a withdrawal."

"Who did she trust?"

Lip caught between her teeth, Lila sat for a silent moment then met Joshua's gaze. "She trusted Miss Emily."

"She cleaned for her, didn't she?"

"She took her to the grocery store, to doctor appointments, wherever she needed to go. But other than gas money, Mama never expected to be paid for those things."

"Did anyone else know about the money?"

Lila shook her head. "Not to my knowledge, but someone could have found out."

Bret stirred in his chair. "I need to get back on duty."

Josh held up a warning hand. "One more question. Why didn't you check on Jennie and Lila when they didn't show up?"

"I tried. I bought a cheap phone and called several times

so my own number wouldn't show on her phone. I also called my parents, but they didn't mention anything about Jennie missing. Not that they kept tabs on the family. I figured Jennie had two sets of plans, and I was plan B. If anyone did look for her in my direction, she wouldn't be there."

"She wouldn't have left me." Lila glared across the table at her cousin.

"I know she'd never do that." Bret heaved a deep sigh. "I am truly sorry, Lila. I should have done more. I even wondered if she decided not to leave at that point and didn't want to risk contacting me."

Bret stood, shoving the chair under the table. He laid a hand on Lila's shoulder. "I came back here last spring after I learned what cousin Buzz did and about the crooked cop that got killed. I wanted to help stop the pattern of violence and crime from the Graingers. My connection was one of the reasons Sam hesitated to hire me. He asked if I intended to take advantage of the position to help my outlaw family. I'll tell you the same thing I told Sam. My answer was a flat-out no."

His gaze shifted to Joshua. Josh returned the glare with one of his own.

"Believe me or not, Canfield, I want answers too."

He turned and walked out of the building, the bell above the door continuing to peal for several more seconds.

"Do you believe him?" Josh asked.

"Yes, for the boy I used to know, but that was years ago." She stared toward the front of the restaurant. "As for the man he is now, I don't know."

The deeper question was could the boy or the man be trusted? Madigan would have been in his late teens at that time and at least ten or so years younger than Jennie. He wouldn't have been the first guy to crush on an older woman and yearning to rescue her from a bad situation. What if Madigan had taken the ferry to PI that night? Did he and Jennie have a last-minute quarrel? Or was she even aware of her in-name-only nephew's interest and rejected him? One thing was obvious after this conversation.

Bret Madigan had been in love with Jennie Grainger.

CHAPTER THIRTEEN

Deep breath. Stay calm.

Megan waited in the open doorway to Erik McCall's office. Hunched over his desk, scribbling on the papers in front of him, he looked busy. Really busy. Maybe too busy for her non-work-related request. She did have an appointment scheduled with him, and he wouldn't have accepted if he didn't intend to honor it.

She ran her palms down the front of her slacks then knocked on the door frame.

Erik glanced at the clock as he stood. A smile flashed on his lean face. "Right on time. Have a seat."

Megan took two steps then stopped. "Okay to shut the door?"

"One of those talks, huh?"

One thing she'd learned since working at McCall Construction was that the owner wasn't *always* as grumpy as he sounded. During those times he was out of sorts, she'd learned how to humor him into a better frame of mind.

"More to keep Kevin from hijacking my time."

"Need me to talk with him?"

"I've already advised him about his erroneous perceptions of his importance relative to everyone else's."

"I bet you did." Erik settled back in his chair, chuckling. "What's on your mind?"

Her throat closed, choked by well-meaning second thoughts.

"Worried if you'll have a job after the buy-out?" He eyed her closely then shook his head. "Or are you here about a raise?"

"A raise would be nice, and it is in a way about money. Not in the way you mean." She took a deep breath. "Here's the situation. While I was trying to locate Mom's parents, I went through a bunch of boxes from the apartment she and Rhys lived in and found some photograph albums."

All good humor disappeared from Erik's expression. "The infamous photos of Kate that I destroyed. Are those the ones you're asking about?"

"Indirectly. I found negatives going back to when Rhys was a baby. He was *so* cute!" Her grin faded when Erik failed to react. "I want to make albums for Rhys and Mom for Christmas and was hoping you would be willing to contribute toward the cost of replacing the photos."

His eyes narrowed. "You have any clue why I destroyed the originals?"

"Because it hurt too much to see her and know she was gone." The answer popped out without the filter she should have used.

Color washed from Erik's features like the tide going out to sea. His lips parted, releasing a rough sigh. "That's some theory you have there."

Too late to backpedal, she met his glare with sympathy but no apology. "It seems the most likely explanation. You were angry at the circumstances. Not with Mom."

He broke the stare-off first. "I regretted it afterwards. It hurt my son that he didn't have any pictures of his mother."

I bet that wasn't the only reason. She managed to keep that thought to herself.

"I wasn't the best father in a lot of ways," he said, giving a one shoulder shrug.

"In some ways, that's probably true. From what I've heard, the Carsons played a big part in Rhys's life, but it's your footsteps he's following now. You gave him the knowledge and love for the business from the time he was a kid. So it seems you did a lot things right."

"That's a benediction I've never been granted before."

Megan lowered her lashes, hiding any reaction to the trace of pain in Erik's voice. She forced a smile. "Hey, single dads deserve respect too. Besides, it's an outsider's viewpoint to take or leave."

"I'll take it." He grinned in a way that reminded her of Rhys. "Question to you. We haven't decided on any staffing changes yet. Are you interested in working at the other office?"

"I'm still considering college next year." Raking fingers through her hair, she grunted. "And I have a boyfriend."

Erik's brows lifted. "Is the boyfriend a reason to stay or go?"

"I don't know. I care about him, but we've only dated for a couple of months. He's older than me and already talking about the future."

"Sounds like he's ready to settle down. Have you talked to your dad about this?"

A hot wave rushed through her, creeping up her neck and face. "Wow, I'm sorry. I didn't mean to dump my personal life on you." She summoned a grin. "You're so easy to talk with."

Erik rolled back in his chair, a hearty laugh rumbling from his chest. "Definitely not something I'm used to hearing."

"It's true as far as I'm concerned. Anyway, I should get back to work." She stood, half-turning before remembering the reason she was there. "About the photos?"

"When are you ordering the copies?"

"I can do it today online. The company will send a postage paid box to me to ship the negatives, but I have to pay first." She laid a copy of the invoice on his desk.

Erik picked up the paper. His eyebrows shot up, and he blew a silent whistle through his lips. "Karma doesn't come cheap."

"I don't mean for you to front the entire purchase. A donation to the cause is all I'm asking."

"I created the mess. I owe Rhys and Kate the replacements." He pulled a card from his wallet and held it out to her. "Go place the order."

"I'll only use it for the copies. I'll pay for the albums and anything else."

"Fair enough." He glanced at the wall clock. "Looks like we've run into time for Kevin's appointment."

"Oh, gee." She scurried to the door, halting to hold up the credit card. "Thank you for this. I'll do that now and bring your card right back. You're the best."

A touch of sadness tinged his smile. "I'm working on it."

Megan opened the door, frowning at Kevin standing in front of his office. Back planted against the wall, arms crossed over his chest. The polite, professional thing to do would be to apologize for running over her allotted time.

He pushed away from the wall, a deep frown creasing his brow. "You cut almost ten minutes into my time. Seems like the rules about respecting time applies to only one of us."

The heck with an apology.

"Wow, how will I ever make that up to you?"

"By taking me to lunch after I finish my meeting with Erik. I'll let you know when I'm ready."

She whirled on her heel, just in time to miss having the door slam in her face.

Lunch? Really? If that jerk thought... Wait a minute. Maybe she'd do exactly that.

❦

Megan shut off the engine then gave Kevin her best smile. "Lunch time. Hop out."

Kevin stared at the weathered exterior of Dottie's Dairy Bar. "Seriously?"

"It's good food and affordable. I don't get to write off lunches at the Lighthouse Cantina like you do."

"Those are working lunches."

She opened the car door. "Think of it as expanding your horizons. Are you coming in, or do I need to leave a window cracked while you wait?"

Kevin mumbled something that was probably better she didn't hear as he got out of the car. He paused at the front of the vehicle, eyeing it with an avaricious gleam.

"Classic BMW convertible." He gave a long, low whistle. "Can't believe I got to ride in one."

She tapped him on the arm. "Play your cards right, and you'll get to ride in it back to the office."

Kevin opened the door, casting a final lingering look at the car. "Graduation present?"

"Hardly. The car belongs to Mom. She's letting me use it while she and Dad are on their honeymoon. She plans on selling it for something more practical."

"Tell her to name her price."

She laughed at the unabashed plea. "It's not practical for winter."

"That's what garages are for."

She gestured toward the menu posted on the wall. "Let's concentrate on lunch for now."

Either the man had a hearty appetite, or he was squeezing every penny he could out of her for the meal. Two loaded hot dogs, chili cheese fries, and a large soft drink. She opted for a single dog and drink, figuring Kevin would offer his fries as a courtesy, and she'd accept.

She held back a chuckle as Kevin adjusted the collar of his polo shirt. Even on Casual Friday, he dressed a little better than anyone else. Then again, so did Mr. McCall. While Kevin's appearance didn't scream "entitled," his air of confidence certainly suggested it.

Seated at one of the bistro tables, they ate several bites before Megan broke the silence.

"Why did you take a job here? You obviously could be making big bucks in a large city."

A shadow flashed across Kevin's face. He took a long sip from his drink then set the cup to one side.

Interesting reaction to a simple question.

"My grandparents own a summer house here. After my parents' divorce was settled, my mother moved here. I came to help her get settled and decided to stay on." His eyes narrowed. "You were the one who identified the man who attacked Erik last summer."

"I did."

He pushed the fries in her direction with a gesture to help herself. She did.

"You probably heard about the history between my father and Erik."

"Just the bare bones of the story." She met his gaze with a

steady look of her own even though she wanted to squirm in her seat. Knowing something so personal about a co-worker and their mutual boss wasn't the most comfortable situation. Still, it would be interesting to hear another side of the story.

"My father and his buddies put Erik in the hospital years ago. When he was attacked last summer, my mother was terrified that Dad had returned here. Even after we learned the perpetrator was an employee Erik had fired, it still took awhile for her to feel safe again."

He flashed a shark-like grin. "Back to your question. While I could be making much more money elsewhere, this buy-out is an opportunity I wouldn't have had elsewhere. I did the research and explored the financial options before presenting it to Erik. McCall Construction has done well this past year due to the projects Rhys has initiated, but that won't last long term. We have to expand to stay in business or people will lose their jobs."

She dragged a fry through the cheese then dropped it to one side of her tray. "I get that this merger—"

"Buy-out."

She rolled her eyes. "—buy-out is necessary. But it irks me that Rhys wasn't involved sooner in the discussions."

"Not my call. In Erik's defense, there wasn't any reason to involve Rhys until it was determined if the move was financially feasible and if Winters was open to negotiation." He heaved a deep breath. "Rhys and I bumped heads at the beginning. As far as I'm concerned, that's history. I respect his knowledge and ability, but I also expect him to respect my capabilities in return."

"I get where you're coming from, and you are the money guy. But it's not a competition between you and Rhys."

"Understood. Now, I need your help with something."

"Sure. What?"

A slight blush darkened his cheeks. "Before she left for her long weekend, Stacy forwarded all the incoming calls from her phone to mine."

A snicker sneaked through her pressed lips, earning a scowl from Kevin. "Sorry, but it does demonstrate the volume of calls she handles."

"She could have found a less passive-aggressive way to prove that point," he grumbled. "Can you fix it?"

She had the code to Stacy's phone. A simple solution that would take less than thirty seconds. "I'll see what I can do."

The relief on his face almost made her regret not letting him stew until they returned to the office.

"Thank you. Now, change of subject. Let's talk about you." He grinned again, a half-crooked smile that relaxed the rest of his features. "Are things serious between you and the deputy?"

Her mouth dropped open. Before she could speak, two hands cupped her shoulders, and a light kiss landed on the top of her head. A familiar scent of aftershave wafted to her nostrils.

Mike Winslow slid onto the seat next to her. "What do you think, Davis?"

Megan caught the gleam in Kevin's eye at Mike's announcement. Oh, crap. Money man had gone into competition mode, and Mike wasn't far behind. All she needed was a battle of testosterone on top of the one between chili dog and fries in her stomach.

"Little to none at all based on the number of times Megan referred to you as a jerk."

Mike ignored the jibe and turned his attention to Megan. "I saw the Beemer outside and thought we could have lunch together."

"We're almost finished, but if you want to join us—"

"We should be getting back," Kevin said, looking at his watch.

Mike's cool glance did nothing to wipe the smirk off Kevin's face. "Change in schedule. I have to work tonight, but I'm off tomorrow."

Megan stuffed the remainder of her lunch into the cup for disposal. "Call me after your shift, and we'll decide what to do."

"Will do." After a squeeze of Megan's hand and a nod to Davis, Mike strolled to the counter to place his order.

Megan turned just in time to see Kevin's gaze flicker from Mike back to her. His smile widened, and he winked. Her conversation with Mike should have cooled any thoughts Kevin had in her direction.

But it hadn't.

Not even close.

CHAPTER FOURTEEN

Lila locked the back door behind Paige and Karen. Her first week at Carson's was finished. This time next week she'd have a paycheck in hand, a sizeable amount compared to how much she would have earned at the Low Tide. If her calculations were correct, she'd even have money left over after paying rent and other bills.

Grabbing her coat and purse from the closet, Lila bit back a grunt at those hard-earned dollars going toward an apartment where she hadn't stayed for days. A waste of money that her conscience couldn't allow to continue. It was time to go home.

Except that dingy little room wasn't home. It was a place she stayed until she could leave PI and make a new life.

Her purse plopped from her hand onto the work counter. She stared at the open door to Paige's office where Joshua was working.

I'm way too comfortable with you, Joshua Canfield.

Cooking dinner together. Cleaning up after the meal. Taking a walk around his neighborhood. All those things adding up to a normality she'd lost years ago. She'd seen the growing awareness in Joshua's gaze. The smile she caught on his face when he didn't realize she was watching him. A touch that lingered but didn't insist.

Attraction simmered on both sides. His slow, easy smile never failed to enchant, and his athletic physique stirred a desire she struggled to resist. Having lived in chaos since her mother's disappearance, Lila reveled in the calm warmth that surrounded him.

A man like Joshua Canfield was a rarity in her world. A protector by nature, a warrior when the cause was right. A good man with a good heart, and that was the lure tugging the hardest.

"Ready to call it a day?" Joshua asked, closing the door to the office.

Lila yelped, this time dropping her jacket to the floor.

Josh walked to the counter. He bent over to pick up the coat. "I didn't mean to scare you."

"I was…" Lila waved one hand "… thinking."

"Good thoughts?"

"Just things. Did you finish what you needed to do?"

Josh groaned. "Not even close. I have another round of test scripts to review before Monday when Ben gets back."

Lila slipped her arms into her jacket. "Will he expect those sooner?"

"Not likely. Ben took Stacy to Richmond for a three-day weekend. I doubt they'll return until late Sunday."

Heat rushed across her cheeks. She tilted her head, letting her hair curtain her face from his view. Those treacherous thoughts so close to the surface teased her with visions of Joshua sweeping her away for an amorous getaway.

As if that would ever happen.

I won't let it happen.

She jerked the strap of her purse over one shoulder then

took a deep breath. "It sounds like you'll have a busy weekend. It's probably a good time for me to go back to my own apartment."

Joshua stopped mid-step to the door. He turned, a slight frown on his face.

"I could use your help."

She stammered for a moment. "I can come over tomorrow morning, if that's convenient."

His frown deepened. "Have I made you feel uncomfortable?"

"No, of course not." Lila hurried to his side, resting her palm on his forearm. "I don't want to overstay my welcome."

"You're welcome to stay as long as you want. I like having your company and knowing you're somewhere safe."

She wanted to stay. She liked his company. She needed to feel safe. No way could she win this argument. Nor did she want to win. Still, she needed to set some boundaries.

"You're right, but I need to get more clothes. I'll also need to go to the laundromat." Money she'd have to spend, but it avoided a trip to Aunt Nan's. She glanced at the wall clock. "If I hurry, I can catch the next bus."

"Save yourself a trip. Use the washer/dryer in the garage. It's included in my rent."

"I still need to get more clothes, and there's no need for you take me. It's the middle of the afternoon. The sun is shining. I'll be fine." Seeing the protest forming on Joshua's face, she added, "You can't go everywhere with me, and I can't be afraid to go by myself."

He whooshed out a slow breath and nodded. Reaching into the pocket of his jeans, he pulled out his key ring and held it out to her.

"Compromise. Drop me off at my place then use my truck to pick up your clothes."

Lila stroked her thumb across the leather strap, and the fragile tie between them grew a little stronger.

"Thank you. I've gotten spoiled not having to ride the bus."

"You're welcome." He tipped his head toward the exit. "Let's go."

After Joshua gave a brief rundown of the controls, Lila backed the truck out of the parking lot. By the time they arrived at his apartment, she felt comfortable driving the vehicle.

Josh hopped out of the cab, standing in the opening. "Want to go out for dinner and let someone else do the cooking?" He hesitated for a second. "If you're tired, we can fix something here."

He looked tired too, but it made sense he also was weary of being in the kitchen. Or was going out a suggestion to give her a break? Before she could answer, Joshua took a step back.

"Think it over, and we'll decide when you get back."

"Sounds good. I shouldn't be long."

"Take care of any other errands while you're out." He closed the door and dashed across the lawn to the garage at the back of the lot.

Lila sat in the idling truck until he was no longer in sight, pretending they were sharing a life together.

⚜

The closer Lila got to Franklin, the less she wanted to be there. The difference between Joshua's apartment and her dingy room was as vast as the one between her childhood home and Aunt Nan's house.

I can't continue staying at Joshua's. If I'm wrong about his intentions, I'll be humiliated and ruin things between us at work. If I'm right, it'll hurt both of us when I leave. Where else can I go?

Rentals were rare except for the ones for tourists which would be out of her price range. What about the B&B where Ben Hampshire was staying? Maisie Porter, that was it. Ben didn't seem like the type of person who would stay somewhere inexpensive, though it wouldn't hurt to go by and talk to the woman. Joshua *had* given her permission to run any errands she needed.

The scent of cigarettes struck her even before she opened the apartment door. The inside reeked of stale smoke. Burn marks scarred the worn fabric in the sofa. The table showed similar burns along with circular stains from a wet bottle or glass.

Cabinet doors in the kitchen stood open, gaps revealing missing glasses and bowls. The toaster and microwave were missing as well. Her gaze shifted to the bed. Rumpled sheets, pillows tossed to one side, beer cans scattered on either side of the bed.

Her hands shook, her knees weakened. She wanted to sink to the floor, but the recent mud stains on the threadbare carpet stopped her.

The bathroom door was open, but she couldn't force herself to look inside. No way would she risk using any of the few items she'd left there.

Lila opened the top dresser drawer and breathed a silent thanks that her belongings looked untouched. She filled the canvas bags she'd found in back of Josh's vehicle with everything from the dresser and carried them to the truck. She made one more trip to empty the remaining items from the tiny closet.

Her fury erupted when she realized the cigarette smells clinging to her and her meager belongings had invaded Joshua's truck. She started the engine and drove to the other end of the lot where the office was located.

Lila charged to the front counter. "Mrs. Yates, I'm moving out. Room 11."

With no change in expression, Glenna Yates fumbled through a stack of cards before extracting one. "Got it. No refunds for the remainder of the month."

Lila took a deep breath. "Someone broke into my room and stole some of my belongings."

"Tough break."

"I wanted to tell you so you'd know when the sheriff's department arrives."

Glenna's mouth dropped open. "I can't have the law snooping around here. It's bad for business."

"The break-in wasn't good for me. I'm getting ready to call them now."

"Hold on." The woman rummaged through a drawer under the counter. When she straightened, she slammed her palm on the desk. "Twenty bucks, and you don't call the cops."

"Forty dollars. I don't call the sheriff, and you can have whatever's left in my apartment."

Glenna narrowed her eyes. "What's left?"

"A few dishes, a bed, sofa. Whatever they couldn't carry away or destroy." Before a counteroffer could be made, Lila held up her phone.

"Deal." Glenna dug into the hidden drawer a second time then shoved two twenty-dollar bills across the counter.

It wasn't much, but it was cash in hand and a small victory.

"Good-bye, Mrs. Yates." Lila pocketed the money and left Franklin Apartments for the final time.

Lila drove to the Crossroads, stopping at the intersection. A turn to the right onto Larkspur would take her to Porter's. One thing for sure was if she did rent a room at the B&B, a car would be essential. She'd put off the purchase, not wanting to risk the vehicle being damaged or stolen from the apartment parking lot. Something she could consider now. More money out of pocket, but an investment in her future. First, she'd find out how much a room at Porter's cost then make a decision after she received her check next week.

Leaving behind those remaining furnishings of her childhood should have hurt more. The sofa could be recovered, the table refinished, but the memory of those scars would remain. She understood now why her mother had been willing to leave so many things behind when planning their escape.

The past holds on in many ways.

Lila hesitated then continued straight toward South Pointe. Moments later, she parked in front of the property where Miss Emily's home once stood.

The surrounding ground lay charred from the fire that had destroyed that beautiful house. At the back of the lot, the shell of a garage huddled in the charred remains next to what had been a lush garden. Her gaze swept across the scorched terrain, halting on an open pit blocked by several barricades a few feet away.

Her chest pounded, blood roared in her ears, and sweat broke out across her brow. She swallowed down the rising bile.

Turn back.

Her feet carried her forward.

Turn back.

Her foot skidded on the uneven ground. She stumbled, regained her balance and walked on.

Turn back.

She stopped a few feet away from the opening. Her pulse slowed, and she drew a deep breath. Coming here was a mistake. Seeing the site where her mother had lain forgotten for years wouldn't provide peace. Not for Lila, and certainly not for Jennie.

A shifting shadow fell across her own silhouette, and she jerked. Before she could spin around, rough hands gripped her shoulders, shoving her toward the open grave.

The scent of whiskey washed across her cheek, and a harsh voice rasped in her ear. "You're next, Lila Grainger."

Drawing a deep breath, she screamed with every ounce of air in her lungs. The grip on her shoulders loosened, and she twisted enough to jab her elbow into the assailant's body. A stomp to the man's instep came next.

"Damn it, Lila. That hurt!"

She spun around to see Jeffy hopping on one foot. Angie stood to one side, a smirk decorating her over-glossed lips. A movement from the far side of the grounds showed Rhys McCall running in her direction. He stopped next to her in a protective stance.

"Lila, are you hurt?"

"No—"

"Hurt?" Jeffy squalled. "Woman, you darn near broke my foot."

"What are you doing here. Were you following me?"

"Don't flatter yourself." Angie waved a hand. "We saw you at the Crossroads in that fancy truck. Jeffy said you must be getting paid something extra under the table. I said more likely under the covers."

Jeffy shot a glare at Angie before offering a fake smile to Lila. "We saw you stopped here and decided to pay our respects."

"That's enough," Rhys took a step forward. "I don't know who the two of you are, but this is private property. You need to leave before I call the sheriff."

Jeffy flexed his shoulders as he wobbled to stand firm. "Think you can make me?"

Rhys chuckled. "Without breaking a sweat."

Angie smacked her hand against Jeffy's back. "Let's go. We got better things to do than stand around with these losers."

Jeffy nodded. "You take care, little cousin. No need to be scared. There's people watching you. I meant to say, people are watching *out* for you."

With a shrill whistle as if calling a dog, Angie motioned for him to follow. They walked away, her hips swaying with each step and Jeffy limping.

"Hey, Lila." Angie paused, lifting one hand in a tapping motion. "Knock-knock. Someone's at the door."

Rhys took a step forward, and they fled. He turned back to Lila. "Are you hurt?"

She shook her head. "I was so relieved when I saw you."

"I was checking the property now that the site's been released."

Lila heaved a deep breath. "I apologize for trespassing. I thought seeing it would—" She pushed back a wave of grief. "I couldn't make myself go any closer. All of sudden, someone began pushing me. He said I was next."

Rhys wiped a hand across his mouth, muffling an exclamation.

"I screamed, jabbed my elbow into his stomach and stomped on his foot. When I got loose, I saw it was Jeffy and his fiancée."

"You gave me a start when I heard that scream."

His concern eased away the remainder of her tension. Joshua and Rhys might not share a blood bond, but they both had a knack for kindness.

"Is that guy a relative?"

She nodded. "My Aunt Nan's son."

"I'm glad you're all right. If you want to stay, I'll hang around as long as you need."

"What I need is for the person who hurt my mother to be punished. I thought it would help coming here, but it didn't. I'm ready to leave."

Rhys escorted her to the edge of the property where she'd parked. "Is that Josh's truck?"

Lila blushed. "Yes, he loaned it to me to run errands so I wouldn't have to take the bus. Stopping here was an impulse, and I'm sorry I did."

"Don't blame yourself. That was a rotten trick from those two."

"I was already on edge from everything else that's happened."

She realized her mistake the instant Rhys's eyes narrowed. Just like his brother, there was something about this man that invited confidences.

"What sort of things?"

No point hiding the truth. He was bound to find out from Joshua. "Last week someone tried to get into my apartment. It was the same day the sheriff had me identify my mother's belongings. Based on that comment Angie made about someone at the door, I think it was her or Jeffy trying to scare me."

"Did you report it?"

"No. We never saw enough to give a description."

"We?"

"Joshua drove me home and was there when it happened. He noticed someone looking through the blinds then trying to open the door. The person ran around the corner of the building by the time he opened the door."

"Have there been any attempts since then?"

She lifted her head, and the lingering scent of smoke

drifted up from her jacket and hair. "I've been staying at Joshua's apartment since then. He was concerned, and I was scared. I went back for the first time today to get more clothes. Someone had been there. Maybe two people. My furniture was damaged. A couple of small appliances and dishes stolen. I reported it to the manager when I told her I was moving out." A small laugh broke free. "I scared her into giving me a small refund on the remainder of this month's rent after threatening to report the break-in to the sheriff."

"Good for you. What about Josh's apartment? Is it secure?"

"There haven't been any incidents, if that's what you mean." She dipped her head, and the next words spilled out. "I don't want Joshua or anyone else hurt because of me."

Rhys leaned against the side of the truck. "I went through something similar last summer. A woman named Vicky Towers stalked me. She broke into my house several times, once while Jamie and I were asleep. Another time, she fired a gun at the car Jamie was driving."

A pang rushed through Lila at the thought of the woman who'd been kind and welcoming to her being threatened. "Was she hurt?"

"Shocked mostly, but she could have been killed because of me. I told her we couldn't be together until the stalker was found."

"You were protecting her."

"I was, but in the process, I hurt her by shutting her out of my life."

"It obviously worked out."

"After she set me straight on a few things. She pointed out I couldn't control or fix everything, and if we were to be a couple, it was all or nothing. It made me realize that whatever happens in life, we're stronger together."

A cool breeze swept across the grounds as the sun dipped closer to the horizon. Lila tugged the car keys from her pocket.

"I'm keeping you from going home to Jamie."

"Jamie and I are going out to dinner tonight." He pushed away from the vehicle. "Why don't you and Josh join us?"

Her mouth dropped open, and she stammered for an instant. "I can't speak for him, but don't you and Jamie want an evening alone?"

A small crease etched his brow. "You know the situation between Josh and me, don't you?"

"That Mrs. Canfield is your biological mother, but Joshua grew up believing she was his?"

"In a nutshell, yes." He gave a short laugh then grew solemn. "Things are awkward between us, but we're making progress. I'd like to hear what it was like for him growing up with Mom. What she was like. I'm hoping if we have dinner together, it'll build on that beginning we made at the wedding."

"I can't promise, but I will ask Joshua." She smiled. "It sounds like fun."

He held the driver's door to the truck open as she climbed in.

"Let's plan on meeting at the Cantina at seven. If you can't make it, you have Jamie's number and can let her know."

"I'll let Jamie know either way."

She started the engine then looked at Rhys as he continued to hold the door.

"You have people who care about you, Lila. You don't have to be strong alone."

A gentle peace settled over her, filling her heart where it had been empty moments ago. She managed a small smile and nodded.

Rhys closed the door then stepped back with a wave. She returned the wave and headed back toward the Crossroads.

Those few minutes spent with Rhys eased away the fright Jeffy's prank had caused. If it was a prank. He claimed people were watching her. Had he altered the wording as another means of keeping her on edge? It wouldn't surprise her if Jeffy and Angie were the ones who broke into her apartment.

Angie. That was the answer. Now that Lila no longer lived at Aunt Nan's house, the bulk of the housework would fall on Angie. The same reason Jeffy wanted her to return to the Low Tide. Since she'd quit, someone had to pick up the slack. All these incidents were juvenile tactics to scare her into returning to Nan's.

The next time they pull one of their tricks, I'll call them out.

The last dregs of tension drained away, replaced by the anticipation of dinner at the Lighthouse Cantina. Another new experience she would share with Joshua.

If he said yes.

❧

Saying "no" had never been an option.

When Lila mentioned the invitation, Josh found himself immediately agreeing. A double date was something Lila probably had never experienced, though his preference would have been just the two of them. They jumped into action to get ready.

A cleaning of the inside of the truck on his part, a load of laundry on hers, then a quick trade-off for the shower.

Tucked in a booth in the back of the restaurant, they enjoyed dinner and casual conversation. Toward the end of the meal, Jamie and Lila excused themselves from the table.

"I'm glad you and Lila could make it," Rhys said. "Jamie was excited when I told her."

"Lila was too. She's fond of Jamie." Forearms resting on the table, Josh leaned forward. "Lila told me what happened at the Adams property. That's another reason I wanted her to have a fun evening out."

"I'm glad I was there."

"What do you make of those two? Do you think Jeff would have pushed Lila into the grave?"

Rhys heaved a deep breath. "The ground was soft from the rain yesterday. I think he intended to push her close enough that she'd fall in on her own despite the barricades. From what I observed, that woman Angie is the more dangerous one of the two."

"Lila told me she thinks the incidents are pranks to get her to move back to her aunt's house."

"Why?"

"Jeff and Angie are getting married and plan on moving in with his mother. Lila figures they want her back to do the cooking and cleaning. Even now she goes there to clean house for her aunt."

"I heard the story from Mike about the bar fight. Is Lila's aunt as crazy as everyone says?"

"Crazy-mean. She called Lila the day of Mom's wedding, all upset about something, begging Lila to come to her. When we got there, she met us at the front steps with a gun."

Rhys's mouth dropped open. "Why?"

"I had to park down the street. Lila was in a panic and took off running, and I followed. Nan said she saw me and claimed she thought Lila was in danger."

"No wonder she's wanting to leave this place."

Josh stiffened. "Leave when?"

"That's what she told Jamie when she asked about buying

her car. I can't blame her for wanting to get away from—"
Rhys's eyes narrowed. "She never mentioned it?"

"No, she didn't." Josh shoved the hurt aside. Lila wasn't
used to trusting others and plans to leave town wasn't the best
news to share with a new employer. Lila seem to enjoy her
new job and might change her mind about leaving, especially
if she broke free from the manipulative chains of the Grainger
clan.

A clan that included a certain Providence Island deputy.

"How well do you know Bret Madigan?"

Rhys frowned. "Not much. He moved here last summer.
Some of the guys meet at the high school for pick-up basket-
ball. He's joined in several times when he hasn't been on duty.
Why?"

"He's Lila's cousin."

The creases in Rhys's brow deepened. "He's related to the
Graingers?"

"His mother, Lila's father and her Aunt Nan were brother
and sisters. Lila went to live with her aunt after her mother
disappeared." Josh glanced around to check that Jamie and
Lila were nowhere in sight before relating Bret's admissions.

Rhys shook his head. "So, what if Bret had a crush on a
slightly older woman? They were related by marriage, not
blood."

"He was in college. She was ten years older with a daughter, and it wasn't a crush. You didn't hear the way he talked
about her or see the look on his face. He was in love with her."

"Even if he was, I don't understand your suspicions. Lila
explained how Bret knew about the shoes."

"What if Madigan came to PI that night?"

"No reason for him to come here if Jennie was going to
meet him the next day."

"We only have his word that was the plan. Maybe she

changed her mind or never agreed to his offer. What if he came here to change her mind and lost his temper?"

"You're going way out on a limb here. If Bret has a guilty conscience, it's probably because he felt he should have done something sooner to get Lila and her mother away from the Graingers." Rhys tapped his thumb against the edge of his plate. "Did you tell Sam about your conversation with Bret?"

"No, for the reasons you just stated. We have no proof."

"After all this time, I doubt there's any way of proving if Jennie was killed there or if someone took advantage of the grounds being prepared for landscaping to bury her body there. It was springtime, and Miss Emily took a lot of pride in her gardens."

"Lila said her mother left her at home to do one errand before leaving. Jennie didn't trust the local bank because one of the Graingers worked there. The only person she did trust was Miss Emily who probably held Jennie's money. That's why she was at Miss Emily's house that night." Josh leaned forward in his chair. "Whoever killed her must have robbed her of all her savings."

"Not necessarily. When we cleared the site, we found a steel vault."

"What was in it?"

"No idea. Before she passed, Miss Emily went to live with her nephew and his family in Tennessee. Sam notified the executor of Miss Emily's estate. The vault's been in holding while he's waiting for a response to claim the property. Because of the body found on the property, Sam filed a warrant to open the vault."

Josh tipped his head in the direction over Rhys's shoulders. "The girls are on their way back."

Jamie dropped a kiss onto Rhys's cheek then slid onto her

chair. "Sorry. There was a line to the restroom. What have you guys been discussing?"

Josh rested his arm along the back of Lila's chair. "Rhys mentioned some guys he knows who get together for basketball."

"Did you play basketball in college?" Lila asked.

"I did in high school along with baseball and track. I didn't have time for sports in college."

"We should watch the guys play," Jamie said. "Shouldn't we, Lila?"

"I'd love to watch."

"Not a good idea, honey." Rhys patted Jamie's hand. "Some of the guys trash talk, and Baby Mac doesn't need to hear that."

"Uh-huh. Sounds like an excuse for a boys' night out. Fine. Lila and I'll have a girls' night."

Josh glanced to the side. The glow on Lila's face wasn't due just to the lights over their table. The tension in her face and shoulders had evaporated. Her body was relaxed, and her smile was contagious. In that moment, he vowed to do everything in his power to convince her PI could be the home of her dreams. A home that included him.

"Or we can tell the guys to clean up their language. I wouldn't mind having Lila and Jamie cheering us on."

"I'm outnumbered—" Rhys broke off as his phone buzzed at the same time as Josh's cell. Only one person would text both of them at the same time.

Josh tapped the screen to read the text.

"It's from Mom. Her parents have returned from their cruise. She and Nick are on their way to Connecticut."

Jamie gasped. "That's wonderful news. Too bad they'll have to cut their stay short at the Inn."

Words froze in Josh's throat. He bit his lower lip, straining to contain his reaction. One look across the table to see Rhys struggling as well broke his resolve. A snort expanded into a chuckle, then a full out laugh from both men.

Jamie shot a blistering glare at both of them. "What's so funny about Dana reuniting with her parents after all these years?"

"Nothing's funny about that." Rhys swallowed back his final chuckle. "It's what you said about the Inn."

"We're picturing the look on Nick's face when he found out his honeymoon at a romantic inn at the bay turned into a visit to his in-laws' house."

Jamie shook her head. "Guys."

Lila smiled. "Brothers."

CHAPTER FIFTEEN

Mike shouldered the door open from the lounge to the deck of the ferry. Coffee cup in one hand, hot chocolate in the other, he held the door for a trio of laughing girls. Each gave him a once-over and a smile, along with a wink from one of them. Not too long ago, he would have pursued that unspoken invitation to chat. Maybe treat them to a cup of coffee before deciding which one to ask for her number.

His only intention now was to find where Megan had stationed herself to watch the waves. She'd nixed sitting in the lounge with their drinks in favor of standing in the sunshine and brisk air. Not that he was complaining. Megan's enthusiasm for the outdoors and willingness to get her hands dirty were two of the many things he found attractive about her. An attraction that had bumped up considerably at the sight of her in the blue silky dress and high heels she'd worn to her dad's wedding.

If asked, he couldn't have said much about the actual ceremony. It might have looked as if he was paying attention, but his senses were centered on the woman beside him, and all he could think was *this could be us*.

Jealousy wasn't a part of his nature, though seeing Megan sharing lunch with Kevin Davis yesterday had sent a jolt through him. Whatever Megan's intentions were, she was a straight shooter who would tell him to his face if she was having second thoughts. Her quick acceptance of his invitation for today swatted away any suspicions. Lunch with Davis had been nothing more than two co-workers sharing a meal.

He found Megan standing not far from his truck. Forearms resting on the rail, hair ruffling in the breeze, face turned toward the mainland just coming into view. His mouth crooked in a half-grin. That was his girl. Always looking ahead.

"Hot chocolate," he said, standing to block the worst of the wind from striking her.

She eased open the flap on the lid then took a sip. "Mmmm. Thank you."

"You're very welcome." He rested one elbow on the railing. "Sure you're not too cold standing out here?"

She shook her head in spite of her red-tipped nose and ears. "After a winter last year in Denver, this is nothing."

"I've never been to Colorado. Did you go skiing while you lived there?"

She wrinkled her nose. "Not my mother's scene, and I didn't have any way to go on my own." Her lips lifted in an impish smile. "Dad and I went skiing several times over the years. Twice in Montana, another time in Iowa."

"Ever been to the Poconos?"

"No, but I heard it's amazing."

"Lot of things to do there besides ski." He scuffed a foot against the metal deck. "If we each can get a couple days off this winter, what about taking a trip there?"

He lifted his cup, stopping half-way to his mouth to watch

Megan's reaction. Her lips parted, her eyes widened, then she took a deep breath.

"Uh... maybe?" She shook her head. "I'm sorry, Mike. That's a crummy answer to a *really* awesome invitation. You caught me off guard, and it's a big step to take, and... I'm still not giving you an answer, am I?"

"Maybe's an answer. Understood that you want to give some thought. How about I check and see what accommodations are available and make a reservation?" Seeing a protest forming on Megan's face, he said, "Easy enough to cancel if we decide not to go."

"Separate rooms?"

"Or a suite with separate sleeping accommodations."

"Won't that cost more?"

"Probably no more than two separate rooms. I'll see what's available then we can decide depending on our work schedules."

He kept his tone light, and the options open.

After a second of silence, Megan kissed the tip of his chin. "Okay."

"Okay it is."

For the first time, the silence that fell between them felt unnatural. Megan was high energy, and any time she was quiet meant she was savoring the experience of that moment. Drawing in every sight and sound to lock in the memory. The quiet now set his cop-senses quivering.

"Something on your mind?"

She didn't meet his eyes immediately. His dread-level rose as she bit her lip, pulled at the collar of her jacket, then finally looked up.

He gazed down at her upturned features. A woman tough but also tender. Did she suspect how much of his heart she held in those two hands? On the flip side, he wondered how much of a place he had in her heart.

A ten-year difference in ages might not mean much if both of them were older. But here he was, a twenty-eight-year-old deputy with a history of serial dating. As for Megan, she freely admitted her dating experience was barely above zero, mostly due to a mother who had been into both serial dating and marriage. Megan was four months passed turning legal, and she had a multitude of options ahead of her before considering a permanent relationship.

"Mike, you're a great guy..."

His heart sank as his stomach rose up to greet it. Was she really about to friend-zone him right here? When the ferry reached Sutton, would they take the next boat back to PI? Or spend the day together as if nothing had changed?

"... and I'm sorry for all those times I called you a jerk."

Sweet relief rushed through him. One corner of his lips lifted in a half-grin. "*Every* time?"

She wrinkled her nose at him. "Maybe one or two exceptions."

"Honey, there's times I am a jerk. Not as much as I used to be, thanks to you."

"Still, name calling isn't the way to handle it."

"We need a code word for those situations."

A giggle spluttered out her mouth. "A code word?"

"Something short and to the point to draw my attention to the transgression."

"Any suggestions?"

He leaned forward, whispering in her ear. "Michael."

The sparkle in her eyes shifted to an icy glare. Feet planted, shoulders set, she drew herself to her full height. Her mouth tightened. "*Michael.*"

Mike pretend-shivered then threw back his head, laughing. "Whew! You just sent a chill through me."

Megan hopped onto her toes and wrapped her arms around his neck. He held her close, savoring the feeling of all being right between them.

The ferry honk sounded, and they jumped apart. Mike dumped the empty cups into the trash receptacle then hopped into the truck. He started the engine while Megan fastened her seatbelt.

"Why haven't you asked me about having lunch with Kevin?"

Mike glanced across the seats while clicking his own belt into position. "When I saw the two of you, it threw me a curve at first. Whatever Davis wanted me to think, I wasn't buying it. You didn't show any interest in him at the wedding, and I doubt that work trip you took Thursday changed your mind. If you had changed your mind, I knew you'd come right out and tell me to my face."

"I would."

He shifted the truck into drive, giving her hand a quick squeeze before returning it to the steering wheel. "Is it okay if I do some macho posturing around Davis?"

"Sure. Go for it." Megan twisted in her seat as the line of vehicles began to move. "Tell me about the farm where we're going."

"McElree Farms. Riding trails. Hay rides. Orchards. Plus the best apple cider donuts. Sam and his family are going there tomorrow. Family fun day, plus Paige picks up fresh produce while they're there."

"Jess will love that." Megan bounced on her seat. "This is going to be so much fun. It's been ages since I've been on a horse. Have I told you about the time Dad took me to a dude ranch?"

There it was. His true competition. Not a pretty rich boy from up North, but Megan's down-to-earth, always-there-for-her father. A protective dad who'd given his daughter numerous adventures was a hard act to follow.

A smile tickled the corners of his mouth. *Look at her. So excited she can't sit still.*

The answer filtered through to him as he drove. Adventures didn't have to be as elaborate as a ski trip. They could be a simple as an impromptu picnic or the challenge of rock wall climbing. He needed to give Megan time to realize that a permanent relationship didn't mean settling down. The world was filled with adventures of all kinds, and they could experience those together.

⌘

Cleaning Joshua's apartment gave Lila a satisfaction that lacked when doing the same at Aunt Nan's house. As much as her aunt complained about people making free with her home, she fussed just as much when any of her sons went elsewhere for snacks or to lounge around. Unless it was to hang out at the Low Tide.

Had Joshua been this tidy all his life? While he had the confidence of someone brought up in wealthy circumstances, he showed no signs of entitlement or expecting special considerations.

Lila returned the vacuum to the utility closet then gave the couch cushions a final fluff. Cushions his mother probably provided in an attempt to give the small apartment a touch of flair. Adding a touch of color while maintaining a sense of masculinity.

She looked around then nodded her satisfaction. The

apartment was clean, and preparations for dinner were underway.

I'm living in a dream world. Telling myself all this is to repay Joshua for giving me a safe place to stay. When it's me pretending this is real.

A small cozy apartment for a couple to start life together. Working together for a future. Setting hopes each year then looking back the next year to see how much they'd accomplished. Their family would grow to one or two more. Maybe even three. Enough to need a house instead of an apartment, but nothing so big that anyone would feel lost or alone.

The tread of footsteps on the outside stairs didn't alarm her. Instead, they alerted her that Joshua was returning home. Already, she recognized the rhythm of his steps when walking, running, or climbing.

Another sign she was getting too familiar, too comfortable with this living situation.

"Finished washing the truck." He stopped to sniff the air. "Wow, something smells great."

"It's meat sauce. I thought we could have spaghetti tonight."

"One of my favorites."

"The sauce needs to simmer another twenty minutes. Plenty of time for you to shower."

"Why don't you go first, and I'll straighten up around here?" He looked around. "Except you already took care of that."

"You didn't leave much for me to do other than the basics."

He glanced into the kitchen area as neat as a meal under preparation could be. "You clean up as you cook too, don't you?"

"Only way to do it." Not that it helped at the Grainger house. The boys seemed to hold a competition as to which one could use the most dishes and leave the biggest mess. "Go ahead with your shower."

He was back in ten minutes, shooing her out of the kitchen. By the time she returned, a salad was on the table, and the spaghetti ready to plate. While they ate, Joshua shared stories of the places he'd worked and lived during his year away from home. Lila drank in any detail, adding the locations to her list of where she'd want to live. How could she choose between coastal Oregon, the wide, open spaces of Montana, or the hills of Tennessee? So many exciting choices for them—

Not them. Just her. Alone.

Appetite gone, Lila pushed her plate to one side. Joshua lost his home and family. After a year of traveling of miles and living alone or with strangers, he found a new home and a more family than he'd expected. She'd lost the two most important people during her childhood. As for the rest of her family, she couldn't wait to put as many miles between them as possible.

"Finished?"

She jerked, staring up as Joshua gestured toward her plate.

"Yes, I've had enough."

"You cooked. I'll clean up."

Lila watched every move he made. Committing to memory the strong set of his jaw, the confident grace of his body, the hint of a smile on his lips. He was every dream come true.

Dreams don't get you anywhere.

Aunt Nan was wrong. How could a person live their life without dreams? Some called them goals or targets, but those words were cold and lacked the soul that dreams inspired. Even when dreams did come true, sometimes reality swept them away, leaving a gap to grieve and a memory to savor.

Dreams hadn't come true for her mother, and they

wouldn't come true for Lila if she let herself believe in illusions.

"How about a movie?" He started the dishwasher. "I don't watch a lot of TV. I'm not sure what channels are available."

"I'm going to pass and turn in early." She stood up and pushed her chair under the table. "We have a busy day tomorrow."

"Lila, wait."

She stopped at the edge of the kitchen.

"Can we talk for a moment?" He gestured toward the living room.

I've made him uncomfortable. I've overstepped.

"Of course."

Lila took a seat in one of the chairs, forcing him to sit on the sofa. Close enough to talk, far enough not to touch. She curled one hand into a fist, pressing her nails into the flesh. A trick she'd learned early in life to distract herself from her emotions.

"Is this something about work?" she asked.

"No. Don't ever worry about your job."

For the first time, Joshua's features showed hesitancy, lessening when the corners of his mouth lifted in a slight smile.

"The first day we met, I felt something I couldn't describe. When we spent that morning on Main Street shopping for my mother's wedding, I realized I was beginning to fall for you. I knew for sure after our date on the ferry."

She squeezed her hand tighter, struggling with the battle whether to run from the room or bolt into his arms. All she could do was manage a single nod of her head.

"I know it's soon, but it's real. We have a chance for a future together. To build a life together. I'm hoping you feel the same and willing to take that chance with me."

If I could, I would take that chance.

But she couldn't bear to drag a good man like Joshua into even the edges of a life that included the Graingers and the Low Tide. He'd suffered too much to have his reputation shredded and his heart broken.

His happiness was here on Providence Island. Hers could never be.

She saw on his face the moment he realized the answer would not be the one he'd wanted.

"I can't say that."

The words were true; the meaning was a lie.

"Can't or won't?"

"Both." She met his gaze with steady one of her own. "I plan on leaving PI as soon as I can save the money to do so. I want to go where I'm not judged by the name Grainger. As long as I stay here, I have nothing."

"You have Jamie. You have Rhys and Paige." He rested his palm on her forearm. "You have me."

"Jamie and Rhys have each other, and they'll have a baby soon. Paige has a husband and a daughter. You have a family that loves you. Everyone will go on with their lives the same as before I knew them."

"Not me." He dropped to one knee before her. "With everything that's happened in our lives, we found each other."

"It was meant to be?"

Her sarcasm bounced off him as if she'd offered a smile instead.

"The two of us meeting at Carson's front door at the same moment seems like destiny to me."

Lila bit back a grunt. How could Joshua have such a positive attitude after everything he'd suffered over the past year?

"Was it destiny that my mother was murdered and buried in an unmarked grave? That you lost a year of your life from your family and never got to see your father again?"

His chest rose as he sucked in a deep breath. She'd managed to shock him, but it didn't give her any pleasure.

"Lila, those deaths occurred because of other people's actions. Most things in our lives happen because of our choices or opportunities. Sometimes unexpected gifts come to us. Call it destiny, miracles, or fate, but meeting you is one of those gifts. I understand why you don't want to remain here. If you chose to leave, I'll go with you. Just say the words."

He never said the word "love"—no doubt to protect his heart—but its purity shone through all the ones he had said. The shell that surrounded her heart for fifteen years cracked. What she hoped for... wished for... wanted with all her being could be hers.

All she had to do was make the most selfish choice of her life.

"I'm sorry, Joshua."

Lila rose before she could see the destruction she'd caused on his face. She paused at the bedroom door, hating her hypocrisy for sleeping in his bed while rejecting him. "I understand if you—"

He stood, features strained, hands tucked in his pockets. Despite every blow she'd delivered, he still managed a quiet, gentle smile. "You're welcome to continue staying here, and your job is for as long as you want it. Nothing's changed."

The kindness in his voice comforted her though she didn't deserve it. Questioning his integrity shamed her and, worse, it hurt him.

"Thank you."

"I'm going out for a walk. I'll lock up on the way out." He picked up his keys from the table by the door. "Good night."

The door closed behind him before she could say those two words. Just as well. There was nothing good left in this night.

CHAPTER SIXTEEN

Dana tucked the Victoria Inn brochure into the glove compartment along with her disappointment. Any other time, the news her parents had arrived home would have elated her. She was excited now, except for the timing.

As busy as her schedule was, she had a flexibility that Nick didn't. His workload had increased due to managing a larger shop with multiple employees. This trip wouldn't have been possible if not for former owner Glenn Thornton agreeing to fill in.

The honeymoon plans had been as much for him as for her. A chance for him to rest, for her to spoil him with undivided attention and to share uninterrupted time as a couple.

They'd checked in and explored the hotel, then debated going into town for dinner. Instead they decided on room service and an early night as the best way to start their honeymoon.

Dana's brother Kit interrupted that early night, informing her that their parents had returned from their months long cruise. With a business trip to England scheduled, Kit wanted to prepare them with the news that their long-thought-to-be-dead daughter was alive before he left. Any chance she and Nick could make the trip to Connecticut, ASAP?

They left the resort well before dawn this morning and had already passed through Maryland, Pennsylvania, and most of New York.

She turned her face toward the window as the passing scenery started to seem familiar. The last time she'd visited her parents was the Christmas before the car accident that sent her living another woman's life.

Whatever basis for James's actions, the majority of the blame belonged to Toddy. Nathan Stoddard fooled all of them into believing he was a benevolent, though cranky, uncle. If James had been honest from the beginning, she would have lived a different life. On the other hand, if she hadn't survived the accident, James and Joshua both would have been killed before Stoddard took his final strike against Dee.

Would you have tried to stop him, Dee? Did money mean more to you than your husband and son?

"We should be at your parents' house in a little over an hour," Nick said, interrupting her thoughts. "You need to stop before then?"

Dana pulled down the sun visor mirror to check her make-up. A few touch-ups before they stopped was all she was needed. "I'm good."

"Beautiful scenery here."

"I love the fall colors. This is my favorite time of year. The winters can be brutal." She twisted in her seat. "Are you okay? I'm—"

"Don't apologize. We're doing something that's long overdue. We've waited months for your folks to get home. If you're not ready to meet them, we don't have to go."

"I want to go. I need to see their faces and hear their

voices. To touch them and hug them. But I feel guilty too. You arranged a wonderful honeymoon for us."

Nick heaved a deep breath. "I was looking forward to the two of us being away from home and work. But this situation has been hanging over your head since Megan located your brother last summer. Now's the chance to get that part of your past—and future—resolved, and I'll do whatever is needed to help make that happen."

Dana leaned her head against his arm for a brief moment. "Thank you."

He threw a quick grin in her direction. "That said, how long do you think we'll stay?"

"It depends on how the visit goes. A couple of days?"

"Today's Thursday, and by the time we get there, we'll have most of today. What if we leave Saturday afternoon and drive back to the Inn? That'll give us the rest of Saturday, all day Sunday and until check-out time on Monday. Only a couple hours drive then we're home."

"Can we get reservations?"

"I made them before we left on that chance. Same room. If you want to stay longer in Connecticut, we can cancel."

"Let's keep it that way for now." She ran a palm down his thigh. "You think of everything."

He rested his hand over hers. "I want my girl to be happy."

"You do make me happy."

She settled in her seat, watching the scenery with an eagerness she hadn't felt moments ago. A wave of déjà vu washed over her, suggesting hints of familiarity supported by snippets of actual memories.

There's so much I want to show Nick while we're here. To see the home where I grew up. Maybe I'll remember more. If I don't, then I'll make new memories.

Memories strobed through her mind as if faded photographs were coming to life. A cornucopia of scarlet, gold and pumpkin blazed against a pure blue sky from the trees standing sentry along the lane. The road opened into a circular driveway, leading to a sprawling white mansion. An occasional glimpse of the Connecticut River could be seen until they drove closer to the house.

"I thought you said your parents were upper-middle class?"

"Yes."

"Honey, we have different definitions of middle class."

"My family's been in this area for generations. The house and land was passed down eventually to my father, and much of the acreage has been sold off over the years. There're families much more wealthy than ours in his area."

"Uh-huh."

"My father was a banker, probably retired now, considering all the travel he and my mother seem to do."

"The property taxes must be enormous."

"Those are paid through...."

Nick parked in front of the house and cut the engine. He rested an elbow on the steering wheel and shifted to face her.

"Through...?"

"A trust fund."

"*Another* trust fund? Why were you living in student housing?"

"I didn't have access to my share of the money until I turned twenty-five. By that time, things had changed."

He glanced at the front door. "Are you sure they're home?"

"We'll need to ring the bell. The housekeeper will let us in."

Nick squeezed her wrist then exited the vehicle. He circled to the other side to open her door.

"Cold," he said.

Dana lifted her face to toward the sun. "Brisk, but I wouldn't call it cold."

He took her elbow as they walked toward the front steps. "I wasn't talking about the weather."

❧

Nick ate his words seconds later as the door swung open. Dana rushed forward to embrace the man standing in the entrance.

"Dad."

"Katie. My little Katie D is home." He held her several seconds, face buried in her neck. When he stepped back, he brushed a hand across each cheek. "Look at you. Just look at you."

Dana touched his face. "I've missed you so much."

"Here I am keeping you on the stoop. Come in."

Once inside, Nick extended his hand. "Nick Warden. I'm Dana's husband."

A frown flitted across the man's face before he returned the handshake. "Chris Dennison. Call me Denny. Hard to think of Katie by another name."

"I know what you mean."

"Let's head to the parlor. Your mother's waiting there."

Following behind Denny, Nick shook his head. Dana didn't seem to find anything unusual about her mother waiting for them to come to her. Maybe he was right about that temperature in the first place.

The parlor wasn't as archaic as the name implied. Despite the wainscoting and ornate fireplace, the room appeared modern but elegant. Carolyn Dennison stood in front of the fireplace and, as they entered, crossed to the center of the room.

"Catherine!" She held out both hands.

Hands, Nick noted. Not arms.

Dana rushed forward, taking one of the mother's hands in hers, embracing her with her other arm. Carolyn responded with several pats on Dana's back.

Pats. Not hugs. Nick bit back another swell of anger.

Carolyn stepped back, her attention shifting to him. "You must be James."

Before Nick could reply, Denny spoke. "No, Carolyn. This is Nick Warden, Katie's new husband."

"I apologize, Mr. Warden. We returned a few days early. The staff isn't due back until the first of the week except for Nina who opened a few rooms for us. Kit was in such a hurry when he told us that Catherine was alive and on her way here. There were so many details, I couldn't process it all." Her lower lip began to tremble. "I wanted things perfect for Catherine's homecoming."

A portion of Nick's ire subsided. "No offence taken, Mrs. Dennison."

Denny slipped an arm around his wife's shoulder. "I'm sure Katie and Nick are fine with the way things are." He glanced to Nick. "Why don't we get your bags? I'll show you to your suite and give you a tour of the house while the ladies visit."

With Dana's assuring nod, Nick left with Denny, but he didn't feel good about it.

"Tell me about your husband," Carolyn said, passing a cup of tea to Dana.

Dana traced her fingers around the rim of the teacup. "I remember this pattern."

"Passed down from your great-grandmother Joanna Dennison."

Dana took a sip of tea. Chamomile. A flavor she hadn't tasted since her marriage to James.

"I met Nick the day I moved to Providence Island last spring." Dana paused, deciding to omit the part of almost being run over that same day she arrived. "Nick owned a small auto repair shop when we met. Last summer, he bought a bodyworks business from a man who was retiring and combined the two services."

"A mechanic," Carolyn murmured. "Your previous husband James hasn't been deceased for long, has he? I believe Kit said he was an attorney."

"That's correct. Mostly estate planning. He's been gone about eighteen months."

"How long have you been married to Mr. Warden?"

"Nick and I were married yesterday." Dana held up her hand, flashing her rings. "We were staying at the Victoria Inn on the Chesapeake Bay when Kit contacted us. That's how we got here so quickly."

"Oh, you're newlyweds." Her gaze shifted upward.

To where a bedroom would be located. Dana bit back a chuckle as she remembered thick walls and heavy wooden doors.

Don't worry, Mother. You won't hear a thing.

"It seems so fast." Carolyn shook her head. "You were always so impulsive."

"There's nothing impulsive about my marriage."

"Oh, Catherine, how can you say that? You defied us to go

to that college in Virginia. Got involved with that McCall man and had a baby when you were just eighteen. Everything that happened since then is because you didn't *listen*."

Memories flooded from that period, this time through the perspective of an adult. Her passion from an early age was design, and her choice of college had been determined through careful research and a scholarship. What she couldn't deny was her emotional reaction when her parents attempted to block her from that path.

"You listened to me, but you dismissed all my choices. You planned which college I was to attend, my course of study, and where to live until I pledged the sorority you selected. Those were your dreams for me, but they weren't mine."

"We wanted the best for you."

Dana caught her mother's hand and pressed it between her palms. The touch soothed the temper burning inside her.

"I know that, Mother. We both dug in our heels when we could have found a compromise. It hurt when you and Dad cut me off, and I'm not talking about money. If we talked, it was because I called. For every two or three letters I sent, I got a postcard or greeting card in return. Rhys and I didn't have a lot, but we had a happy life. I had a scholarship and a job. Erik helped too. He provided what he could for his son. Despite the situation between us, he did for Rhys and me what you and Dad refused to do. You lost knowing your grandson except for a few days that last Christmas because you couldn't let go of the past."

"We thought if we held firm, you'd come home. It was pride on my part. I had so many hopes and dreams for you. So many things I wanted for you. Then you were gone, and there were no more chances to say the words you deserved to hear." Carolyn dabbed at the corner of her eyes with a linen napkin. "We were wrong."

The tension that had risen since beginning the trip to her childhood home subsided, replaced by another part of her past shifting into place.

"I understand, Mother."

Carolyn sank back against the cushions, her features tired and her complexion faded. "Do you, Catherine? How could you?"

"When James sent Joshua away to keep him safe, I went a year without knowing if he was alive. We've all made decisions for what we felt was for the best. We've all suffered because of one man's greed. I'll never get those years with Rhys back. Nor those years with you and Dad." She rested a hand on her mother's knee. "One thing we're not going to do is waste another moment."

"I want that too, Katie. I want to enjoy your visit and celebrate—" Her lips trembled, her eyes glistened. She swallowed and pushed away those displays of emotion with all the resolve of her New England heritage. "—celebrate having my daughter back."

"Let's start with showing you my family. Your family now, too." Dana reached into her purse and pulled out her tablet. She angled the tablet for both of them to view. "These were taken at our wedding. This is Nick and me."

A soft gasp fell from Carolyn's lips. "Oh, Catherine, you look so beautiful. Your husband is quite handsome too."

"Yes, he is." She swiped to the next image. "This is Rhys and his wife Jamie. Does he look anything like you remember?"

"All grown up, but I see signs of that little boy. He still has your face, except for that beard. Have you talked to him about shaving? He'd looked much better without the facial hair." She rushed on without waiting for a reply. "His wife is lovely."

"She's beautiful inside as well. She and Rhys are expecting a baby in the spring."

"Oh, a baby on the way. I'll be a great-grandmother. Imagine that. Boy or girl?" "

"Boy." Time to change the subject before her mother started planning Baby Mac's future. "This is my other son, Joshua."

She waited, silently daring her mother to challenge Joshua's role.

"He's also handsome though he doesn't look like our side of the family."

"Joshua takes after James. He reminds me of his father in so many ways."

"Hmm. Now that I think about it, he does favor the Colby side of the family. I don't know if you remember, but my sister Anna was married to Roger Colby."

"Colby is Joshua's middle name." Dana chuckled. "I can't count how many times I've said 'Joshua Colby Canfield' over years."

Dana continued through the photos. Megan. Paige. Sam. Then Jess and Robert.

"She's adorable, but where's the little boy?"

"Robert is the dog. Jess named him. Don't ask me why." Dana lifted one hand, chuckling. "His full name is Robert Samuel Carson. Jess has an incredible imagination."

"Is that why she thinks you and your husband are her grandparents?"

"Oh, no. She figured it out on her own and drew a family tree to prove it."

Dana watched as Carolyn's lips moved silently. Her thumb tapped each finger on her hand as if trying to connect each relationship. Truth, in this case, came from the loving heart of six-year old.

"It'll make more sense when you see Jess's drawing." She held up the tablet. "We may not be related by blood or even marriage in some cases, but we are family."

"Yes, we are." The tight lines in Carolyn's face relaxed. She stood, smoothing non-existing wrinkles from her dress. "I imagine you and your husband would like to rest before dinner. Nina assured me dinner would be ready by seven. We'll meet here at six-thirty for appetizers and cocktails. Is that acceptable?"

"Sounds wonderful. Which room are we staying in?"

"The Buttercup Suite. Second floor, facing the river." Carolyn paused in the doorway, a frown creasing her brow. "Do you remember where that's located?"

She did. Vaguely.

"I'll find it." She picked up her tablet. "First, I need to let the kids know we arrived and see what they're doing."

Carolyn lingered in the doorway. A second later, a sob broke free. She rushed forward, arms extended. Dana bolted to her feet and into her mother's embrace.

"I'm so happy you're home, Katie."

"Me too, Mom. I love you."

⌒⌒

Dana scooted onto a stool at the kitchen island to enjoy her morning coffee. Having forged a fast bond the previous evening, Nick and her father left for a walk after the morning meal. Carolyn bustled around the room, cleaning up the remains from breakfast.

"Catherine, toast and coffee is not a proper breakfast. You'll be hungry before we have lunch. Skipping meals at your age—"

Dana sucked in a deep breath. "Fruit, Mother. If you have fruit, that would be—"

Her cell phone rang with a request for a video call from Rhys. From the corner of her eye, she saw Carolyn moving around the kitchen.

"Hi, honey."

"Good morning, Mom. Last night you mentioned going to an old family homestead?"

"It's a museum now in Mystic. We're heading there in an hour or so."

"Can you take pictures? I'd like to see it."

"I'd planned on doing that very thing."

"What do you think about enlarging and framing some of the photos and hanging them in the lobby of The Dennison?"

"I love that idea!"

"I can't take credit. Jamie thought of it."

Dana looked up to see Carolyn standing at the end of the counter. Hands folded in front of her, a wistful look on her face.

"My mother is in the kitchen with me. Would you like to talk with her?"

"Sure. Hand her over."

Dana held out the phone. Carolyn patted her hair and adjusted the collar of her blouse before taking the phone.

"Good morning, Grandmother."

"Good morning to you, Grandson. I told Catherine when she showed me your picture that I could still see the face of that little boy."

He winked. *"My mom's face."*

"Can you remember anything about your stay here?"

"I remember jumping on a bed. Mom told me to quit, and you said it wasn't hurting anything. I remember riding the tricycle you and my grandfather gave me down a long hallway. There might

have been some mention about scuff marks on the floor, but... I don't remember much about that part."

"Anything else?"

Elbow propped on the counter table, Dana smiled at the hopeful look on her mother's face.

"The room I remember the most was large. It had a brick floor, and the walls were windows."

Carolyn gasped. "You remember the Lookout Room?"

"I had to stand on my toes to see out the window. Granddad found a step-stool for me to stand on so I could see the ocean."

"That wasn't the ocean, dear. It's the Connecticut River."

"Sorry, Grandmother. You tried to trick me back then. Not falling for it now."

Carolyn's mouth dropped open, and Dana reached for the phone. "Stop teasing your grandmother, and I'll let you see that room again."

"Sorry, Grandmother."

Following her mother, Dana identified the rooms they passed on the way to the back of the house. Most of which Rhys couldn't recall. When she stepped to the doorway of the Lookout Room, she slowly panned the camera.

"I remember this!"

Both women laughed at his exclamation.

Dana showed him the bricks in the floor and the three-legged wooden stool that had lifted him to see out the windows. Despite the cold morning air, she opened one window so he could hear the waves crashing against the rocks and see the spray dancing in the sunlight.

"I have one thing I bet neither of you remember," Carolyn said.

Motioning Dana to follow, she walked to the doorway. She leaned forward and pointed to several markings on the frame.

A straight line marked the height of a child along with Rhys's name and a date.

"When I measured how tall he was, Rhys told me I had to do it again the next time he visited..." Carolyn's voice began to quiver. "...so I could see how much he'd grown."

"I remember that too."

From the look on Carolyn's face, Dana knew her son couldn't have given her a better gift than that memory.

"I'll take a picture of that," Dana said. "I hear Nick and Dad in the kitchen, so we'll be leaving in a few minutes."

"Can you get a picture of the ocean outside the window for me too?"

Carolyn whirled around, mouth opening.

Dana winked at her mother. "I'll get one of the river for you too."

"Thanks. Have a good day. Love you."

"Love you too."

"I see Rhys is as mischievous as he ever was." Carolyn paused in the doorway. "Hurry and take your photographs, dear. I'm going upstairs to finishing getting dressed. Your breakfast is waiting on the counter."

She was getting a bit hungry and should hurry. If a fruit plate was sitting on the counter, there was good chance Nick and her father would make inroads before she had a chance. She snapped several photos from the window then kneeled beside the door.

The frame had been covered with a clear coating to preserve the markings. She traced her fingertips over the pencil marks. *I remember this now.*

Rhys standing straight, his face beaming with pride at the attention. She'd made similar marks on the door frame inside the closet at their apartment. Erik had scoffed the first time she asked him to hold their infant so she could make the initial mark. Trying to get their little wiggle worm to hold still had them both laughing. From then on, she'd noted his height on every birthday and half-birthday, and sometimes holidays or whenever he wanted.

This one measurement was the only one left of her son's childhood, but it was the one tangible reminder that her parents had of that short time with their grandson.

She took a picture then headed to the kitchen to see if any fruit was left.

⁓

The visit passed in a whirl. Visiting places from Dana's past. Showing Nick historical sites connected to her family. Walking the grounds with her father. Sharing time with her mother. Pieces of her former life blended with the new.

They left just after lunch, Carolyn having pleaded for one more meal together, something she nor Nick could refuse. Traffic was light, and they were making good time on their way back to Fairburn.

Dana bounced in her seat. "Are we there yet?"

Nick scoffed. "Brat. You know we're still twenty minutes from the Victoria."

"I know, but I'm excited. Do you think my parents will come to our house for Thanksgiving? Dad loved the idea."

Nick shrugged. "The decision is in their hands. Either way, we'll celebrate the holiday. I'm leaning toward they will come."

"Why do you think that?"

"Your mother mentioned it was a lengthy trip for them to make. I suspect she was trying to play on my sympathy so we'd agree to celebrate there. I mentioned that after taking that long cruise, an eight-hour drive to Virginia would be a snap and suggested they rent a limo with a driver and come down in style. I also pointed out there was no way all of us could arrange time off work to make that trip, and Jess was looking forward to meeting her great-grandmother."

"In other words, she has decided but doesn't want to admit it."

"Sounds about right."

"Nick, do you think I'm bossy?"

"You're asking that question now? Happy honeymoon to me."

She punched his arm. "Bad timing aside, do you?"

"No, and I'm not saying that so you'll put out tonight."

"Tonight? What if I want you sooner?"

He grunted. "Fine, Miss Bossy. As soon as we get checked in, I'm all yours."

Dana giggled. "Answer the question."

"Let me guess. Your mother said that? Speaking of bossy, she would know."

"She didn't come right out and say those words, but she mentioned several times how often I talked with the kids. How they're adults and don't need my ongoing supervision."

"You remember our first night together?"

She scooted in the seat and ran her palm up his arm. "Vividly."

He shot back a grin. "Thanks."

"What's your point?"

"I no more than agreed to go upstairs when you grabbed my hand and raced us up the steps. While I was admiring your backside, I thought 'bossy little thing.'" He shrugged. "You didn't hear me complain, did you?"

Her lips tipped into a smile. "No, I didn't."

"Sweetheart, you're a strong-minded woman. I like that you don't take guff off anyone. Dealing with clients and contractors you've had to be assertive. You and I have bumped heads a number of times. Got mad, talked it over, and put it aside. Do the same with this."

The sign for the Victoria Inn came into view. Nick turned onto the road leading to the hotel.

"You're right. That's gone and forgotten. The next two days are all about us."

Nick stopped at Valet Parking and shifted into Park. He leaned over and kissed Dana's lips.

"Happy honeymoon, Dana."

She kissed him back. "Happy honeymoon, Nick."

CHAPTER SEVENTEEN

Lila sat on the couch, waiting for Joshua. Her stomach churned, her throat ached, but not as much as her heart. What hurt even more was the shame she bore for inflicting pain on a man who'd been nothing but kind to her.

Kindness that had turned into love. Something she'd dreamed about but never thought would happen until he spoke the words that promised all his todays and tomorrows. All the things she'd ever wanted could be hers with a simple 'yes.'

How could she accept his offer when it meant separating Joshua from his family? He'd lost a year with his mother and lost his father forever during that time. He finally had a family again. An adoring mother, a stepfather who respected Joshua enough to ask for his mother's hand in marriage, a growing relationship with his brother Rhys, a sister, a sister-in-law, and a soon-to-be nephew.

Refusing Joshua had been the hardest choice she'd ever made. Look at the chaos she'd brought to his life over the past week. What would his life be like if he were tied to her family? She couldn't put that yoke around his neck.

Staying in his home tied Joshua to her family grief. If she had a lick of self-respect, she'd release him from his sense of obligation toward her. But moving to the B&B would put Maisie Porter in danger. If the incidents hadn't been a ploy for her to return to Aunt Nan's house, where else could she go?

I'm scared, and there's nowhere else I'll feel safe.

Unless she left PI. Going to an unknown location to start a new life the way she and her mother had planned.

The closet door in the hallway clicked. Joshua walked into the living room, pulling on his jacket. He smiled, but a sadness remained in his gaze.

"Ready?" He picked up her plaid coat, holding it for her as he'd done every morning.

"Yes," she said, sliding her arm into the sleeves.

During the drive, she stared out the window at the mists that draped the streets. She could have been sitting on a bench waiting for the bus instead riding in a warm truck. One more way she was taking advantage of Joshua.

Before she could change her mind, Lila slid her phone from her pocket.

Hi Jamie. Is your car still for sale?

She tapped her thumb against the edge of phone. Jamie probably wasn't even awake yet. Seconds later, a notification chime sounded.

Yes. R U in a hurry? I have appts today & need my car. Ckg with R about sharing his.

Here she was again, thinking only of herself. No excuse for being this selfish. Before she could send a reply, another message arrived.

R said no prob. Tomorrow work 4 U?

Yes! Thank you!!

Yr very welcome. Talk to U tomorrow.

Lila sent a smiley emoji in response, then eased the phone into her pocket. One step closer.

✎

The staff at Carson's seemed determined to suck every drop of Ben's vacation glow from existence.

Paige was her usual exuberant self, bouncing from one idea to another before he could finish with the first one. He settled her down with a request to put those ideas in writing. Supposedly to keep him organized; in actuality, to keep her occupied and out of his hair.

Thankfully, Aaron was out on delivery runs. His energy and his mouth ran non-stop. Cheerful kid, but exhausting to be around.

Lila appeared calm except for being on the edge of tears every time she looked at Canfield.

Josh's usual laid-back self crumbled under the grim set of his jaw and the longing looks he kept casting at Ms. Grainger. The dynamics between the two suggested problems of a personal nature, confirmed by Canfield's bark of 'mind your own business' when he'd asked.

The saving grace was Karen. She raved how the process made the work easier, and her honest desire to conquer the system struck a chord with Ben. When she accidentally mentioned an issue at home, he listened, even reassuring her after she realized what she'd done.

"Don't be so hard on yourself. You didn't know anything about this system last week and look how much you've learned. As far as your other situation, dump the guy."

"I want to be fair. Dale says he need time on his own to decide what he wants."

Ben shrugged. "Don't buy that excuse. Things might not

have been perfect, but it sounds like he had a good life. Home. Wife. Family. You deserve better than putting your life on hold."

Karen frowned. "You only know my side of the story."

"I can see the way he made you feel."

She sat up a little straighter, a hint of hope blooming in her eyes. "I have to get up front and help, but I'll give a hard thought to what you said."

Ben flashed a thumbs-up. "If you can spare her, ask Lila to come back."

Moments later, Lila joined him at the front office table. He slid her set of test scripts in front of her.

"You didn't initial and date the steps as you completed them."

"I made a check-mark."

"I need your initials and the date." He held up one hand. "It may seem unnecessary to you, but it's a quality process I follow for all projects. No exceptions."

"I'm sorry. I've been distracted lately. I'll take care of this right away."

Ben sat back in his chair. "Have you heard of circular thinking?"

Her brow knitted at the question. "No."

"Terminal objectives?"

"I heard you mention it."

"How about the story of the kid with a hole in his bucket?"

"Still, no." Her expression shifted to something just short of impatience.

"This kid needs to haul water, but the bucket has a hole. He needs to cut the straw to fill the hole. His knife is dull, and the whetstone to sharpen the knife needs water which he can't get because of the hole in the bucket."

"Why doesn't he take the whetstone to where the water is?"

"Because he's caught in that circle. People get caught up in thinking there's only one way to achieve an objective. Like taking a road trip. There's several routes, and you decide if you want speed, scenery or no tolls. All of them get you to the place you're going."

Lila's features tightened. "I get your point, and I don't appreciate your interference. I can't believe Joshua told you our private business."

"What he told me was to mind my own business. The thing is, when my buddy's heart gets stomped on, it becomes my business." Ben stood, pausing beside Lila's chair. "I'm heading out to lunch. I'll be back this afternoon to pick up the scripts."

He speed-walked through the kitchen before Paige noticed him and out the back door. A smile erupted at the sight of Stacy's car turning into the alley at the far end of the block.

If she had a morning anything like mine, maybe we can have lunch at her apartment.

⌒

The lunch crowd dwindled away, and Lila returned to the back office table. She scribbled her initials and date on each line on the test script. Her shoulders stiffened, and her hand froze next to the final line.

Initials. Which made her think of... Engraved letters. Like the ones inscribed in her parents' wedding rings with her own added after her birth.

J&J+L

John & Jennie plus Lila.

The pen dropped from her fingers as the image of the ring she'd seen at Aunt Nan's house flashed through her mind.

"I never looked for the inscription."

She'd never had a chance to do that. Nan had commandeered the ring, putting it on her own finger.

Lila bolted from the chair and rushed to the kitchen door. Slowing her pace as she entered, she stepped to the doorway of Paige's office.

"I need to leave... it's personal... Maybe an hour?" She rubbed her forehead. "A little longer if I miss the bus."

Paige studied her for a silent moment. She opened her desk drawer then held out a set of keys. "Take my Jeep."

Lila forced a deep breath. Even if the lunch rush was done, leaving work in the middle of the day was irresponsible. She glanced at the clock. Today was one of Aunt Nan's day shifts at the hospital. She had time to get to her house and check for the ring before her aunt got off work.

She closed her hand around the keys. "Thank you, Paige. I'll be careful."

Paige rose and circled the desk. "I don't know what's upset you, but let me get Joshua. Or Ben if he's still here."

"Ben's not back from lunch, and Joshua hasn't returned from his walk. I'll be fine." She managed a smile that wouldn't fool anyone then hurried to the back door.

Lila avoided the main roads, sticking to the side streets going through the residential areas. The lack of traffic compensated for the slower speed. She parked on the opposite side of the street from Aunt Nan's home.

Nan and Jeffy's cars were gone. None of the neighbors were in sight. If any of them were watching through the window, they'd assume Lila was there to clean or cook.

Keeping an even pace, she strolled up the front walk then inserted her key into the lock. She opened the door, pausing to listen for any sounds. Nothing except for the rumble from the refrigerator.

She called out a greeting. "Aunt Nan, are you home? It's Lila."

Receiving no answer, she closed the front door. A quick search showed no one in the kitchen or bathroom, and she continued to Nan's bedroom.

The room was dim, the shades drawn, the bed unmade. A hint of *White Diamonds* underscored with mothballs scented the air. Lila walked to the dresser where Nan's jewelry box sat. With all the drama over the ring, it wouldn't be in the main compartment. She ran her fingertips along the lower rim of the box, jiggling the frame until a faint click sounded.

Thank you, Uncle Mick. Good grief, Aunt Nan would have had a fit if she'd known her husband had shared that secret with Lila. Her heart thumped, and her hand stilled over the box. She eased the drawer open to reveal a ruby ring resting on a bed of faded black velvet.

Lila glanced around the room. With the shades down, it was too dim to see the engraving. She slid the ring on her finger and eased the hidden compartment back into place. A chill swept through her body.

What if I'm wrong and stealing jewelry that doesn't belong to me?

If she was right....

I have to get out of here.

With her luck, Aunt Nan's shift would be cut short, or Jeffy would stop by. She wouldn't be able to explain her uninvited presence. She dashed to the front door. Once outside, she kept an even pace to the car. No need to draw attention from neighbors who might be monitoring any activity on the street.

Her gaze dropped continually to the ring on her left hand. The ruby glistened and the gold glittered in the daylight. For once, every light was green, giving no opportunity to remove the ring and check the band.

She parked Paige's vehicle in the assigned spot. Unable to wait any longer, she slid the ring off her finger and held it up before her.

J&J+L

Oh, my God. It is Mama's ring.

She threaded the ring back onto her finger. Fighting back the acid taste of bile rising into her throat, she stumbled out of the Jeep. Stopping at the door, she rummaged in her pocket for her pass card. Behind her, a car passed then stopped. Lila glanced over one shoulder.

Nan stalked around the side of her car. Shoulders set, hands clenched, features tight with a barely contained fury.

"I heard you made a trip to my house." Her glare dropped to Lila's hand. "Find what you were looking for?'

Lila whirled, scrambling to swipe her pass card. A sharp pain exploded against her head. She fought the darkness, kicking her feet to no avail. She was lifted then dropped. Daylight disappeared with the bang of metal. She closed her eyes, pushing back the nausea from rocking of the car.

I'm in the trunk.

Aunt Nan's going to kill me, too.

⌒

Josh rubbed a hand against his neck as he paced the length of the island. "How could you let her go off by herself?"

"She's an adult," Paige snapped, waving her hands. "She was determined to leave. I thought letting her have my Jeep would be safer than the bus. She refused to let anyone go with her."

Josh winced as Paige's voice cracked. "It's not your fault. I have a bad feeling about this."

"So do I, after hearing what that scuzzy cousin did to her over—"

The security alarm buzzed. The back door jerked open to reveal Ben Hampshire, face pale, chest heaving.

"Canfield. Lila. Now."

Josh bolted across the kitchen, Paige on his heels.

"My Jeep's here," Paige said. "Where's Lila?"

"Kidnapped by that crazy aunt." Ben broke into a jog. "Move it, Canfield. Stacy's waiting at the corner to see which way she went."

Josh raced after Ben, his long legs allowing him to catch up within seconds. He dove into the back seat of Stacy's car while Ben took the front passenger seat.

"She's headed toward Old Main," Stacy said, making a left turn.

Josh scooted to the middle seat, his gaze searching the road ahead.

"How do you know?"

"I saw her make a right on Portsmouth. That's a straight shot to Old Main."

"We need to catch up before she reaches the Crossroads."

Ben shifted in his seat to look at Josh. "Stacy was driving me back to Carson's after lunch. We got there in time to see Nan slam down the trunk of her car before peeling out. I recognized the ID number on the pass card on the ground as the one I set up for Lila."

"We're coming up on the Crossroads," Stacy said, easing the car to a stop at the intersection. "Her car's nowhere in sight."

"Her house?" Ben asked over one shoulder. "Or the Low Tide?"

"She wouldn't take Lila where other people—Oh, God."

His throat swelled, and he struggled to breathe. "Go straight. She's taking Lila to Miss Emily's property."

༺⁂༻

The scent of earth enveloped her. Something small with many legs crawled across her arm. She struggled to sit up, but her wrists and legs were bound. Her eyelids fluttered open. She was on her back. Nan Grainger stood above her on one side, the open pit that once held her mother's body on the other.

"About time you woke up. You can't take a knock in the head, that's for sure." She scattered a shovelful of dirt across Lila's prone form. A spiteful act of contempt.

"I'm due back at work. People will be looking for me. You won't get away with this."

"You're a Grainger, and those town people don't give a damn about you, girl. I've gotten away with way more than this."

"How did you know I was at your house?"

"Angie called me. She was in your old room. For once, she was good for something besides lazing around. She saw you take that ring." She shook her head. "I should've gotten rid of it a long time ago."

Nan planted the edge of the shovel in the ground then leaned an elbow on the handle. "I had big plans for you. I was going to teach you how to take over once I was gone. My mistake thinking I could toughen you up. You're weak, just like Jennie. Fitting, ain't it? Burying you where I laid your mama out."

Lila squirmed onto her knees. "You killed her, didn't you?"

"No more than she deserved. If she hadn't been so greedy for *the finer things*, John wouldn't have taken that job in Sutton. He'd've stayed here and helped the family."

Lila sank onto her bound legs. "My father loved his job. He wanted to give us a better life."

"Wanting got both of your folks killed. If he'd been here where he belonged, he wouldn't have been in that car wreck. Jennie started getting sneaky. I knew something was up. I had people watching. When she left the house that night, I followed her. She was all gussied up in her new clothes. Pretty little Jennie wasn't so pretty after I popped her neck."

Nan stared in the direction where Miss Emily's house once stood. "Lucky break for me that night. The ground was plowed for some fancy landscaping. Didn't have to do much digging. Harley came and helped. I could always count on him." Her gaze shifted back to Lila. "Till one of those people you hooked up with caused him to go to jail."

"He tried to rob the restaurant and threatened a little girl at gunpoint."

"Wah-wah. I bet she got over it, didn't she?" Nan shook her head. "You brought this on yourself, Lila. Getting high-and-mighty. Shacking up with that Canfield boy. Stealing my property."

"That ring belonged to my mother."

"Belonged to a Grainger before that."

Nan gazed into the pit, her eyes glazed as if viewing something long past. A smile creased her lips, a haunting smile that sent a shiver through Lila's veins.

"I always wanted a daughter. Didn't seem right that I had nothing but boys. When I learned Jennie was planning to take you away and I'd never see you again, it ripped me to the core. Best of part of my day was coming home. You had the house cleaned and dinner started. Just a bitty thing, but I could count on you. Remember how we used to play card games and talk?"

"I remember."

I have to keep her talking. Paige has *to realize something's wrong when I don't return.* A lump rolled in her stomach. *Will anyone think to look here?*

"All those times have to mean something to you, Aunt Nan. More than what you're doing now."

Nan blinked several times then wiped a knuckle across one eye. "You're the only person in this whole family I ever loved, including Mick and the boys. Now, you've betrayed me and stole from me. I can't trust you anymore. I should've put you in the ground right away, but I wanted hear your voice one more time." She jerked her head in quick nod. "Best to get to it. Come tomorrow, they'll be pouring concrete."

"You want to hear my voice?" Lila demanded. "Fine. I'll scream until my last breath."

"Go ahead. Ain't nobody coming to save you." She pitched a shovelful of dirt onto Lila's face. "Don't hear no screams."

Lila spluttered, falling back. Rough hands rolled her onto her stomach. She kicked her feet, struggling against the boot planted on her back. Tears streamed down her face, wetting the dirt beneath her head. Her body shook with sobs.

"One quick tap then I'll roll you in the hole." A sob—or a chuckle—sounded. It could have been both. "Good-bye, little Lila."

She steeled herself for the blow, praying that the end would be quick, and she wouldn't awake to find herself partially buried.

I love you, Joshua. I'm sorry I never told you.

A roar sounded above her. Her body jerked, waiting for the promised blow.

Joshua raced across the yard, leaping to catch the shovel before it descended. Nan spun, landing a vicious kick to his shin. Ben Hampshire charged from the side, barrelling into the woman. They tumbled to the ground. Nan recovered first, fist raised as Ben rolled to his feet. Shovel in hand, Joshua rushed toward them.

"Stand back!" Stacy yelled. Feet planted, she extended both arms. A crack filled the air. Nan screamed and dropped to the ground, her body twitching from the shock of the taser.

Ben wiped an arm across his face. "Damn it, Stacy. I told you to stay in the car."

"As if." She tugged the handcuffs from her pocket and tossed them to him. "Cuff her before I zap her again for trying to hit you."

Joshua dropped the shovel and rushed to Lila's side, helping her to sit up. He cupped her face, brushing away the tear-stained dirt. His mouth tightened at the swelling at her temple.

"How did you know?"

Head bowed, he loosened the ropes around her ankles then started on the ones around her wrists. "Ben saw Nan closing the lid of her trunk when Stacy drove him back from lunch. He found the pass card you dropped. We took a chance she was coming here."

The final knot loosened, and the ropes fell to the ground. Lila threw her arms around Joshua, sobbing into his neck. "I thought I'd never see you again."

He cradled her against his chest, smoothing her hair to one side. "I wasn't giving up until we found you."

In the distance, the sound of sirens grew closer. Another pop of electricity exploded behind them along with a scream from Nan.

"Watch who you're calling names, *Hannah*, because I can do this all day."

Lila pushed away from Joshua's chest. "I want her punished, but not like that."

"It's to keep her contained until the sheriff gets here." He looked over one shoulder at Ben who shrugged.

Flashing lights appeared, and the sirens silenced. Seconds later, the sheriff, two deputies and a paramedic rushed toward them. After Tom Hunter secured Nan, the paramedic removed the probes and evaluated her. Stacy surrendered the weapon to Mike then walked with Ben to join Joshua.

Lowered onto one knee, Sam examined the Lila's injuries. "Owen'll check you over after he finishes with the prisoner. How are you feeling?"

"Shaky. Thirsty. My head hurts."

Sam pushed to his feet. "Anyone else injured?"

Josh shook his head. "I'm okay. What about you, Ben?'

"I'm good."

Stacy wrapped an arm around Ben's waist. "So am I."

Sam motioned to Tom who jogged across the grounds.

"Go with Owen to take the prisoner to Memorial for evaluation then book her. I'll take Lila to the ER in my cruiser. Tell Mike to go back to the office." He turned a stern gaze on the others. "He'll meet the three of you there to take your statements."

Josh bristled at the order. "I'm going with Lila. She needs someone with her."

"No, you're not." Sam jerked his head toward Stacy. "You can come with Lila. I'll take your statement while Lila's being checked."

Stacy tossed the car keys to Ben. She nodded to Sam. "Let's go. Lila doesn't need to stay here any longer."

Josh fumed as Sam and Stacy helped Lila to her feet. He

should have been the one helping her, keeping her calm, and reassuring her that she was safe. He took a half-step forward, stopping as Ben nudged his arm.

"Let's go. The quicker we give our statements, the sooner you can get to the hospital."

Supported on either side, Lila paused in front of him. "I'll be fine."

He held her gaze, needing that connection. "I'll be there as soon as I can."

⁓

Josh scraped his thumbnail against the label on his beer bottle. "I made the trip to take Lila's purse and change of clothing to Stacy's apartment. She could have let me in at least long enough to see Lila."

"She was sleeping." Ben glanced around the Lighthouse Cantina dining room. "Quiet here tonight. You want another round before we go?"

Ignoring whatever Hampshire was blathering about, Josh rolled the bottle between his palms. "She's awake now. Plus, Paige, Jamie and Megan are there. But I can't be?"

Ben grabbed the bottle and set it to one side. "Lila's dealing with physical and emotional trauma. She probably doesn't want you to see her while she's coping with everything that happened today. You'll get your turn to comfort her. Right now, she needs support from her female friends."

Josh eased back in his chair and scowled. "Stacy told you to say that, didn't she?"

One side of Ben's mouth lifted in a half-grin. "Yeah, except for leaving out the part about you being a big baby."

"What if I don't get that chance?"

"Why wouldn't you?"

"She's planning to leave PI."

"I thought she took the job at Carson's because she needed the money. Doesn't sound like she can leave anytime soon."

"Except there might be money in a vault found in the rubble on Miss Emily's property. Rhys said the heirs haven't claimed it. Since Jennie Grainger's body was found, Sam filed for a warrant to open the vault."

"Still don't see the problem. If you stay and Lila leaves, you've lost her. If you go with her, assuming she wants you, you can still come back to visit family."

"She doesn't want to separate me from my family. If she's stays, there's still the Graingers to contend with."

Ben snickered. "Obviously you haven't put your best effort into changing her mind."

Jerk. Sometimes it was easy to forget how much of one Ben could be. Time to turn the tables.

"Is Stacy the reason you haven't moved on?"

Ben swiveled his head to gaze around the dining room. "As quiet as it is, you'd think we wouldn't have to wait for the check."

"Is that a yes?"

A whoosh of air rushed between Ben's lips. "If Stacy gets transferred to the mainland when McCall's completes their buy-out of that other company, it changes things for us."

"You can work anywhere."

"True, but I've built up enough business here to keep me busy and out of trouble. I can start over again, but will things be the same between Stacy and me?"

Josh shrugged. "Probably, unless you act like a big baby."

"Bite me." Ben stood, dropping several bills on the table. "I'm heading out."

Josh shook his head. *What's my life come to that I'm taking love life advice from Ben Hampshire?*

CHAPTER EIGHTEEN

Lila wandered through the quiet apartment. Stacy had left for work according to a note left on the kitchen counter. She sat down on one of the bar stools, reveling in the peace that surrounded her.

I should be sad, and I still am about Mama. Although yesterday had been devastating, it did sever the remaining threads tying her to Aunt Nan and the rest of the Graingers. Paige's husband Sam couldn't have been more compassionate in his questioning. Having Stacy at her side helped too.

One thing she hadn't expected after sleeping a couple of hours was the gathering Stacy arranged. So much for her plan of lying in the dark, staring at the ceiling. Food and the company of the other women had been exactly what she'd needed.

Paige assuring her that her job was safe, even offering an additional day or two off.

Jamie bringing the title to the car and handing over the keys, assuring Lila the down payment could wait for a day or two.

Megan providing several college catalogs plus a list of online colleges.

A tinge of guilt trickled through those good thoughts. *I should have called Joshua instead of texting. I didn't thank Ben either.*

The bigger problem was where to go. Accepting Stacy's offer to stay with her would mean interfering with whatever arrangement she had with Ben. Porter's B&B also was out of the question due to the cost of the room plus gasoline back and forth to work. That left Joshua's apartment. Now that the danger was over, it wasn't fair to encroach on his privacy either.

Her mother's plan for their future warred with Ben's story of circular thinking. He had a point. She didn't have to check off each step before moving to the next. Her mother must have saved for years before realizing the dangers of staying. Jennie Grainger took a leap of faith in hopes to provide a better life for Lila, never recognizing the evil that stood in her way.

I don't need to wait any longer. Nothing's going to stop me from my dreams.

She packed her belongings, silently thanking Joshua for sending more than she'd needed, although that could be Stacy's influence of 'a girl needs options.' She wrote a thank-you message at the bottom of Stacy's note, then picked up her tote, purse, and keys.

Chilled by the morning air, she shivered until the heater warmed the interior of the car and the defroster cleared the windows. She drove off the parking lot. If she'd timed it correctly, she'd get to the terminal before the next boat left.

∽

The tap of Josh's shoes broke the morning quiet as he walked to his truck. He started the engine then sat until the defroster cleared the windshield before pulling out of the driveway.

Lila cared for him. Her reaction yesterday when she confessed her fear of never seeing him again proved it.

A little over a week ago, he didn't know her. Today, the pain of being without her cut him to the core. He'd come to PI to find a home again, to carve out a place in his mother's new life and try to connect with a brother who lost the life Josh got to live. What he hadn't expected was to find a woman who brought joy to his life. Her smile warmed his heart, sweeping away the loneliness that had held his life in stasis.

Now that Nan was in jail, he hoped to convince Lila to stay on PI. She'd have a family who would love and support her. He heaved a sigh. Maybe the bad memories outweighed the promise of better ones. If Lila was determined to leave, Josh was ready to pack up and go with her. He'd miss his family, but not as much as he would miss Lila.

Josh parked on the lot at the Canfield building then walked down the alley to Carson's. Paige's car was the only vehicle there. It was too early for Lila's shift, though she usually came in early with him. Or was she still recovering from yesterday?

He took a deep breath then swiped his card through the reader.

"Morning, Paige."

Paige looked up from her phone. "That was a strange call."

"Karen?"

"No, Lila. I called to let her know she didn't have to come in today if she didn't feel like it."

"And?"

"I heard a horn blow. Lila said she couldn't hear and would

call back." Her face crumpled into deep lines of worry. "Josh, I think she's at the ferry terminal."

"I'm going after her." He bolted for the door.

"Are you parked down the street?"

At his nod, Paige pulled her keys from her pocket. "I'll drive. Quicker than going to yours."

Ten minutes later, they hadn't reached the terminal. Josh stretched, eyeing the morning traffic. He grabbed the door handle.

"I'll go on foot from here."

"I'll park somewhere on the terminal lot," Paige said. "Tell her we love her and don't want her to leave."

Josh gave a jerk of his head and swung the door closed. His long legs ate up the distance as he edged around early morning joggers and dashed between openings in traffic. Cars slowed to a stop as the line to board the ferry halted. Another blast of the ship's horn blared through the air, signaling its departure.

He stumbled to the overlook, searching the outgoing vessel for Lila's car. None of the cars in view were hers, which proved nothing. Squinting through the morning sun, he scanned the parking lot and the cars lined up for the next trip.

Nothing.

Forearms resting on the railing, Josh bowed his head. Even if he could make the next sailing, there was no way he'd know which way Lila had gone. Unless she went to stay with the Madigans? Maybe guilt had prodded Bret to convince them to do for Lila what they hadn't done for her mother.

Was he the one now chasing a dream? Maybe Lila hadn't said good-bye for a reason, not wanting to be put on the spot for another confession of love from him.

I never said the actual words. I didn't want her to feel guilty or obliged. I should have said the words in my heart. I love you, Lila Grainger, and I'm not giving up on us.

Straightening, he gave a last longing look at the ferry in the distance before turning to leave. The click of heels on the wooden boardwalk caught his attention. He turned, and his breath caught as Lila walked toward him.

Words caught in his throat as he broke into a jog. He caught her in a tight embrace and buried his face in her neck.

"What are you doing here?" She drew back, her gaze sweeping across his face. "Did something else happen?"

"Paige said you called. She heard the horn from the ferry." He shook his head and swallowed hard. "I thought you'd left."

Her jaw tightened. "You thought I'd walk off my job with no notice? That I'd leave without saying good-bye?"

"I was running on fear." He cupped her face. "I thought I'd never see you again."

With the echo of her words from yesterday, Lila relaxed. She took his hand from her face and gestured with the other toward the ocean.

"Remember the promise my mother gave me for the future?"

"Leave Providence Island and find happiness." Not an exact quote, but bookends for the plan.

"One of the last things she said to me was 'we're going to be happy.'" Her lower lip trembled. "I've held those words to my heart since then. I planned and saved toward the day I could leave. I wouldn't let anything get in the way of that plan."

Josh choked back a sob forming in his throat. Maybe it would have been easier if Lila had left without a good-bye. Living through a countdown until that day would be a greater heartbreak. He had to tell her what was in his own heart. Not to pressure her, but if she ever did think back to her time on PI, there would be one good thing for her to remember.

"Did you ever hear of circular thinking?"

Caught off-guard by the question, he coughed the sob aside. "No, but it sounds like something Ben would say."

"He did say it. Along with terminal objectives and other words I have no idea what they mean. He dumbed it down to a story about a little boy with a hole in a bucket."

"I remember that. I always wondered why he didn't take the whetstone to the water to sharpen the knife."

"I said the same thing. It made me realize my life was locked in a cycle I'd made. I have a job I love. I have friends who care for me. I have a wonderful man who loves me." She tilted her head to look up at him. "And I love him."

Her face glowed in the morning sunlight. The chill that had yet to burn away tipped her cheeks and nose in pink. The ache in his heart began to ease.

"When I said I couldn't tell you that I wanted the same things you did, it was because I didn't want to make a promise I thought I couldn't keep."

"And now?"

She moved so they stood face to face. "I want your face to be the last thing I see each night. I want to hear your voice first thing every morning. I want to spend every day of my life with you." She took his other hand. "Joshua Canfield, will you marry me?"

Joy brighter than the sunline caressing the horizon soared through his veins. "I love you, Lila Grainger, and nothing would make me happier than being married to you."

"I still want to go to college. I can take online classes for a start. And I want babies."

"Babies who will never doubt how much they're loved." He

tipped her head upward with a knuckle under her chin. "Because their parents love each other."

His phone rang, breaking the mood. "That must be Paige." Josh pulled the phone from his pocket.

"Well?"

"All is good. I'm with Lila. We'll meet you at Carson's."

"I want to hear everything when you get back."

Lila leaned forward, tilting the phone. "I'll give you a hint. Guess who's getting married?"

A scream split the air. Josh jerked the phone back. "We're on our way now."

He ended the call then grinned at Lila. "She'll never give us any peace and is probably calling Jamie."

"Happiness is meant to be shared." Lila linked her arms around his neck. "If it gives her joy to tell others, I don't mind."

"As long as she doesn't tell my mom. I want to be the one to give her that news."

"We should go."

"Wait a minute." Josh lifted a hand toward a woman walking toward the terminal. "Excuse me? Would you mind taking our picture?"

The woman's pace slowed, and her gaze shifted from Josh to Lila.

Josh grinned and held out his phone. "She proposed, and I said yes."

The woman's wary expression shifted to amusement. "A proposal on the boardwalk at sunrise. That's a romantic story to tell your children one day." She set down her tote bag and took the phone.

They stood arm-in-arm, smiling for the camera. When Lila nestled her head against his shoulder, Joshua rested his head upon hers.

"I love you, Lila."

"I love you, too."

She wrapped her arms around his neck and lifted her face; he caught her in a tight embrace and lowered his mouth to hers. The kiss lasted until the clicks from the camera finally caught their attention.

The woman held up the phone, a wide smile on her face. "Is a dozen pictures enough?"

Lila hid a giggle behind one hand while Joshua stepped forward to take back the phone. "Yes, thank you."

"Would you mind telling us your name?" Lila asked. "For the story we'll tell our children."

"Naomi." She picked up her tote. "Best wishes to you both."

"Thank you, Naomi."

Josh tucked the phone back in his pocket. "We should get to work. Where did you park on the lot?"

Lila shook her head. "I parked a couple blocks down on the next street. Parking on the lot costs money. It's free on the street until eight a.m."

He held out one hand. "It's closing in on eight. Let's get walking. I'd hate for your car to get a ticket on its first day."

⁓

As much as Lila loved her car, she handed the keys to Josh with a request for him to drive. During the ride back to Carson's, she watched the scenery and the people walking to their jobs. The streets were decorated with the colors of fall and coming signs of Halloween. Despite the construction on the new Dennison building, Towne Square also looked ready for the season.

Most of all, she savored the sight of the man next to her. If not for him, and if not for Ben, she would never have seen this day. Instead of sunshine and the autumn colors surrounding her, it would have been layers of cold, damp dirt topped by a slab of concrete.

I'm alive, and I will never take my life for granted.

"I love you, Joshua."

He sent a quick grin in her direction. "I love you, too, and I love hearing that."

"Good, because I don't want a day to go by without saying that to you."

He parked the car into the assigned space. Lila hopped from the vehicle and skipped to the door. "I forgot to get my card back."

"Ben might have it unless the sheriff kept it for some reason. Ben's coming in this morning to make sure everything's working the way it should. More so to ease Paige's mind."

"Of course. She has a lot riding on these changes."

Joshua swiped his card and held the door open. They'd barely cleared the entrance when Paige rushed toward them.

"You're getting married!" She grabbed Lila's hands and jumped up and down.

"I know it seems quick."

Paige waved one hand in dismissal. "Pshh! It didn't take any time for Dana and Nick or Rhys and Jamie to get together. Though the two of you are breaking the record to get engaged."

"Take a deep breath, Paige." Joshua chuckled as he pulled off his jacket.

She did exactly that, then ramped up again. "I'm still excited, but I'll try to control myself. We need to get cracking on our orders, but first, Sam needs to talk with both of you. He's at the table out front."

Lila clutched Joshua's forearm, fighting the shadow that swept across her vision. "Nan escaped?"

"No, sweetie. She's locked up. It's about the vault they found on Miss Emily's property." Paige glanced to Joshua. "And a few other things."

Lila sucked in a deep breath of her own. She managed a small smile, mostly to reassure Paige. "Let's take care of that so we can get started on the lunch orders."

Sam wasn't alone at the table. Ben Hampshire sat in the chair opposite him. Both men rose to their feet.

"Hello, Lila," Sam greeted her. "How's your head today?"

"The swelling has gone down, and the headache's barely there."

"Good." He gestured to one of the empty chairs. "There's a few things we need to discuss. I thought you'd be more comfortable here."

"One thing first." Lila turned to Ben. "I didn't get a chance to thank you yesterday. If it hadn't been for you—" A rush of tears flooded her eyes, and the words choked in her throat.

"Stacy and I were there at the right time."

"It was more than that. You didn't ignore what you saw. You found my pass card and figured out what happened. You helped save me." She took a step closer. "Stacy gave me a one-time pass to do this."

She grazed Ben's cheek with a light kiss.

He grinned and winked. "You're welcome."

Joshua arrived with the extra chair, placing it at the end of the table.

Sam frowned. "We don't need another chair."

Paige plopped down next to him. "Yes, we do."

"Don't you have things to do in the kitchen?"

"Karen just got here, and Aaron said he could come in

early." She tapped a drumroll on the tabletop. "Let's get started."

"You're not needed here."

"I'll find everything out at some point so you might as well let me listen now."

Sam shook his head. "No secret where Jess gets it from."

Paige blew a kiss in his direction. "Get started."

Lila clamped a hand over her mouth as the two exchanged mock glares. A glance at Joshua showed he was amused as well. Ben stared into his coffee mug, looking bored.

"Getting down to business," Sam said. "We obtained a warrant to search Mrs. Grainger's house. We found several unregistered firearms. One of which matches the make of the gun used to kill Nathan Stoddard."

Joshua shifted in his chair, forcing himself not to look in Ben's direction. "You're saying Nan Grainger killed Toddy?"

Lila rested her palm on his forearm. Her cousin Buzz tried to kill Joshua's mother. Harley threatened Paige, Megan and Jess at gunpoint. Now, Nan was connected with the man who almost succeeded in murdering Dana Canfield.

"We're running ballistics tests to confirm that, but she's already confessed."

Ben sat forward. "How did Nan Grainger meet someone like Nathan Stoddard?"

Josh bit the inside of his mouth. *How can he sound so innocent?*

"According to her, Detective Kyle Lansing made contact with someone at the Low Tide who directed him to Nan as a person who 'got things done.' He needed someone to eliminate Dana, and she told Buzz to take care of it."

"Why would she kill Buzz?"

"She claimed he was holding onto money Lansing paid

him, and she killed Lansing because he was setting her up to take the fall."

Lila nodded. "Aunt Nan never tolerated disloyalty."

"As for Stoddard, her story is he told her to meet him for a pay-out which turned out to be a set up to kill her. She beat him to the draw."

Paige looked at Lila. "Does your aunt know anything about guns?"

"Definitely. She served in the military for over ten years." Her voice hardened. "She killed my mother with her bare hands. I have no doubt she'd shoot a person with no hesitation."

"What about Vicky Towers?" Ben asked. "Was she connected to Stoddard or just a random stalker who fixated on Rhys McCall?"

And Wallace has no idea Ben is clicking off each connection to him... and me.

Sam rested an arm along the back of Paige's chair. He took a long sip of coffee before replying. "According to Nan, the woman 'got in her business.' She refuses to say anything else about that murder. Oh, and that three-shot pattern—" Sam pointed two fingers to his chest then one to his head. "—she claims to have seen it on some true crime show and thought it would convince law enforcement to look elsewhere for a suspect."

"That fits too," Lila said. "She loved watching those type of shows."

"She calls it her Hat-Trick." Seeing the frowns around the table, he said, "Quoting, 'She shoots, she scores.'"

Ben rolled his eyes.

"Do you believe her story?" Josh asked.

"There's gaps in the some of the details. Nan's fixated on giving interviews and making plans on how she'll rule the roost in prison." Sam tilted his head toward Josh. "What tipped the balance was the description your mother gave after Lansing was killed."

Lila stared wide-eyed at Joshua. "Your mother saw Nan?"

He shook his head then looked at Sam. "What did she see?"

"Dana never got a good look at the person other than a fleeting glance through the front window of her building. The description was tall with blond hair. Assumption was the shooter was male. The clincher is the recording from Dana's phone. Lansing said a portion of a name before he was hit. H-A-N."

"Hannah." Lila gave a soft gasp. "How would he have known that name?"

"Lansing was a detective. He would have checked backgrounds before engaging with any of the Graingers." Sam's gaze shifted to Ben. "At first, we thought Lansing might have said 'Ham.'"

Ben's eyes widened. "You thought I shot that guy?"

"Sam!" Paige twisted in her chair. "You never told me that."

"No reason to." Sam turned his attention back to Ben. "You fit the description but there was nothing else to tie you to the murder. We also considered you when Vicky Towers was murdered since both of you were staying at Maisie Porter's B&B and came up empty. You're a guy who came to PI, decided to settle down, and open a business. Nothing suspicious other than not much of a digital footprint."

Ben shrugged. "I keep a low profile because many of my contracts are high-security."

"As I said, there's holes in her story but the mayor likes it. So does the state police and the prosecutor. It closes out four murder cases plus the attempted murder on Lila."

"What happens to my aunt?"

"State police are on their way here. They'll transfer her to a more secure location." Sam hesitated for a second. "I'm passing on this message because I'm obliged to do so. Mrs. Grainger wants to see you before she's transferred."

Josh half-rose from his seat. "Absolutely not!"

No way would that woman lay eyes on Lila again. Whatever hateful words or pleas for sympathy Nan Grainger planned to say could remain buried in her cold, evil heart.

Lila's hand stroked his forearm, her gentle touch breaking though his fury. He sank down in his chair.

"I have nothing to say to my aunt, Sheriff. Even if I went to confront her, she'd take it as a sign that she still has control." Her shoulders sagged. "I will feel better, though, when I know she's gone."

"I have something else that might make you feel better too." Sam slid a cardboard envelope across the table.

"I'm not needed for this." Ben nodded to Paige. "I need your feedback on the mobile app."

"Um..." Paige looked from the packet to Lila then Ben.

"I can't finish without your approval. I have another appointment in less than an hour and won't be available until tomorrow." He shrugged. "Up to you."

She scrambled to her feet. "Let's go."

*

Lila touched the ribbon surrounding the cardboard envelope. Across the front surface, a shaky hand had written *To Lila*.

"We notified Miss Emily's heirs after McCall Construction found a vault in the ruins of the house. Her nephew never arranged to take possession, and it's been in holding since then. After your mother's remains were found, I requested a warrant to allow us to open the safe. I emailed a copy of the signed warrant to Miss Emily's nephew and the attorney on record. We opened the safe this morning. Molly recorded the session, and the contents were inventoried. That envelope was included in the safe."

"Why would she put only my name on the flap?"

"No idea," Sam said. "Might be more answers once you open it. What I need from you is a signature of receipt." He pulled a folded sheet of paper from his jacket pocket along with a pen.

"Don't you need to see what's inside?"

"No, ma'am. Our inventory shows one envelope of that description which I'm delivering to you. What's inside is your personal property."

Lila read the release then signed her name.

"I have a feeling there's money in that envelope. If the bank gives you any problems, have them get in touch with me." Sam replaced the receipt in his pocket, switching it for a card. "The forensics lab is releasing your mother's remains. This is the number to call to discuss final arrangements."

Josh slid the card in front of himself. "We'll give them a call."

Sam grinned. "I hear congratulations are in order for you two."

Lila laughed. "I asked, and he said yes!"

"Good for both of you." Sam chuckled then turned to leave. "I'll get Paige to let me out."

Lila waited until Sam entered the kitchen then turned to Joshua. "Can you put the envelope in the safe here for now?"

"Don't you want to open it?"

What other secrets had Miss Emily hid all these years? Was it money? Or perhaps something sentimental such as pictures or a letter? Or another piece of news that would change her life? Whatever it was contained in the packet, she was content to let it remain hidden for a few more hours.

"Later. When we're alone."

~

Josh made it a point to remain in the kitchen until Ben was ready to leave. He waved him toward the back door.

"This way, buddy. I'll let you out."

Ben's eyes narrowed. "I'm headed to the Canfield building to meet with Jamie. I'm going out the front."

"I'll let you out the front."

Josh followed Ben out the door, side-stepping to stop him. "You said you got rid of that gun."

"I said I took care of it. Meaning I kept it in a safe location until it was needed."

"You have no qualms about that woman taking the fall for four murders she didn't commit?"

Ben glared at the sheriff's department across the street. "That woman is more than eager to take credit for those four murders. Over the course of her miserable life, she's probably committed that many and more. Consider this justice for the ones who didn't deserve it the way Stoddard and the others did."

Josh ran a hand over his neck. "You're right. Greater good and all that."

"We defeated evil, and you got the girl. Good job on our part, although I hadn't expected the old gal to take credit the way she did. I'd love to have seen the look on Hunter's face when she confessed."

"I would have enjoyed seeing that too." Josh scuffed his foot against the pavement. "Straight life for you now?"

Ben flashed a smug know-it-all grin. "The mayor asked for

a consultation about their computer system. Wallace wants input on additional safety and security options now that the Main Street area is booming. All legit."

"Congratulations." Josh took several steps back. "I have to get back inside, and you have a meeting. Catch you later."

Ben lifted a hand. "Same."

He waited until Ben reached the corner of Carson's then gave a short whistle. Ben turned.

"Take it easy, Hat-Trick."

For once, Hampshire lacked a smart-mouthed response. He lifted one hand, flashing a gesture other than the one Josh expected. Thumbs up.

What a great day. We did defeat evil, I did win the girl, and I got the last word with Ben.

CHAPTER NINETEEN

Dear Jennie,

How exciting that you're ready to start a new life. Now that you're on your way, I feel free to confess that I tucked some extra money in with your savings. All I ask is the occasional card or letter to keep in touch. Love to you and darling Lila.

Miss Emily Adele Anderson

Dear Lila,

One day this package will come to you. I will be gone by that time.

I never believed the stories told about dear Jennie. She is a good woman and loving mother. I have to refer to her in the present tense. To believe anything else is unbearable.

How I wished the courts would have let me take you instead of your aunt. Your family refused to allow me to see you or to let you visit me. It broke my heart.

I've continued to save over these years. I made up my mind to hold these funds rather than letting others take it for their own greed.

I pray this gift will reach you at a time it serves you best. Be good to yourself and follow your dreams.

Much love,

Miss Emily

Sitting cross-legged on Joshua's bed, Lila laid the letter on the nightstand. She picked up the photographs Miss Emily had included. Several of Lila and her mother or Lila and Miss Emily. A few of all three of them, and one of that grand lady by herself.

I miss you, Miss Emily. It broke my heart, too, when I couldn't see you again.

Not that the fault fell totally on Aunt Nan or the other Graingers. *When I got older, I could have made the effort, and now it's too late.* A visit would have meant so much to a woman who'd loved and never forgot her.

A tap sounded on the bedroom door.

"Come in."

Joshua entered, and she patted the bed.

He sat down and wrapped an arm around her, resting his cheek on her head. "You okay?"

She wiped away a final tear. "I am. The letters were sweet. One to my mother, and the other to me. They sounded like she was talking to me. There were photographs, too." Tears began to stream again. "Oh, Joshua, I got to see my mother and Miss Emily again."

"I want to see those pictures and hear stories about them." He straightened. "First, I want to talk to you about the money. It came to almost twelve thousand dollars."

Lila's mouth fell open. "How can that be? Even with Miss Emily adding some of her own money?"

"Your mother saved a considerable amount on her own.

According to Miss Emily's notes, she added fifty dollars a month of her own money, sometimes more. Over the years, it added up."

"Miss Emily was right about the timing." Lila picked up the letter addressed to her. "She wrote, 'I pray this will reach you at a time it serves you best.'"

"It would have helped you sooner."

"No, it came at the perfect time. She knew the Graingers would spend anything they got their hands on. Even if it came two weeks ago, it would have been the wrong time." She rested her head against his arm. "I might have left and never met you."

"I don't even want to think about that."

"I know you have money from your family, but it means a lot that I can bring something into our marriage." She held up a hand, knowing Joshua was about to protest. "Two women I loved very much made sacrifices to leave this gift to me. I want it to count."

"Agreed on one condition. That you take a couple hundred and spend it on yourself." This time Josh was the one to hold up a hand. "Promise me."

She nodded. Reluctantly. "Agreed."

"Are you sure you feel like going to my mom's tonight?"

"Absolutely. We need to tell her about our engagement before she hears it from someone else."

"Mom has a safe at her house. I don't want to leave this much money in the apartment overnight." He glanced at the bedside clock. "We need to leave in about fifteen minutes. Does that give you enough time to get ready?"

Lila uncrossed her legs and eased off the bed. "I'll be ready."

"I'll wait in the living room."

When the door closed, Lila rummaged through her

meager collection of clothing. Everything looked too cheap or shabby to meet Joshua's mother socially. For this evening, the black slacks she'd worn to Mrs. Canfield's wedding and a second-hand sweater purchased two winters ago would have to do.

As much as it pained her to spend hard-earned money, she'd have to buy new clothing rather than risk embarrassing Joshua with a threadbare appearance. She'd set a strict budget and—

Be good to yourself.

She sank onto the bed with a silent chuckle. Once again she'd fallen into the trap of thinking in circles. A bad habit, but one she would conquer. Just as she had to conquer her nerves over meeting Mrs. Canfield as her future mother-in-law.

~

When Lila left the apartment to go with Joshua to his mother's home, she hadn't expected to spend the next day with her future mother-in-law. All thanks to another crazy combination of events that had marked her life for the past week.

What a difference in families. The Canfields-McCalls-Wardens didn't hesitate to change their plans to help one another. So unlike her family. Unless it benefited a Grainger, members of that clan disappeared whenever a need occurred.

She drove down the ramp at the Sutton terminal then followed the signs to the main road.

"Turn right at the end of the parking lot," Dana said, checking the directions on her phone. "DMV Customer Service Center is five miles down that road."

"That's easy enough to find," Lila said. "Have you heard how Jess is feeling?"

Dana dropped her phone into her purse by her feet. "She's feeling better but still has a slight fever."

"With Paige not able to come in to work, I feel bad taking another day off. The bank and DMV could have waited."

"It could have, but we found a way to take care of it now."

Lila smiled to herself. Another defeat for circular thinking. "It was sweet of Megan to take a day off from her job to help out at Carson's."

"Between you and me, I think she misses working there. But her job at McCall's is full-time and pays more."

"She mentioned saving for a car. I hope she wasn't upset that Jamie sold her car to me."

"Not that I've heard. I think she's looking forward to going car shopping with her dad." Dana laughed. "Of course, the more money Megan saves, the more Nick has to match."

"Thank you for going to the bank with me."

The transaction might not have gone as smoothly even if it had been Joshua with her instead of his mother. The name Dana Canfield plus being the owner of one of the bank's largest accounts gained them immediate access to the manager. Any suspicion of being a Grainger with a large amount of cash was eliminated when Dana explained the funds were a bequest from the late Miss Emily Adams.

"You're very welcome." Dana gestured to a building ahead on the right. "We're coming up on the DMV."

Less than an hour later, they left with new plates and registration card. As a thank you, Lila insisted on treating Dana to lunch.

"This has been a productive morning." Dana took a sip of iced tea then dabbed a napkin to her lips.

Toying with the napkin in her lap, Lila said, "I have a question to ask, and I hope you won't get upset."

"I doubt that I will, but go ahead."

Every interaction with Dana Canfield had been pleasant, even friendly. Any reserve on the part of Joshua's mother was probably due to Lila's imagination.

"Last night at your house, you and Joshua were talking. You looked at me then a few seconds later, he became upset. I don't want to start a marriage with tension between us. If you have reservations about me, I want to know."

Lila bit her bottom lip, steeling herself for anything from fake reassurance to icy acknowledgment. Instead, a quizzical look flashed across Dana's face followed by a sad smile.

"I asked Joshua if he wanted my former engagement ring from his father." Dana hesitated, then said, "I supposed Joshua told you about the identity switch with his biological mother?"

"He did, but why was he upset?"

"He declined the offer, and I understand why. Technically, it's something his father gave to Joshua's biological mother. Joshua felt it would be disloyal to me to accept it and for you to wear a ring that he has no emotional connection."

"I understand that. Joshua asked if I wanted to wear my mother's ring. I'll always treasure that ring because my father gave it to her. Right now, I can't forget that Aunt Nan took it off my mother's finger." Her lip trembled, and her voice quivered. "Keeping it as some sort of trophy."

"Her ego caught up with her. If you hadn't seen that ring at her house, she would have continued to get away with murder."

A wave of gratitude washed through Lila. "Your description helped too."

Dana frowned. "When did I give a description of your aunt?"

"So much has happened, Joshua must have forgotten to tell you. The description you provided when Detective Lansing was shot."

"I didn't see the person. Just a glimpse through the window. Tall, blond, male."

"My aunt is almost six-feet tall, probably two hundred pounds. Her real name is Hannah which the detective half-way said during the recording you made. When the deputies searched her house, they found a gun that matched the one that killed Mr. Stoddard. The sheriff said they're running ballistic tests to confirm if it is the murder weapon."

"What did your aunt say?"

"She confessed to killing Buzz, the detective, that Towers woman, and Nathan Stoddard." Lila snorted. "Nan thinks someone will write a book or make a movie about her."

"I didn't see that coming." Dana's hand shook as she reached for her glass. "What do you say we talk about something more pleasant?"

Lila nodded, mulling over her next question. She'd spent a good portion of the money she'd allocated for today at the DMV. Still, she would get paid on Friday, much more than what she usually earned. Then again, next week's pay would be less due to the fewer hours she was working this week, and she still had to pay her first installment to Jamie.

She swallowed away any hesitation. "Dana, if you're not in a hurry, would you mind if we did some shopping for clothes before going home? I'd love to have your help."

"I'd enjoy that very much."

Tears appeared in Dana's eyes, discreetly dabbed away with her napkin before they could fall.

Lila gulped, rushing to console the other woman. "I'm sorry. I've upset you. If you'd rather go home—"

"Not at all. I'm touched that you asked me." Dana briefly rested her palm on the back of Lila's hand.

"This will sound forward considering we haven't spent

much time together, but I hope we can have the kind of relationship you have with Jamie."

"I want that too. When I moved to Providence last spring, I was alone. I met Nick and reunited with Rhys. I gained a daughter when Jamie married my son. Paige and Sam became part of our extended family with Jess claiming grandchild status. Joshua came home, and I have both my sons." Her hand moved to her throat. "I see how happy you make him, and that's the greatest gift you could give me."

"I think you and my mama would have been good friends."

"I'm sure we would have. I hope you won't mind if I think of you as a daughter."

A warmth grew inside her, melting the final piece that had remained frozen for over fifteen years. "I would love that."

"Back to your original question about shopping." Dana reached for her purse. "There's an outlet near here where we can get some great bargains."

"Sounds wonderful." Lila picked up the check and slid out of the booth.

This afternoon, she'd keep her promise to Joshua to buy the things she needed and follow Miss Emily's advice to be good to herself.

Within reason.

CHAPTER TWENTY

Rhys slowed his father's boat then made his way to the bow to set the anchor. "We passed the three-mile mark."

Joshua took Lila's hand. "Are you sure you want to do this? We can apply for a permit to bury your mother's ashes in your father's grave. They can be together."

Lila sat to one side, facing the water. She looked up from the urn nestled next to her feet. "My parents have been together for years. I just didn't know it."

With a nod, Josh moved to join Rhys in attaching ropes to the side and bottom of the urn. They lifted the container over the side of the boat. After Joshua removed the lid, they lowered the urn. When the vessel touched the water's surface, they eased the bottom rope upward. Ashes mixed with rose petals fanned outward, riding on the gentle waves and washed in the golden rays of the early evening sun.

Once the urn was emptied, they lifted it back onto the boat.

Lila raised a pink rose to her lips. She kissed the fragrant bloom then tossed it onto the ashes as they were carried outward toward the ocean. She turned into Joshua's waiting embrace.

"She's free."

She buried her face in his chest as sobs racked her body. Her knees weakened, and they both eased onto the deck. A deep sob broke free from Joshua, his grief—whether shared for the loss of her mother or for his own losses—mingled with hers.

Rhys lowered himself onto one knee. Wrapping his arms around both of them, he rested his brow against his brother's bowed head, holding them as long as they needed.

CHAPTER TWENTY-ONE

Thanksgiving

Cell phone in hand, Dana rushed down the steps from her bedroom to the kitchen. She stopped in the doorway, smiling at the flurry of activity. Pies, cakes, and cookies decorated the breakfast nook table. Paige stood at one end of the island, assembling a bowl of potato salad. Jamie worked on rolls while Lila prepared the dressing.

"The ferry just left Sutton," Dana said, swiping a grape from the fruit tray. "My parents should be here in a little over an hour."

"It's too bad they couldn't make it here yesterday," Paige said.

"Connecticut weather." Dana lifted one shoulder in a 'what can you do' gesture. "I'm glad the roads cleared up so they could make the trip safely."

Lila nodded. "That's what counts."

Dana looked around. "Where's Megan? Is she watching the game with the guys?"

"She was going to try to put the leaf in the dining table,"

Jamie said. "I told her the guys would take care of it. But she wanted the table to look good for your parents' arrival."

Paige glanced toward the formal dining room. "That's a huge table as it is now."

"It belonged to James's family. He made me promise to never get rid of it. Nick doesn't care for it, and I'm not in love with it. I'm hoping Joshua will want it once he settles in a house."

Paige chuckled. "It'll have to be a big house."

Dana stepped to the door leading into the dining room. A muffled word she couldn't make out sounded from under the table.

"Megan?"

A hand appeared, gripping the edge of the table. Hair messed, face flushed, Megan rose to her knees.

"What are you doing?"

"I couldn't get the table to open. I was checking underneath."

"Honey, that's a two-person job, plus the leaf is heavy. I'll get some man-power out here."

"Great. I'm going upstairs to comb my hair... and stuff."

"Are you all right? Did you bump your head?"

"No!" She pushed to her feet. "I don't want to look like a slob in front of your folks. I'll be right back." Megan darted out of the room. Seconds later, her footsteps sounded on the stairs.

Paige stood in the doorway. "Good luck getting any of the guys out of the man cave."

Jamie laughed. "Don't you mean Nick's study?"

"Huge black leather couch. Big screen TV. Wet bar. Juke-box." She snorted. "It's a man cave."

"Get the linens ready for the table. I'm going in."

Dana walked down the hallway, gave a quick tap on the

door before opening it. Five men sprawled on the couch and chairs, attention focused on the TV.

"Excuse me."

Nick tipped his head in her direction, gaze still fixed on the game. "Yeah, honey?"

"I need two volunteers."

Josh lifted a hand. "One second, Mom" at the same time Rhys asked, "Can you give us a couple minutes?"

Sam nodded. "Almost half-time."

"I need to earn some good-will points, Mrs. Canfield." Mike stood and stretched. "What do you need?"

"Thank you, Mike. You—" She raised her voice. "—will get first pick of the desserts. With thirteen people dining here, good luck to the rest of you."

Rhys leaped from his chair, and Joshua followed close behind. Dana pressed herself against the wall while the three men spilled out of the room. They tackled and wrestled their way down the hallway. Josh blocked Mike who then attempted to elbow crawl into the kitchen. Rhys leaped past both of them.

"Winner!" he shouted.

"Good for you," Dana patted his cheek. "All three of you into the dining room. Joshua, you know how to unfold the drop leaf. Mike and Rhys, get the extra seating from the storage room. After you wash up, set the table. Linens, china, silver. The works. I want to see a perfect formal setting within the next twenty minutes."

She stepped back inside the kitchen to watch and listen.

"You know how to do that?" Mike whispered to the other men.

Josh nodded, moving to one end of the table. "Drilled into my head at a young age."

Rhys moved to the other end. Each gave a tug, exposing an opening with a drop-down leaf.

"Guys, there's only room for twelve. How do we fit in an extra setting?"

Josh nodded to Rhys. "Ask the architect."

"Megan and Mike have a fight, and she kicks him out."

"Or Nick kicks him out for calling Mom 'Mrs. Canfield' instead of 'Mrs. Warden.'"

"Aw, crap. I forgot."

Josh clapped a hand to his forehead. "Wait a minute. There's a matching bench the length of the table when it's closed. Jess is little. She won't take up much space. We can use that and fill the remainder of the space with chairs."

"Won't that bench/chair arrangement on one side of the table upset Mom's aesthetic sensibilities?" Rhys shot a teasing glance toward the kitchen.

"I'll bear up under the burden." Dana chuckled from the doorway. "If you'll hurry and get the seating set up, I'll let you off china duty."

Mike swiped an arm across his brow. "Okay, guys, lets move."

They rushed down the hallway to the storage room. Dana moved back to the island. "I like Mike."

Jamie smiled. "Megan will be glad to hear that. Any particular reason?"

"He's still scared enough of me not to get mouthy like the other two."

Paige snorted. "More like he's too scared of Megan to upset you."

"That's a good possibility." Dana joined in the laughter then looked around. "What needs to be done? I feel like I'm not doing my share of the work."

Lila glanced around the kitchen. "We're in good shape. I

put the dressing in the oven. Everything else has to wait until closer to meal time."

"Can you check on Jess?" Paige asked. "She's been pinned to the front window for the past half-hour. I shouldn't complain since I know where she is and what she's doing."

"I'm surprised she's not watching football with Nick." Jamie covered the rolls and set them to one side to rise.

"I'll check on her."

Dana walked to the living room to find Jess kneeling on the couch. Her head rested on crossed-arms as she looked out the window.

"Watching doesn't make time go faster." She sat down then rubbed a hand across Jess's back.

Jess swiveled, snuggling against Dana's arm. She heaved a deep sigh. "I know." A second later, she bolted up, blinking her eyes. "But I *don't* need a nap."

"We all might need one after we eat."

"Maybe. I'm excited about tomorrow, Granna. Uncle Josh is getting married, and Lila will be my new aunt."

Dana dropped a kiss on the top of Jess's head. "You're getting to be an expert flower girl, aren't you?"

"Sure am. I love my new dress Uncle Josh and Aunt Lila bought me. Mom said I should wear the one I wore at your wedding to Granddad, but it would look funny in the pictures if I wore the same thing. They offered. I didn't ask."

"That was sweet of Josh and Lila."

"It was fun going shopping with them." Her voice dropped to a whisper. "I got to see Lila's dress too. It's *so* pretty! Uncle Josh didn't get to see it. It's a surprise for him."

Jess's smile and the sparkle in her eyes faded. "Granna, are you sad that Uncle Josh's daddy didn't get to see him get married?"

Dana thought back to her conversation with Joshua on her

wedding day. *You remind me so much of your father.* James would have been overjoyed to see this day. Except it wouldn't have taken place here, and the bride would be some other woman. The love between Joshua and Lila gave her both joy and sorrow. An abundance of joy because he'd had found a woman he loved and who loved him. A touch of sadness that he too was taking another step away from her to forge his own family.

"Yes, it makes me sad, but James will be here in my heart and in Joshua's."

Jess sat silent for a moment then nodded. "That makes me happy."

She patted Jess's knee. "What also makes me happy is my parents will be here for the wedding."

Jess's eyes widened and her mouth formed silent 'oh'. "Will there be cake like before? Or will we have leftovers from today?"

Dana chucked and patted Jess's knee. "There will be cake and flowers. Which means we'll have plenty to do tomorrow."

"I love my family." Jess's gaze swept around the room until she reached Dana. "Do your mom and dad understand they're my great-grandparents?"

"They do."

"I drew a new picture showing how we're all related in case they didn't know." She gave another big sigh and slid off the couch. "I'm going to go watch the game with the guys. Call me when they get here, okay?"

"Will do."

Dana watched until Jess skipped out of sight. She shifted positions to look out the window.

I love my family too.

Slumped against the wall in her bedroom, Megan clutched the leather-bound journal to her chest.

I can't show this to Mom. Not today with everything else she's dealing with. Her parents visiting. Joshua getting married tomorrow.

She opened the cover, re-reading the inscription.

To Katie. My love. My forever. James

"Why did you call her Katie? Why didn't you have the guts to talk to her, face-to-face?"

Instead of saying it in a book in a box bolted to the bottom of a dining room table.

Do I tell Dad? Show it to Rhys? I can't tell Mike. Even though that crazy woman confessed to killing all those people, Sam might take it for evidence. Mr. Canfield's been dead a year and a half. Giving it to Mom can wait. I'm not ruining Thanksgiving.

Megan walked to her dresser. She tucked the book in the back of the bottom drawer under a stack of summer clothes. Time to get downstairs before someone came to check on her.

She halted at the door, stung by her own hypocrisy. Was she any better than James Canfield? Keeping another secret by hiding it away? A measure of her resentment for the man faded. He did what he had to protect his family.

She gave one last glare at the dresser.

I'm not ruining Joshua's wedding either.

~

Dana leaped from the couch as a sleek luxury car pulled into the driveway. Ever the gentleman, her father exited first. He walked around the car, opening the door for his wife. They stood for a moment gazing at the house then walked toward the front steps.

Jamie had the family assembled at the far end of the living

room by the time Nick and Dana escorted her parents into the house.

"Oh, my." Carolyn touched her throat as she viewed the gathering. "I understand why you said it would be easier for the two of us to make the trip."

"We'll keep the introductions orderly," Nick said. "After that, no promises as to the level of chaos. Denny, if you'll hand over your keys, we'll take your cases upstairs."

"Thank you, Nick," Denny said, passing over the keys. "We're eager to get the reception line started."

Mike stepped forward. "I'll help with the cases."

Carolyn lifted a palm to stall his departure. "And you are, young man?"

Mike flashed the smile that helped him win first place in the Lighthouse Cantina Man-of-the-Month poster contest last June. He took Carolyn's hand in his and gave a slight bow.

"Deputy Michael Winslow. I'm here as Megan's guest, and I am pleased to meet you, Mrs. Dennison."

A light flush crossed Carolyn's cheeks. "Likewise, Deputy. Thank you for your kind assistance."

"My pleasure, ma'am. Please call me Mike." He paused to shake Denny's hand before following Nick outside.

"What a charmer," Carolyn said. "You'll have to watch Megan around him."

Dana nodded. "Don't worry about Megan. She keeps Mike in line."

The introductions continued. Fervent hugs for Rhys, Jamie, and Megan. Handshakes for Sam, Paige, and Lila. An affectionate smile for Jess who performed a sweet curtsy.

"Where's Joshua?" Dana asked, looking around the room.

Sam nodded toward the foyer. "He went out to help Nick rearrange the cars in case I got a call and had to leave. Mike's carrying the luggage upstairs."

Dana turned to her parents. "Do you want to go upstairs and rest or freshen up?"

"Game's on in the back, Denny, if you want to join us," Nick said as he returned.

"There's a snack tray in the fridge," Jamie said.

"Thanks," Sam said. "I'll take it to the den on my way."

"Football and snacks." Denny rubbed his hands together. "I'm up for that."

"One moment, dear." Carolyn said. "There's one more person we need to greet."

Joshua paused in the foyer to drop several sets of keys into a bowl then continued into the living room. He took the hand Dana held out to him.

"Mom, Dad, this is my son, Joshua. Honey, these are my parents."

He shook both their hands. "Nice to meet you."

"Sit down, Joshua. We'd like to get to know you better. Your grandmother Anna and I were sisters."

"Which would make you my great-aunt."

"To be correct, I'm your grand-aunt. However, since your maternal grandparents are deceased—"

"Cut to the chase, Carrie." Denny leaned around his wife to look Joshua straight in the eye. "You're Katie's son which means you're our grandson."

Carolyn huffed. "I was about to say that very thing with the caveat of whether Joshua is comfortable with that designation."

Josh grinned. "Thank you. Since you're comfortable with it as well, yes, I'd like that."

"What about your other grandparents?" Denny asked.

"My grandparents on my father's side also are deceased."

"You're all alone," Carolyn whispered, squeezing his hand.

He shook his head. "I have my mom, and the rest of the

family you just met. In case Mom didn't mention it, Lila is my fiancée. Your visit is good timing because we're getting married tomorrow."

Carolyn turned a stunned look to Dana. "What time is the ceremony? I need time to shop. Joshua, where are you registered?

"We're not, and don't worry about a gift. We're happy you're here to celebrate with us."

"Mom, don't fret. It's an evening wedding. In the morning, we'll go to the Main Street Village and check the shops. You can see the renovation work Rhys and I did there."

"It'll have to do until we get home. If I'd had more notice—"

"Anything is appreciated." Josh paused. "I'm not sure what to call you."

Jess skipped half-way into the room. "Excuse me. May I come in?"

Dana held out her hand. "Of course, you may."

"I'm just in time!" She scooted onto the sofa between Dana and Carolyn.

"Time for what, sweetheart?"

"To pick names for my new great-grandparents. Josh might give them wrong names."

Josh gave a gentle tug to her ponytail. "Wouldn't want that."

Seeing her mother's confused expression, Dana provided an explanation. "Jess asked Nick and me what grandparent names we wanted. Nick is Granddad, and I'm Granna."

Denny leaned forward. "Sounds like a keen idea. Every-body calls me Denny, so how about Grandpa Denny?"

Jess whispered the name then nodded. "I love it!"

He pushed to his feet. "Good job. Which way to the game?"

Dana heard Josh's low chuckle and fought back one of her

own. "Left through the kitchen, down the hallway, last door on the left."

Denny hustled across the room. Carolyn's mouth opened, her comment aborted as Jess tapped her arm. "I have the most wonderful idea for your name."

"I was thinking perhaps Grand'Mère."

Jess blinked several times. "Here's my idea. Gigi. Because G is for great and G is for grandmother."

Josh grinned. "What do you say, Gigi? It's got that French vibe you wanted, but it's way cooler."

Carolyn sniffed, though the corners of her mouth lifted a few degrees. "Yes, well, cool is something to which I do aspire."

Eyes wide, Jess stared up at her. "Does that mean yes?"

Carolyn gave a light laugh. "It does indeed, dear. I believe I can carry off the name Gigi with no effort. Now that's settled, I brought something I want to share this evening with everyone."

"I love surprises." Jess clapped her hands.

A tickle ran across the nape of Dana's neck. "What is it, Mom?"

"Pictures of you." Carolyn beamed, clapping as well. "Baby pictures through high school."

Josh wrapped an arm around Dana while shooting a wink to Carolyn. "Way cool, Gigi."

❧

Friday

Josh paced the length of the dining room, an easier task now that the table had been reduced to its original size. Hands in pockets, Ben lounged against the door frame opening from the foyer.

"Nervous?"

"I'm trying to think of a word that describes how I feel. Happy. Ecstatic. Blessed."

He halted mid-step. "Thank you for everything you did. I wouldn't be here—"

"Don't get maudlin, Canfield." Ben held up one hand. "I know you didn't approve of my methods. I did some of those things to save my hide as well as yours."

"Straight and narrow from here?"

Ben winked. "Sure."

Rhys entered from the kitchen. He stopped in front of Josh to adjust the other man's tie. "Ready, little brother?"

"Couldn't be more ready." Josh dared a quick glance at Ben.

Ben stiffened, a haunting shadow dancing across his face.

Enough of the secrets.

"Hey, Rhys. Little brother is what Ben used to call you, isn't it?"

Rhys half-turned, his gaze shifting from Ben to Josh. "What are you talking about?"

If Ben had the power, his look would have dropped Josh where he stood. Still, it was amusing to see his silver-tongued friend totally speechless.

"I'm sorry, Ben. It slipped out. I know you wanted to tell Rhys yourself." He shifted his gaze to Rhys. "Back when you and Mom lived in that campus apartment."

Rhys shook his head. "No, that kid's name was Cody." His eyes widened as he studied Ben. "You're Cody?"

Ben nodded.

"I don't understand. Why didn't you tell me?" He looked at Josh. "Does Mom know?"

Paige swooped into the room. "Ben, Rhys, get to your seats.

Josh, take your place up front." She sped out as fast as she'd arrived.

"We'll talk later." Rhys moved toward the doorway. "I can't wait to get caught up with you."

"It's quite a story," Ben said. As soon as Rhys walked away, he whirled on Josh. "Why did you do that?"

"No more secrets. Like it or not, we're your family."

✧

Joshua stood at the front of the fireplace. He rocked on his heels until he caught the slight frown on Gigi's face. He winked then clasped his hands before him in suitable solemn pose. Maybe he should have had a best man to keep his energy focused.

"Nothing to be nervous about." Reverend Lawson patted his shoulder. "Just a few more minutes."

Not nervous. Happy. More than he could contain.

Fragments of his home life flashed through his memory. Happy times but cocooned from an ultimate danger none of them had expected. For over a year, he'd lived on the run, alone and scared, hiding to save his life and even taking two lives to save Ben. He grew up in a way that his comfortable childhood never prepared him for. His safety net vanished, but his world grew larger and brighter. Perceptions altered, awareness expanded. Despite the lies and the pain and the secrets, he became a better man.

A man worthy of the woman who would pledge her life to his in a matter of minutes.

His glance landed on Gigi as her confused gaze wandered around the room at the multitude of flowers in lemon yellow, tangerine, and dusky pink. She leaned toward her daughter, her attempt to whisper failing.

"Why does it look like spring in here?"

"It's their theme."

"But it's November."

"They know." Dana patted her mother's knee as a signal to drop the subject.

Catching his mother's eye, Joshua winked. His mom knew what she was doing when she suggested Nick take her parents for a tour of PI along with shopping on Main Street while the wedding preparations were underway.

Head bowed, he closed his eyes and shut out the sounds surrounding him.

Jennie, I hope you don't mind me calling you by that name. I promise I'll love Lila every day of our lives together. I'll keep your promise, too, to give her a happy life. He swallowed back the lump rising in his throat. *If you see my dad, tell him I miss him and love him.*

The music cued, and he straightened, gaze shifting to the doorway on the left.

Clad in a pink dress with a white sash, Jess entered, face beaming as she scattered rose petals with each step. Seconds later, Lila appeared, hand tucked into the crook of Nick's arm. A satin and lace dress, a few shades darker than the blush on her cheeks, skimmed over her slender figure. Her hair was pulled away from her face, cascading in loose curls down her back.

He managed a nod to Nick before taking Lila's hand.

I love you. I cherish you.

What came out of his mouth was, "I do."

In the length of a heartbeat, Lila echoed those words. "I do, too."

Amidst the chuckles that swept across the room came a high-pitched giggle from Jess and a gasp from Gigi. Reverend

Lawson stepped forward, amusement wreathing his lined features.

"As you can see, the bride and groom are committed to this union. However, for our guests, we'll proceed with the long version." His brown eyes twinkled as he looked to Joshua and Lila. "If that's acceptable with the two of you."

"Absolutely, sir."

"Yes, please."

They listened to each word he said. Sealed the meaning of those words in their hearts as they spoke their vows. A blessing and a kiss later, they were married.

They stayed long enough for cake and champagne, conversation and congratulations, and at least a dozen or more photographs to make his mother happy.

⁂

Lila stretched her legs, watching as the high beams cut through the darkness. She wasn't familiar with the roads on this side of PI, but it seemed like they were headed away from his apartment.

"Where are we going?"

"I'm taking the scenic route."

"Joshua, it's pitch dark. We can't see a thing."

"We can see the stars and the moon. The best I could do considering we can't get away for a honeymoon at this time."

"The stars and moon are beautiful. I'll always remember this night." She gave a soft sigh. "I love you, Joshua."

He squeezed her hand. "I love you, Lila Canfield."

I'm Lila Canfield.

Hearing her new name for the first time spoken by Joshua was one more gift this day had bestowed.

She rested her palm on top of his leg and kicked off her pink shoes.

"Let's go home."

THE END

If you enjoyed *Crossroads,* please consider writing a review to help others learn about the book. It's the best gift you can give an author.

Thank you for your support!

To learn about my new releases, go to my website, http://www.diannawilkes.com.

The story continues in *Boardwalk* (Providence Island Book 5):

EXCERPT FROM BOARDWALK

Chapter One

Car keys jingling in his hand, Ben Hampshire stopped in the doorway to the dining room. His landlady, Maisie Porter, sat at the table, waiting for him to drive her to her friend Yolanda's house. Realizing Maisie was unaware of his presence, he watched as the early evening sunlight cast the elderly woman in a golden glow. With her white hair and cornflower blue eyes, she looked like a modern-day Mrs. Claus.

Chauffeur duties weren't the usual arrangement for a tenant, but the two of them had moved into a more personal relationship during the year he'd lived at Porter's Bed-and-Breakfast. The privacy provided by the third-floor suite along with the incredible meals Maisie cooked were two of the reasons he'd remained in residence for almost a year.

Maisie not only opened both her home to him, she'd also opened her heart. She was the grandmother he'd never had and his strongest supporter when suspicion fell on him for the murders that occurred on Providence Island last year.

He *was* guilty of shooting those four individuals. In his

defense, each one of them deserved it. Law enforcement would disagree, but Ben considered his oath to protect Dana Canfield and her family took higher priority.

Ben shoved those thoughts away. He was settled in the first home he'd had in ages, dating a hot redhead, and becoming a respected part of the community as "the IT guy."

He tapped on the door frame. "Ready for your girls' night, Maisie?"

The Fab Five—Maisie and four other women from her church—had planned an over-night baking and crafting party. Based on the two bottles of wine protruding from the tote bag next to her chair, the meeting appeared to be leaning more toward the party side.

Maisie gestured toward the chair next to her. "We need to talk."

Her smile lacked its usual warmth, and the sparkle in her blue eyes was missing. A quiver ran through his stomach.

"What's wrong? Are you sick?"

Maisie lowered her brows. "Ben Hampshire, do I *look* like I'm sick?"

That flash of spirit spurred Ben to sit down. "No, ma'am."

"I've put off having this talk with you, and it's long past due." She pushed a rectangular piece of paper in front of him.

His confusion cleared when he realized it was his payment for next month's rent. No reason for Maisie to be nervous about asking for an increase.

"I'm fine with whatever you charge. Give me the amount, and I'll write a new check."

She placed her palm over his hand. "Ben, it's time for you to move out."

For one of the few times in his life, Ben was speechless. When she pulled her hand away, she took a piece of his security with her.

Maisie sighed, her gaze traveling to a point somewhere over his shoulder. "I'd planned on shutting this place down last year. Then you came, and with all the murders, I felt safer with you living here."

He edged the check back in front of her. "If it's money—"

She shook her head. "When Clyde and I moved into this house, we fixed it up with a back porch. A place where we could see the sun rise and set and watch our children playing. Except we never had any children, and Clyde passed away a few days before our thirtieth anniversary. I've lived here alone all the years since then except for guests that came and went. I never expected you to stay as long as you have, but I'm happy you did. It's been good for both of us, don't you think?"

His throat swelled with that unexpected U-turn in the conversation. He didn't do emotions, and Maisie was bringing out feelings he'd locked away ages ago. He managed a small nod.

She slowly tore the check in quarters. "That's why I'm not going to let you waste your life the way I've done with mine."

His mind reeled as he recalled Maisie never denied being sick. If that was reason for this change, he'd make sure she had the best doctor and the best care available. If it was money, he had enough to keep her in comfort. Whatever the cause, he'd find it and fix it. What he needed to do now is find a way to comfort her.

"What do you mean you've wasted your life? You have friends, your work at church, your garden—"

"And I have you, a blessing I never expected." Her thumb toyed with one scrap of the torn check. "Before you came here, each day was the same as the next, and the weeks rolled along with little change. As much as I love this old house and my garden, I need excitement and purpose in my life. The girls and I talked, and we decided to shake things up."

Half of him wanted to laugh at the idea of the Fab Five going rogue; the other half cringed at that same thought.

"Change up how?"

"Travel. Road trips. Cruises. Maybe even start a little business on Main Street." A hint of pink bloomed in her cheeks, and the sparkle re-ignited in her eyes.

Ben mulled over those options. They sounded good on the surface, but plenty of room existed for trouble. Before he could inject a dose of logic, Maisie rolled ahead with her explanation.

"First thing on Monday, I'm listing my house with Elliott Realty. Yolanda has a ranch house on Cypress. Sandy and I are going to move in with her. Tina's selling her house and moving in with Deloris. After we get the traveling bug out of our system, we'll decide what to do next."

"Selling the house is a drastic move. Why not wait to see if these living arrangements work out?"

"We discussed that but decided to go with our gut, and…" She fixed a stern look on him. "…before you suggest buying this house, I'm telling you it's a flat no. You need to take the next step with the young woman you've been seeing."

Nope. It was one thing for Maisie to redesign her life. He could manage his own just fine. "We're not at that point—"

"No excuses. Besides you spend more nights away than you do here." Her gaze softened, and an affectionate smile touched the corners of her lips. "I've seen how your face lights up when you get a message on your phone from her. That smile you get doesn't lie. You're in love with this woman."

A line of sweat broke out across his brow, and his head spun from the deft switch in topics. "I'm not—"

"You're in love whether you want to admit it or not. I have no doubt she's in love with you as well. You both need to move ahead while you have the chance. Life takes things away when we least expect it."

Something he knew too well. The last time he'd said "I love you" was to his fiancée before she died in his arms. At least Maisie had those thirty years with Clyde. He'd promised Betsy twice that many.

Maisie gave a quick wink before standing. "I can't go on forever being your culinary side-piece. After all, a woman has her pride to consider."

Ben jerked, knocking his keys from the table to the floor. "Jeez, Maisie!"

"Would you mind carrying my tote to the car? Don't forget I'm getting a ride with one of the girls tomorrow morning." She patted his shoulder as she passed. "I'll bring brownies home for you."

Ben stood in stunned silence as Maisie headed toward the front door. *What just happened?* In a matter of minutes, he'd lost his home, was ordered to move in with Stacy, and witnessed his kindly landlady morph into a wanna-be Golden Girl.

Maisie did deserve fun and enjoyment in life. While ninety-five percent of him agreed with her plan, the other five percent sulked over having his comfortable life disrupted. He eyed the vacant doorway then chuckled.

Culinary side-piece. Good one, Maisie.

He grabbed his keys and her tote. As he walked to the car, he practiced what to say to Stacy.

And what to do if she told him no.

～

The Fab Five settled into their favorite spots in Yolanda's living room with conversation fueled by fresh-baked cupcakes and glasses of wine. The "have you heard" topics lasted longer than Maisie expected before the question she'd dreaded was asked.

"Did you talk with Ben?" Deloris, a retired librarian, had a voice that could range from angelic to drill sergeant. A quality which served her well in her years of dealing with the public. As always, her tone with Maisie was gentle.

"I did." Maisie set her glass to one side then reached for her craft bag.

"About time," Tina grumbled. "He's a grown man. You should have kicked him out of the nest months ago."

"Uh, Tina." Yolanda waved one hand in a circle. "Maisie runs a Bed and Breakfast. It wasn't like he was mooching."

"I think he's sweet." Sandy placed another brownie on her plate. Just past fifty-years old, she was the youngest of the widows.

"Remember how he helped us set up the booth for Founder's Day last summer? The Fall Festival booth in October. The Christmas booth in December." Deloris ticked off each event on her fingers.

Maisie dropped the yarn and crochet hook onto her lap. Her lower lip quivered. "Oh, girls, I'm going to miss him."

"It's not as if he's moving away." Sandy scooted closer to Maisie on the couch and patted her knee. "He'll continue to take you out to dinner once a week, won't he?"

"I hope so." Maisie swallowed back a sob. "He doesn't talk much about his past. I know his mother passed away when he was young, and his father didn't seem to be very involved in his son's life. This was the first home Ben's had in a long time, and I told him to leave. I hurt his feelings."

"You did it for the right reasons," Sandy said.

Deloris looked up from her knitting. "Who he's dating?"

"Stacy Andrews." Maisie picked up her crochet hook and began a row of double-chain stitches.

Tina snorted. "That redhead with the RBF?"

Deloris frowned. "What's an RBF?"

"Resting Bitch Face."

"I want one of those!" Sandy exclaimed. She huffed at the reactions ranging from surprise to censure. "Well, I do. You try being five-foot two with a squeaky voice. I'd love to have an expression that says "back off, buster." I wouldn't mind having a figure like hers too."

"She doesn't mind showing it off with those short skirts." Tina glanced around the room for agreement, frowning when none appeared.

Yolanda nodded. "If I had a figure like that, I'd wear my skirts half-way to Heaven's Gate."

"I've met Stacy," Maisie broke in before Tina counter-argued. "She's a lovely woman. She gives off all those clues that says she's in love with him too. Touching his arm while he's talking. Straightening the collar of his shirt. Watching when he walks away—"

Sandy fanned her face. "I've done that *so* many times!"

Tina slapped a palm on her knee. "Sandra Lynn Armstrong, how many glasses of wine have you had tonight?"

"Just one. I'm little, and it doesn't take much."

"Wine or not," Deloris said, her voice shifting into the drill sergeant range. "We all can agree that Ben is an attractive man—"

Sandy sighed. "Tall... blond hair and blue eyes..."

"—and we want to see him happy. Maisie's done all she can do. What happens next is out of our control."

Maisie nodded toward the crocheted stitches. "I have enough faith in those two getting together that I'm starting a baby blanket."

Tina shrugged as she walked toward the kitchen. "If your plan doesn't work out, you can always donate the blanket to the church bazaar."

Maisie hid a smile as she continued to whip out another row of stitches. *It'll work. This time next year, I may be rocking a little baby Ben.*

⁓

After dropping Maisie off at Yolanda's house, Ben drove by the house recently purchased by Joshua Canfield and his wife Lila.

Canfield had planned for the future with that purchase. Three-bedroom Cape Cod, large back yard and—best of all—an apartment over the double-wide garage. The unit was smaller than Ben's current suite, but it was an option. If need be, he'd make it work.

Just his luck Stacy was out of town on business. Now that Maisie had planted the idea in his head, he wanted the conversation over with.

Is this the way you intend to discuss the matter with your lady?

He grunted at the imaginary scolding. Admitting he was in love with Stacy—which he wasn't ready to do—meant opening the heart he'd shut down years ago. What was wrong with leaving things as they are? He was happy with the arrangement; so was she. They enjoyed their time together and appreciated their time apart.

Logical decision. Subject closed.

Emotions drop-kicked logic to the side. This wasn't a piece of software he could code to give him the solution he wanted. Once he broached the subject with Stacy, everything changed. A "yes" meant acknowledging a relationship and implied a future. A "no" opened another door, one possibly leading to an end. An option he wasn't prepared to face.

Ben headed for the Crossroads on his way back to the B&B. Moments later, his phone chimed.

Stacy's ringtone.

He flipped on the blinker and turned into the parking lot for Warden's Garage. Shoving the car into Park, he pulled out his phone. Recalling Maisie's observation, he tugged down the rear-view mirror.

A stupid grin reflected back at him.

Crap.

He shoved the mirror back in position then checked the text.

May or may not see you tomorrow. More meetings. My fault for carpooling. A flame and demon emoji followed the text, an obvious reference to CFO Kevin Davis. Seconds later, another text arrived.

I miss you accompanied by hearts and fireworks.

Hearts.

Ben scrolled through every text they'd exchanged. Had they been saying "I love you" all this time, just not in words?

He shot a quick glance at the dash clock and did a quick calculation. If he caught the next ferry, he could be in Frostburg by nine p.m. The stupid grin grew wider as he reached for the gear shift. His hand froze as a movement from the back of the lot caught his attention.

A man lay face-down, one arm outstretched. In the not-yet-dusky light, Ben saw blood staining the back of the man's body and the ground around him.

He bolted from the car and raced across the lot. His breath caught as he recognized Glenn Thornton, the man who'd sold his body shop to Nick Warden.

Dropping to his knees, Ben located the entry site of a

gunshot. He pulled off his fleece hoody and rolled the man onto his side, pressing the jacket against the wound. He fumbled with his cell phone with the other hand.

"Sheriff's Department. What's your emergency?"

"A man's been shot. Parking lot of Warden's Garage on Old Main near the Crossroads. He's lost a lot of blood."

"I'm dispatching EMS and a deputy. I need you to stay on the line—"

Ben disconnected the call and shoved the phone in his pocket. He needed both hands to keep a firm pressure on the wound.

"Mr. Thornton... Glenn. Can you hear me?"

A moan. A flutter of eyelids.

"It's Ben Hampshire, Maisie's tenant. You're safe, Glenn. Help's on the way."

His mouth moved. A second later, his eyes opened. Fingers on one hand curled and flexed the air. "Evie—"

Ben clasped Glenn's hand. Thornton was too far gone to save, and he needed to know he wasn't alone.

"Tell—" He coughed, spluttering blood. "Evie—"

"I'll tell her you love her."

A peaceful smile crossed Glenn's lips, and his body began to relax. In the distance, the sound of sirens grew louder. Ben tightened his grip as if touch would tether the man until help arrived.

"Talk to me, Glenn. Did you see who shot you?" Shooting a man in the back was a coward's way. Thornton deserved justice, and Ben needed that name.

For a brief instant, the haze cleared from the man's eyes. Ben leaned forward, straining to listen over the scream of the sirens and shouts of the deputies and EMTs. With his final breath, Glenn whispered one word.

Nick.

ABOUT THE AUTHOR

Dianna Wilkes is an award-winning contemporary romance author, known for the Providence Island mystery series.

Reading has always been an important part of her life. "I learned to read when I was four years old," she said. "Writing my own stories seemed a natural progression."

Dianna holds a B.A. in Visual Communication and a M.Ed. in Instructional Technology. She worked as an Education Consultant for a medical technology company before leaving the corporate world to write full time. Despite all that nerdy stuff, she loves creating stories of romance and mystery with touches of humor.

When she isn't writing, Dianna is deep in researching various twigs and branches on her family tree or fulfilling entries on her travel bucket list.

Facebook:
www.facebook.com/DiannaWilkesAuthor/
Website:
www.diannawilkes.com

Made in the USA
Monee, IL
27 June 2021